A Big
Fat
Greek
Murder

The Goddess of Greene St. Mysteries
by Kate Collins

Statue of Limitations

A Big Fat Greek Murder

A Goddess of
Greene St. Mystery

A Big
Fat
Greek
Murder

Kate Collins

KENSINGTON BOOKS
www.kensingtonbooks.com

First Printing: December 2020
ISBN-13: 978-1-4967-2435-9
ISBN-10: 1-4967-2435-6

ISBN-13: 978-1-4967-2436-6 (ebook)
ISBN-10: 1-4967-2436-4 (ebook)

10 9 8 7 6 5 4 3 2 1

Printed in the United States of America

This book is dedicated to my son, Jason, and my daughter, Julia. Together, we're the Three Musketeers, able to accomplish anything.

Everybody's got a plan until they get punched
in the face.
—Mike Tyson

IT'S ALL GREEK TO ME
by Goddess Anon

This has to be a fast post because I'm due at a rehearsal dinner in an hour, and I have yet to change. Lucky me, you say? Sounds like a good time? "Humbug" is my reply. Getting all dolled up after a day of work so I can spend my evening pretending to be overjoyed for a happy couple is not my idea of a good time. Lest ye forget, I was once one-half of a so-called "happy couple."

It won't be easy for me to watch the soon-to-be-wed duo entwine arms, sip champagne, and promise to be loyal to each other forever because I know that forever is a long, long time.

I realize it seems I've soured on marriage, but I haven't completely given up. I keep hoping to find my Prince Charming out there somewhere. But who knows where that will be? Surely not here in my small Michigan hometown. I can't even find a decent white wine, let alone a white knight—unless my luck is changing. I don't be-lieve in miracles, but there does seem to be a certain magic in the air lately. Who knows? Maybe it could hap-pen tonight.

Look at the time, and I still don't have a clue as to what I should wear. How does one attract a white knight? Black, perhaps?

Till tomorrow, this is Goddess Anon bidding you adio. P.S. That's Greek for good-bye. Wish me luck!

CHAPTER ONE

Friday

I posted the blog, closed my laptop, and turned in my chair to look at the small bedroom closet overflowing with clothes from my former life. Somewhere in that mess was the dress I'd be wearing to the rehearsal dinner.

A white knight. *Hmm.* Dark wavy hair, strong jaw, soulful eyes that seem to look through me, melt me like butter . . . and there was Case Donnelly once again creeping into my thoughts. After inviting him to meet me for a drink after the rehearsal dinner, and his nonchalant excuse, I cursed myself for taking the chance. A white knight was out there somewhere for me, but clearly it wasn't Case Donnelly.

I took a deep breath and began the hunt for my black dress.

Fifteen minutes later, after one last look in the bathroom mirror, I kissed my ten-year-old son, Nicholas, good-bye, blew a kiss at my youngest sister, Delphi, who'd stayed home to babysit, grabbed my purse and a lightweight coat, and hurried out to my white SUV for the ten-minute ride to the Parthenon, my grandparents' diner.

My phone rang through the car's speakers, and I tapped a button to answer, "Hello."

"Thenie, it's Dad. I need your help."

"I'm almost at the Parthenon, Pops. What's up?"

"Mrs. Bird is out back pecking at the new rose bushes and demanding to see you, Delphi is babysitting your son, and I've got a line of customers out the door. I know you promised your mother that you'd help out at the diner, but I could really use your help."

"Might I mention again that we need seasonal employees?"

"You can lecture me when you get here."

"I can't make it right now, Pops. I'll call Delphi. She can bring Nicholas with her."

"Thanks, but we need a landscape consultant or we're going to lose Mrs. Bird's business."

"Let Delphi ring up the customers. You can handle Mrs. Bird."

"That's not the answer I was looking for."

"I'll be there as soon as I can, Pops."

Landscape consultant was on the opposite end of the spectrum from my former job as a newspaper reporter in Chicago. The vibrant tourist town of Sequoia was equally distant on the spectrum from the bustling Windy City that my son and I used to call home. The two cities shared the same water, but the breeze blowing east from Lake Michigan felt different. It smelled different, fresher perhaps.

If circumstances hadn't forced me to move back into the big family home, I'd still be running around the city, interviewing people and sitting at a computer until late at night to turn in my "noteworthy" articles. Instead, I was able to be outdoors working with plants and flowers and the cheerful people who came to our garden center to buy them. And at last, after one month of working in the office, learning the ins and outs of the business end of the operation, my dad felt I was ready to try my hand at landscape design. Turned out, I loved it.

I parked my car in the public lot on the block behind Greene Street and scurried up the alley. I entered through a back gate in the high fence and made my way to the outdoor eating area. With white wrought-iron tables and chairs, a concrete patio floor painted Grecian blue, white Greek-style columns on each corner, and blue-and-white lights strung around the entire perimeter, Yiayiá and Pappoús could not have made it look cozier or more inviting.

At least I thought so. But the guests didn't seem to be enjoying it. In fact, there was a distinctly unhappy *vibe* in the air, as Delphi would say. My mother was standing in front of the kitchen door, worrying the thick gold Greek bracelet she was never without. As I approached, my feet already hurting, Mama said, "It's not good, Athena. The groom-to-be hasn't shown up, and no one can reach him. What are you wearing?"

My mother had on black slacks with a Grecian blue blouse, or, as Mama referred to blue, "the color of the Ionian Sea." Unfortunately, I hadn't gotten the memo, so I was the oddball in my short black dress and strappy black heels. And no prince in sight. "I didn't know there was a dress code."

I glanced around at the tables, full of worried, whispering guests. "Maybe he got cold feet. Did he show up for the rehearsal?"

"They're having the wedding rehearsal after the dinner because some of the family members had to work."

"Why such a big crowd for a rehearsal dinner?" I asked. "Usually it's just for the wedding party."

"The Blacks decided to include the families of the wedding party," Mama said. "They're wealthy, and they pay very well. I wasn't about to question them on their decision."

I scanned the area, making mental notes. The wedding party was gathered at the head table, where Mandy, the bride-to-be, in a yellow silk dress, was being consoled not only by her bridesmaids, but also her parents and my oldest sister, Selene. Mitchell, the bride's twin brother and best man, stood directly behind them, checking his watch and looking perturbed, while maid of honor Tonya stood off to the side, talking quietly on her phone.

"What about the groom's parents?" I asked. "Have they heard from him?"

"His parents aren't here," Mama said. "Apparently, they declined the invitation."

My sister Maia joined us, breathless with news. "I just heard that two of Brady's groomsmen have gone to his apartment to see what the holdup is. He lives down the road, so it shouldn't take long—and aren't those my heels, Athena? And why are you so dressed up?"

Mama licked her thumb to wipe away a smudge from under Maia's eye, causing my sister to roll her head to the side. "Never mind about her outfit," Mama said, "and good for those brave boys. Yiayiá and Pappoús will be pleased. You know how upset they get if their food gets cold. Hold *still*, Maia."

That was so typical of our Greek family—more concerned about the guests missing a meal than the bride-to-be missing her groom.

Submitting to my mother's ministrations, Maia rolled her eyes, while I tried to hide my smile with a cough.

Maia was born after me; we were the two middle sisters of four, all named after Greek goddesses—Selene after the moon goddess, me after Athena, goddess of war and wisdom, and Maia after goddess of the fields. The exception was our youngest sister, Delphi, who was named in honor of the Oracle of Delphi. Stymied that she wasn't a "goddess," Delphi had long ago decided that she had the gift of foresight and was a true modern-day oracle. The remarkable thing was that sometimes she got her predictions right.

Also remarkable was how much Maia, Selene, and Delphi looked like our mother, shortish in stature, with fuller curves, lots of curly black hair, and typical Greek features. I, on the other hand, took after my father's English side of the family, inheriting his light brown hair, slender body, oval face, and softer features. In family photos, I was the gawky, pale-skinned girl in the back row standing beside the tall, pale-skinned man.

Selene broke away from the inconsolable bride and headed in our direction, an exasperated look on her face—coincidentally, the same expression Mama was wearing. Because she was also part of the wedding party, Selene wore a black-and-white sheath dress and heels instead of the waitress outfit.

"Selene," Mama said, "go back and ask the bride's mother whether we should serve the appetizers now. These poor people have to eat something."

"I just came from there," Selene replied, looking even

more exasperated than before. "I don't think they're in
any mood to—"

Mama gave her "the look," and Selene did an about-
face, slipping away obediently.

My grandmother joined our little group then, asking if
she and Pappoús should start serving the lemon rice soup
known as *avgolemono* (pronounced "ahv-lemono").

"No, Yiayiá," I said. "We're waiting for the groom to
arrive."

"Still?" she asked in her high, raspy voice. "But the
people need food."

Maia looked at me, trying to suppress another eye roll.
I couldn't help but laugh, rubbing my grandmother's
back to calm her down.

"Why you laugh?" Yiayiá asked with a scowl. Standing at a mere five feet high, she wore a black blouse, a
long, full, black-print cotton skirt, and thick-soled black
shoes. The only brightness in her outfit was a blue—
excuse me—Ionian Sea–colored scarf that wrapped around
her white hair, wound into its usual tight knot at the back
of her head.

"It shouldn't be long, Mama," my mother said to her,
shooting us a glare. "We expect them at any moment."

"*Endáksi*," she said with a sigh and a shrug. *Okay.*
Wearing her usual world-weary expression, she headed
back into the kitchen to share the news with Pappoús.

Suddenly, the two absent groomsmen came jogging
around the corner of the restaurant, out of breath and
wild-eyed. "Brady," one gasped, holding his side, "he's
been hurt. Badly."

"Taken," the second groomsmen said, bending over to
gulp air, "to the hospital."

As the guests rose to their feet in concern, the bride

gathered her full skirt and ran toward the two men, grabbing onto the shirt front of one. "Trevor, is Brady dead?"

In between gulps of air, Trevor replied, "He was—unconscious—when the paramedics—took him away."

Mandy took a step backward as though she'd been pushed. "Then he's alive?"

"We don't know," Patrick, the other groomsman said, "We found him on his apartment floor with a pair of—"

"Patrick," Trevor snapped, giving a subtle nod in Mandy's direction.

"With a pair of what?" Mandy cried, grabbing his shirt front again. "Tell me. With *what*?"

Trevor's chin began to tremble, and a tear ran down his cheek. "Scissors in his back."

There was a collective gasp. My mother made the sign of the cross. Maia's mouth dropped open. Selene froze in place. I spotted Tonya, the bridesmaid who'd been on the cell phone, turn to give the other bridesmaids a knowing look, and I instantly filed it away.

"The police are on their way, Mandy," Patrick said. "They'll be able to tell you more."

The bride-to-be collapsed in a puddle of yellow silk, sobbing hysterically, "Brady's dead. I know he's dead. What will I do? Oh my God, what will I do?"

Her parents helped her to her chair and sat on either side of her, rubbing her hands, while her brother strode toward the two groomsmen to have a whispered conference. My mother hurried over to talk to the bride's mother, who was consoling her distraught daughter. That was when I spotted Selene, her face ashen, slip around the guests and disappear into the kitchen.

Before I could follow her, Mama returned to say quietly to us, "I just spoke with Mandy and her parents.

They're going to stay here until the police arrive. Maia, go tell Yiayiá and Pappoús we'll start serving the soup afterward."

"Maia, wait!" I called, as she started toward the kitchen. "Mama, no one is going to stay for dinner. This is supposed to be a celebration."

"But they must eat!" she cried. "Think of all the food waiting for them."

"Athena is right, Mama," Maia said. "They've just had horrible news. They're not going to sit down and dine now."

Mama put her hand over her forehead. "Then go tell your grandparents that, Maia."

"I'll tell them," I said, and headed inside to deliver the message and find out why Selene had slipped away.

"Yiayiá, Pappoús, the dinner has been canceled," I announced. "The groom was taken to the hospital with a serious injury."

Pappoús stopped stirring the soup, and Yiayiá straightened, putting one hand on her lower back. Almost in unison they said, "But the people have to eat!"

"It's not appropriate to serve food when there's been a calamity," I explained.

"Calamity is right," Yiayiá said grumpily, eyeing all the food.

"The groom is injured, sure," Pappoús said in his thick Greek accent, "but what about the others?"

"They'll be going home soon." I glanced around but didn't see my sister. "Yiayiá, did you see Selene come through the kitchen?"

"She's sitting out there by herself," Yiayiá replied, nodding her head toward the swinging doors to the diner.

"Maybe you can talk to her. She won't tell me what's wrong."

I found my sister in a booth in the empty diner, staring blankly into space. She had scooted to the far end, with her back to the wall and her feet hanging off the edge. I slid in opposite her and reached for her hand.

"What's wrong, Selene? You look like you just lost your best friend."

Her gaze shifted to mine, and I saw fear in her eyes. Just as she was about to speak, my mother stepped into the room and clapped her hands. "Girls, the police are here. They want everyone outside except for Yiayiá and Pappoús. *Páme!*"

As soon as Mama left, Selene bent her head and sobbed. I hadn't seen my oldest sister cry since we were children, and it startled me. Selene had always been strong and bold, the fearless firstborn, a role model for her sisters. Now she wept as though her heart was broken.

"Selene, what is it?"

"Stay with me, Athena," she sobbed, reaching for my hand. "Don't leave my side."

"I won't, but tell me why."

"The scissors in Brady's back? I think they're mine."

CHAPTER TWO

I sat back in shock. "*Your* scissors were used to stab the groom?"

"They disappeared yesterday," she said in a frightened whisper. "What if they're mine? What if someone stole them? You know I'll be the first to be suspected."

"That's not possible, Selene. You can't even step on a spider, let alone stab someone."

With a trembling lower lip, she said, "Thenie, please listen. If they *are* mine, then *my* fingerprints will be on them. *My* DNA. You know the police will think I stabbed him."

I massaged my eyes, thinking. Selene was the most requested stylist at the popular Over the Top hair salon, especially for wedding parties, but there shouldn't be any reason to assume her scissors were used. "First of all, if Brady survived the attack, he should be able to tell the police who it was. Second, you don't have a motive. You don't even know Brady. And, third, you were at the hair salon, so you didn't have the opportunity."

Selene looked up at me with big, watery eyes. Her hands trembled in her lap. She opened her mouth as though to speak, but no words came.

"What, Selene?" I asked. "Talk to me. What's going on?"

She inhaled deeply and blurted, "I do know Brady."

"Because of the wedding?"

She shook her head.

"You don't know him *that* well, do you?"

Again, she held back her answer. I had a bad feeling deep inside my stomach, and I leaned forward. "How well do you know Brady Rogers?"

She finally blurted out her response. "He was my workout coach at the gym, but I couldn't stand him. I quit going to the gym because of him. He was a bad guy, Thenie, and I had to let his manager know. I think I almost got him fired."

"Okay," I said, thinking quickly, "but that's a very weak motive for murder. And you have an alibi for today, right? You were at the salon?"

She looked down and shook her head. She didn't seem ashamed, just in shock as the bad news began to pile up. "I was off today. I spent the day at my apartment until I came here to help Mama serve."

I wanted to tell her that things would be okay, but as I stared at her, I realized that I was now the one with an open mouth and no words. It wasn't out of the ordinary to not like a workout coach or file a complaint, but she didn't have an alibi, and that was most definitely a concern.

"What, Athena? What are you thinking?"

"I don't want you to worry, Selene. If they want to

question you, I'll be right there to make sure they do it properly. When I was a news reporter, I dealt with the police all the time."

"You promise you'll stay with me?"

I held my hand over my heart. "Goddess's honor."

"Athena?"

I turned to see Bob Maguire, a tall, slender, redheaded police officer, standing in the doorway, holding one of the swinging doors open. Maguire was well acquainted with my sisters and me because we'd all attended the same high school. He and I had become friends because we'd both been shunned by the popular kids. Bob had been the class clown. I'd been the class nerd.

Regardless of our friendship, my concern now was how best to protect my sister, so I slid out of the booth and stood in front of Selene so he wouldn't see her tear-streaked face. "Hey, Maguire. What's the news on the groom?"

"You both need to come outside," he said.

His somber look and tone scared me. I smiled and gave him a thumbs-up. "We'll be right out."

As soon as he was gone, Selene said, "He's got bad news. I know he does." She was trembling so hard her teeth were chattering.

"You can do this, Selene. You're goddess of the moon, remember? Fearless and beautiful."

She lifted her head at that and dried her eyes with her fingertips. "You're right. I can do this." At that, she scooted out of the booth, took a deep breath, and squared her shoulders. "Okay, warrior goddess, let's go."

Arm in arm, we walked back outside to find Officer Gomez waiting for us.

"Miss Spencer," he said curtly, giving me a nod.

"Officer Gomez," I said in the same tone.

"Wait here with me, please," he said, "while Officer Maguire makes an announcement."

Selene grabbed my hand and held it tightly.

Officer Juan Gomez, a humorless, twenty-something cop who was fairly new to the force, hadn't liked me since I'd gotten in the way of a police investigation by hiding a man wrongly accused of murder. He'd liked me even less when that man, Case Donnelly, and I had un-covered the true killer's identity before the detectives had.

I glanced around to see Maguire and a third officer talking with Mandy Black and the bride's parents. Mrs. Black had her arms around her distraught daughter, pat-ting her shoulder to calm her while their guests sat frozen to their chairs. The only other movement came from the blue-and-white lights around the patio swaying in the evening breeze.

As the third officer escorted Mandy and her parents out to a waiting car, Maguire stood at the head table, fac-ing the seated group, and said in a loud voice, "Folks, may I have your attention please? I'm afraid we have bad news. The bride has asked us to tell you that her fiancé, Brady Rogers, has passed away."

As horrified gasps ran through the crowd, Selene sagged against me, and it was only by sheer effort that I was able to hold her up. Immediately, Maia was on her other side, helping to keep her on her feet.

"Let's get her to a chair," I said.

"Don't let Mama see her," Maia whispered to me.

"Don't let Mama see who?" Mama asked. "Selene, give me your arm."

"Where are you going?" Gomez snapped to the four of us.

"Right there," Mama said, pointing to the long, empty banquet table three feet away. "Our feet hurt. We're going to sit down."

Gomez gave a curt nod and stepped back, somehow sensing he'd never win a battle against our mother.

We sat down as Bob Maguire held up his hands to get everyone's attention. "You'll all have to remain here for a little while. We'll let you know when you can leave."

"Óxi!" Yiayiá wailed from the kitchen doorway. *No!* She raised her hands to the heavens as though her worst fear had come true. Muttering to herself that the guests were going to starve, she returned to the kitchen.

"I'd better help her pack up the food," Mama said and rose from her chair to bustle in after her, which meant we'd probably be eating chicken, rice, moussaka, pastitsio, and baklava for at least the next week.

I noticed two officers having a hushed conversation with Mandy's bridesmaid, Tonya, then Gomez came over to our table and asked my shivering older sister, "Are you Selene Spencer?"

Selene took my hand again and squeezed it. "Yes."

"Where do you work?"

"At Over the Top hair salon."

"Are you missing a pair of hair scissors?"

She nodded, squeezing my hand tight enough to make it tingle.

"Do you know Brady Rogers?" he asked.

She gave another quick nod and squeezed so hard my pinkie started to go numb. Hello, nerve damage.

"You'll have to come down to the station with us for some questioning."

Selene gripped my hand so hard I winced and pulled it free. "I told you," she whispered.

"Hold on," I said to Gomez, flexing my tingling hand as I got to my feet. "Why can't you talk to her here?"

Gomez stiffened his mouth into a hard line, refusing to answer, but I guessed what the answer was. Someone in the bridal party had informed the officers that the scissors may have belonged to Selene. I could see the three bridesmaids standing in the corner, watching Gomez talking to us. It was all happening too fast. Too coincidental. My intuition was telling me something was seriously off.

Gomez said again. "Selene Spencer, come with me, please."

Selene made a sound like a kitten mewling. Maia put her arm around her shoulders, while I caught Maguire's eye and motioned for him to come over.

"What's up?" Maguire asked quietly.

"Your partner wants to take Selene to the station for questioning," I said.

"Ma'am, they're just routine questions," Gomez said.

I stared him straight in the eye and said, "Then read her the Miranda rights."

"She hasn't been charged with anything," Gomez responded.

"My sister isn't going anywhere until she's been read her rights, and since you don't want to do it, I will." Turning back to Selene I said, "Selene Demetra Spencer, you have the right to remain silent. Anything you say can and will be used against you in a court of law. You have the right to an attorney. If you cannot afford an attorney, one will be provided for you. Do you understand?"

Gomez got the message. He had just been informed

that I wasn't about to let the cops or anyone else run roughshod over someone I loved.

"Selene," Maguire said kindly, "if at any point you don't want to answer the questions or want a lawyer, all you have to do is say so."

She gave a quick nod of her head.

"If you'll accompany me," Officer Gomez said, trying his best to put on a polite face, "the squad car is out front."

"I'm going with her," I said, "as her legal representative."

"When did you become a lawyer?" Gomez asked.

His snide attitude was really getting under my skin. "Then I'm going as her personal representative."

"Me too," Maia said.

By the twitch in his cheek muscle, I could see that Gomez was struggling to keep his temper under control, but I didn't care.

"I've got this, Juan," Maguire said. "Athena, you're welcome to accompany your sister. Maia, you'll need to stay back and explain to the rest of your family what's going on."

"Please do that, Maia," Selene said. "They'll be worried."

"Tell them Bob Maguire will be there with us," I added, then gave Gomez a pointed look.

Throwing me a chilly glance, Gomez led the way to the squad car parked in front of the Parthenon, lights still flashing. A group of passersby had gathered to see what the trouble was.

"Everyone's going to see us," Selene whispered, trying to keep her head turned away.

"Maguire, could you shut off the lights?" I asked, as we climbed into the back seat. "We're drawing a crowd."

"No problem." He switched the lights off, started the engine, and buckled his seat belt as Gomez shut the back door and got into the front passenger seat.

I could feel Selene shaking as we made the quick trip to the police station. I considered calling my ex-boyfriend Kevin Coreopsis, a newly hired defense attorney, but decided to wait to see what their questions were first. Leaning close to my sister, I whispered, "Keep your answers as brief as possible. Yes and no are the best replies. Don't offer any details that aren't absolutely necessary. Okay?"

"Okay," she whispered.

We were taken to a large room filled with desks and officers typing reports and talking on the phone. Maguire positioned an extra chair for me near Selene, then he took a seat at his desk and turned on his computer, while Gomez leaned nonchalantly against a file cabinet to our right, arms crossed.

"Selene," Maguire began, "may I call you Selene?"

"Of course, B—," she started, then whispered to me, "Should I call him Officer Maguire?"

"Bob will do," he said. "We're keeping this informal. I'm going to type notes as you answer questions, okay?" At her nod, he said, "What brand of scissors are you missing?"

"Equinox."

He gave a slight nod, as if that was the answer he was expecting. I took it as a bad sign.

"Tell me when you last saw your scissors."

She glanced my way, and after I gave her an assuring nod, she said, "Yesterday before lunch."

"When did you notice them missing?"

"After lunch."

Before she could elaborate, I gave her foot a gentle nudge.

"I understand that the bride and her bridesmaids were among your customers. Is that right?"

"Just the bridesmaids. Mandy was there, but she used another stylist because we were so busy."

"Did Mandy's stylist report her scissors missing, too?"

"No. In fact, I had to borrow her spare pair."

Maguire halted his fingers on the keypad. "Tell me what happened when you got back from lunch."

"I had a customer waiting, so I called her over to my station, and we discussed what she wanted me to do. Then I washed her hair and brought her back to start cutting. That was when I noticed that my scissors weren't on my tray. I looked in the drawers, I asked the other stylists if they'd seen them or picked them up, and I even checked our break room, but they were gone."

"Could they have fallen into a trash can?" Maguire asked.

Selene shook her head. "I looked in the trash can next to my station. Believe me, I looked everywhere. Good scissors are expensive."

Maguire kept going. "Do you know Brady Rogers?"

"Yes."

"How?"

"In April, I signed up at Fitness First, the gym over by the marina, and he was my workout coach. I stuck it out for a month, but I didn't like Brady, so I quit."

I knew her answer would spark more intense questioning, so I nudged her to remind her to not give so many details.

"Why didn't you like him?" Gomez asked.

"He expected too much from me."

"Meaning?" Gomez asked. I knew he was looking for a way to trip her up.

Selene looked embarrassed as she spoke. "He made advances toward me."

"Did you tell him to stop?" Maguire asked.

"Yes, but he said I should stop whining."

"Did you have any contact with him after that?" Gomez asked.

"No."

"Did he ever ask you why you'd quit the gym?" Gomez asked.

"No."

"Do you have any idea how your scissors could have ended up at his apartment?"

"No."

"Is it possible one of the other stylists borrowed your scissors?"

"They wouldn't have without my permission."

I patted her hand to let her know she was doing a good job.

"Are you willing to take a lie-detector test?" Gomez asked.

"Yes!" Selene said before I could stop her.

"Okay, time out," I said. "If you're going that route, Officer Gomez, we want to consult with a lawyer first."

"Then we'll skip that for now," Maguire said. "Do you know where Brady Rogers lives?"

"No."

"Did he ever ask you out on a date?" Maguire asked.

Selene hesitated, and Gomez perked up. "Yes," she

said slowly, "once, but I didn't like him, so I told him I was seeing someone."

"Are you seeing someone?" Gomez asked.

"Irrelevant!" I cried, standing.

"We're not in a courtroom, Attorney Spencer," Gomez said dryly.

"What did Brady say when you told him you were quitting the gym?" Maguire asked.

"I didn't tell him. I called the office and told them that he'd behaved inappropriately. They had me fill out a complaint form."

"Did he try to persuade you to come back?" Gomez asked.

Selene glanced down. I felt a knot begin in my stomach.

"Miss Spencer, I asked you a question," Gomez said.

"Yes, he called me. He must've gotten my phone number from the office, because I didn't give it to him."

"What did he say?"

"That I had hurt his reputation at the gym, and he wanted to make it right."

"Why do you think he did that?" Maguire asked.

"I don't know, but it didn't seem genuine," she answered.

Gomez prodded further. "How did he behave inappropriately?"

Selene hesitated again. She looked at me for help, so I chimed in, "She already told you how."

Ignoring me, Gomez said, "In other words, you called the manager to get Brady into trouble."

"No, he got himself into trouble," Selene said, showing some of her old fighting spirit. "I made a phone call to cancel my membership and was asked to fill out a complaint form. That was it."

Maguire smiled at that, then said to his partner, "I don't have any more questions."

"I have just one." Gomez paused, studying Selene through narrowed eyes for a long moment before he asked, "Did you have an affair with Brady Rogers?"

"No!" Selene cried. "I told you I couldn't stand him. Besides, I would never do that to Mandy. She's my friend. Athena can vouch for that."

"My sister doesn't lie," I said to Gomez with a scowl. "Selene and Mandy have been friends since high school, as Officer Maguire can testify. Right, Bob?" I turned to give Maguire a pleading look.

"I think we have all we need from her, Juan," Maguire said to his partner.

Gomez motioned for her to stand. "You'll need to step over to the counter to be fingerprinted."

Selene was about to get up, but I grabbed her arm and said to Gomez, "You do understand that if the scissors are hers, her fingerprints will be on them."

Talking to me as though I were a five-year-old, Gomez replied, "Yes, and if anyone else handled them without gloves on, their fingerprints will be on them, too."

His smart-aleck answer brought out my Greek temper. I pulled out my phone and scrolled through my contacts. "I'm calling our attorney right now. And as soon as you fingerprint her, we're leaving."

As Selene accompanied Gomez across the room, I stepped away from the desk for privacy. As much as I hated to do so, I put in a call to Kevin on his personal cell phone line. When he answered, I explained what had happened, and he was gracious enough to set up an appointment for Selene at eight in the morning, an hour before she started work. Then I called Maia and told her to come get us.

"Okay, Miss Spencer," Gomez said, returning with Selene, who looked as though she was ready to throw up, "your sister is free to go home, but as I warned her, she can't leave town."

"On what basis?" I asked.

Selene grabbed my hand as Gomez said, "On Mandy Black's accusation that your sister had an affair with Brady Rogers and then murdered him."

CHAPTER THREE

As Selene broke out in sobs, I stared at Gomez in shock. "Murder? You've got to be kidding. Didn't you hear a word of what my sister told you?"

"We're required to follow up on Miss Black's report, Miss Spencer," Gomez said. "You know that."

"I'm going to be sick," Selene murmured, her arms wrapped tightly around her body.

I was so furious I couldn't think of what to say. I put my hand on Selene's shoulder and looked at the two officers in total shock. In an instant, Selene's life had been turned upside down.

"Athena, take her home," Maguire said. "We can talk to her tomorrow if we need anything else." He pulled a business card out of his shirt pocket and handed it to me. "If you have any questions, feel free to call."

I glanced at it and saw that he'd written his personal

cell phone number on it. I attempted a smile of gratitude and slipped it into my purse.

As we stood on the sidewalk outside waiting for Maia, I put my arm around my terrified sister. "We're seeing Kevin first thing in the morning. He'll help us."

"How can Mandy think *I* murdered Brady?" she cried, wiping her eyes, "or would *ever* have an affair with him? It doesn't make sense."

"That's exactly it, Selene. It doesn't make sense, so we'll get it straightened out."

"Look at this." She held out her hand to show me how it was shaking. "How can I cut hair shaking like this?" Her eyes widened. "What if the police come to the salon to arrest me?"

"Listen to me, Selene. No one is going to charge you with murder as long as I'm able to draw a breath."

As Maia pulled up to the curb in her silver Honda Civic, Selene threw her arms around me and hugged me tightly. "I'm frightened, Thenie. I think I've been set up."

"I know, and now *you* know that I'm here for you. I won't rest until I find out why this is happening. So what do you say we go back to the Parthenon and have a big glass of wine?"

"That sounds wonderful," Selene said as she got into the passenger seat. As I buckled up behind her, she sighed and leaned her head against the headrest. "I could use some of Yiayiá's baklava, too."

I couldn't help but laugh, and that started Selene laughing.

"Hey, don't forget to include me," Maia said, glancing at me in her rearview mirror.

"Did you tell the family what happened?" Selene asked.

"Yep," Maia replied, "and they're all at the diner, waiting anxiously to see you."

Selene dropped her head into her hands. "More questions."

"We'll step in if you feel overwhelmed," I said. "Just try to enjoy your wine and baklava, and picture this all being over tomorrow."

My phone dinged. I pulled it out of my purse and saw a text from Case: **RU free for lunch?**

It was a shock to hear from him, not to mention wonderful to have something else to think about. I texted back: **Sounds great. Pizza food truck in the plaza?**

Case: **As long as I can pick out my own pizza.**

Athena: **Funny man. See you at noon.**

Despite everything that had happened that evening, I couldn't help but smile at Case's text. While working on a very tricky murder investigation, we'd argued over what kind of pizza to order. He was a classic pepperoni guy, whereas I preferred a gourmet spinach-and-goat-cheese pie. The handsome, dark-haired, thirty-five-year-old was still fairly new to Sequoia. Case had traveled here from Pittsburgh a month ago to find an ancient, invaluable statue called *The Treasure of Athena* that had been stolen over a century ago from his great-grandfather's museum in Crete, Greece. As a top-notch research specialist, Case had tracked the statue from Greece to England to the United States and then to Sequoia.

One night while I was alone at the family's garden center, I'd heard a noise in the outdoor garden area and found a strange man kneeling at the base of that same statue, trying to open a hidden compartment with a switchblade. Frightened, I was about to call the police, but he'd persuaded me to listen to his story before I made a judgment. I'd done so warily, and when he'd finished, I'd had to admit his mission was admirable.

But the very next day, Case had been accused of murdering the assistant of the deceased real estate tycoon who'd owned the statue before us. After Case had convinced me that he didn't kill the man, I'd agreed to help him find the real murderer and hid him on the *Páme*, my *pappoús*'s fishing boat. I then had him grow a close-shaved beard, had given him a new hair style, and convinced him to exchange his city attire for that of a Greek fisherman. Being a quarter Greek hadn't hurt him, either. He'd fooled everyone, including my family.

We'd become very close during those weeks of working together, but I'd had no desire to take our relationship any further. I had a son to think of. Plus, I'd just escaped a ten-year marriage to a heel who'd left enough emotional scars to make me wary of ever marrying again.

Still, I couldn't deny the strong chemistry between us, although I'd tried after we'd almost kissed. It had been an electrifying moment, a feeling that my life was about to change forever, followed by elation when he told me he planned to stay in Sequoia. Then he went back to Pennsylvania to move his belongings and somehow fell off the radar. We'd texted a few times after that, and I'd asked him how the move was going. His reply was always that he was tying up loose ends.

I had been on the verge of writing him off—and then his most recent text came in. Now I was elated yet at the same time guarded. Lesson learned.

Maia parked her car in the parking lot across the street from the Parthenon, and we all got out. Just before we entered the diner, Selene said to Maia, "Give me a minute to pull myself together."

"Okay," Maia said. "I'll let them know you're on your way in."

Selene grabbed my wrist and held me back. "I need to tell you something."

Her somber tone pulled me out of my elation over Case's text. The look in her eyes was frightening. Was there more to her story than she'd let on?

Trying not to betray my anxiety, I said, "Go ahead."

In a hushed, hurried voice, Selene said, "As you know, Mandy and her bridesmaids were at the salon the day my scissors were taken—actually, right before I went to lunch. Two of the bridesmaids, Joni and Paulette, were sitting in the waiting area nearby while I finished a client's hair, and Tonya had stepped outside to make a phone call. That was when—"

"Selene, slow down," I said, loosening her grip on my wrist. "You're shaking all over, and you're cutting off my circulation."

"I'm sorry, Thenie."

As I rubbed my hand to bring back the feeling in it, she took a steadying breath and continued. "Anyway, that was when I overheard the two bridesmaids whispering between them that Mandy had learned just a week before that Brady was having an affair. They said she was so upset she was threatening to kill him."

"And then your scissors went missing."

She looked down and nodded, obviously unwilling to accuse her friend.

"Did either bridesmaid say you were the one Brady had been seeing?"

"They were discussing who it could've been but never

mentioned me. Now that I think about it, the way they were looking at me as they were discussing it was almost like they were gauging my reaction, like they thought it was me."

"Did they say how Mandy found out about the affair?"

"No."

"Why didn't you tell the police all this?"

Selene's eyes welled up. "I don't know. Mandy and I are friends. It was just gossip, but thinking back . . ." She trailed off.

"Clearly, Mandy doesn't feel the same way, Selene. You don't owe her any loyalty. You need to let the police know what you overheard, or at least tell Bob Maguire."

"No lectures, Thenie. I'm not going to tell the police. It's their job to investigate Brady's death."

"You don't understand how they work. They latch onto the most likely suspect, and if they have enough evidence to convince the district attorney that they've found the killer, they don't look any further. That's why you have to be up front with them."

She took me by the shoulders and looked me straight in the eye. "Listen to me, Thenie. I'm not going to tell them something I can't verify, and you have to swear you won't either."

I wasn't about to make that promise, not if my sister's future was in jeopardy. So instead I asked, "Why are you protecting Mandy?"

"Because what if the police trip me up and it just makes me look even more guilty? It's my word over hers, and she's got a whole group of friends who will back her up."

"Then we let the evidence do the talking for you. Don't you think it's a little too coincidental that your scissors went missing after Mandy was at Over the Top? Do you see where I'm going with this?"

She dropped her hands and looked down.

I sighed, trying to rub away the building tension in my forehead. "Let me look into it. I won't tell the police anything unless you give me your approval."

"Okay."

"Now let's get inside before Mama sends out a search party."

"Promise you won't say anything to the family. I don't want them to worry."

"Mum's the word." I put my arm around her. "Come on. I haven't seen Nicholas all evening."

As we entered the Parthenon's main dining area, we saw Maia and Delphi coming toward us at a trot. They had indeed been sent to lasso us in. They led us to the outdoor dining area, where we found our parents, grandparents, and my son waiting.

As soon as Nicholas saw me, he ran up and wrapped his arms around me. "I missed you, Mama."

"I missed you, too, Nich—Niko," I said, hugging him back. I just couldn't get used to his newly adopted Greek name. But he liked it, so I made the effort.

"We've got a surprise waiting for you and Aunt Selene," he said, practically dancing in place.

"Show me," I said.

I glanced over and saw that the rest of the family had circled Selene to take turns hugging her before leading her to a chair at one of the long tables, now cleaned of all traces of the dinner. Nicholas and I sat at the end together, watching as Yiayiá brought out a big pan of baklava and Dad poured tall glasses of Greek wine.

Selene hadn't taken one bite of dessert before Mama started asking her for details. I sat quietly as Selene gave them her edited version of the events, ready to jump in if Mama got too nosy. But, instead, Selene's recounting had the desired effect of calming everyone down, all of them assured that the police would be on the hunt for the real killer.

While the family chatted, I went to talk to my dad, who was looking for more wine in the kitchen. He waved his hand at me, knowing already what I was about to say.

"I know. Your sister was in trouble, and family comes first. No need for apologies."

"Thanks, Pops. Did you have to close the garden center early? Did we lose Mrs. Bird's business?"

"Considering Selene's troubles, I did close early. And you know Mrs. Bird. She's all beak and no bite. But I had a long line of angry customers who probably won't come back."

"Are you at the very least considering a seasonal employee?"

"I am now," he answered dryly.

Spencer's had always been a family business, and he liked it that way. No outside hires, ever. I put my hand on his arm. "Let me find someone. It'll make things easier for us, especially now that Selene might need my help, too."

He eyed me curiously. "And why would Selene need your help?"

I smiled and shrugged off his question. "You know, family comes first."

"Uh-huh. Well, then, I'll leave the new hire up to you." As he walked out with the bottle of wine, he added, "As long as you deal with Mrs. Bird tomorrow."

I smiled, but when he left, my thoughts immediately switched back to Selene, and I began to make a mental list of people I needed to talk to. I knew better than to believe the police investigation would be impartial, especially after the district attorney got his hands on the case. As I'd experienced both in Sequoia and in Chicago, once a DA had a viable suspect, he or she often became single-minded in wanting to prove that person's guilt and close the file on the case. I was not going to let that happen to my sister.

Saturday

Spencer's Garden Center was hopping with customers the moment we opened the big red barn doors at nine. Over a century ago, Spencer's had been a horse barn on the very northern edge of Sequoia, the last building on Greene Street. Now, with a brand-new arched roof, big picture windows in front, a high-beamed ceiling, cream-colored shiplap walls, and a shiny oak floor, Spencer's was one of the most attractive buildings on the mile-long stretch of tourist shops.

Just inside Spencer's sat my namesake, a tall marble statue called *The Treasure of Athena.* My *pappoús* had famously purchased the statue at the Talbot estate sale, which had ultimately led me straight into a double homicide investigation. He'd originally wanted to put it in the Parthenon's front entrance, but the statue had been too large for the small diner. So it came to Spencer's.

After learning that the statue was worth a small fortune, being a one-of-a-kind by Antonius, a Greek sculptor, I'd tried to convince Pappoús to sell it, but he loved the statue too much to part with it. So now it greeted customers coming in to buy their garden supplies.

The statue had also become something of a local attraction. After Case and I had solved the Talbot murders, Case, along with the local newspaper, had dubbed me the Goddess of Greene Street, and after that people would come in to take pictures with the statue, and sometimes even with me. I liked to think I'd not only brought a killer to justice but had also brought quite a bit of new business to the old barn.

Beyond the statue, on the left side of the shop, stood the wide, L-shaped checkout counter, and through a doorway behind it, the office where I worked, plus a kitchenette, a bathroom, and a conference room. A wide aisle down the center of the barn led past rows of indoor plants, flowering annuals and perennials, and vegetables on one side, and garden supplies, tools, and decorative pots on the other. Beyond that was a big selection of patio tables and chairs; and all the way at the back sat a long, oak-plank conference table, which we used when Spencer's hosted the monthly Greek Merchants Association (GMA) meetings.

A glass door at the back opened onto our outdoor garden area, situated on an acre lot. Just outside the door, hanging lanterns encircled a cement floor in a ballroom-sized area. There we sold stone, clay, glass, and cement garden sculptures, water fountains, large decorative planters, wrought-iron benches, and all types of patio furniture.

Beyond the cement were the flowering shrubs, yews, small evergreens, and saplings common to most garden centers. The outdoor area was also home to Oscar, our young neighborhood raccoon, who liked to nibble on nuts

A BIG FAT GREEK MURDER

that Delphi kept in a cabinet especially for him. Oscar also liked to steal shiny objects, which we'd learned the hard way.

After finishing my accounting work for the day, I decided to do some preliminary sleuthing, so I did a search for Mandy Black and found a link for her Facebook page. On it were photos of her with Brady and with her bridesmaids. I also saw a picture of her brother, Mitchell, with the caption *Best Man* and lots of photos about the wedding flowers she was considering. Nothing seemed out of the ordinary.

I opened a new tab and did a search for Brady Rogers, which also gave me a link to his Facebook page. There were selfies of him with Mandy, with his groomsmen, and one that appeared to be of him with a bunch of guys at a party. Bachelor party perhaps? There were also many videos promoting himself as a workout trainer at Fitness First. Nothing looked out of the ordinary there either.

I glanced up and caught my dad casting me questioning looks as he came in to refill his coffee cup. It hadn't been the first time, either. Something was up.

"Hey, Pops, is everything okay?"

"Now that you mention it"—he walked over to the door and shut it—"I couldn't help but wonder why you've been so quiet all morning. What's going on in that creative brain of yours?"

"I was just looking for seasonal help."

When he started around the desk, I quickly switched screens.

He stood behind me for a moment, then said, "Are you investigating Brady Roger's death?"

I looked up with an innocent smile. "No. What made you think I was?"

He reached forward to tap the big monitor. "Because you have these two tabs open, one of which says Facebook Mandy Black and the other says Facebook Brady Rogers."

I felt heat rise in my face. "I was just . . . curious."

"Then you're not investigating the murder?"

"Me?" My hand moved immediately to a loose strand of hair. I stopped myself before I started to twirl it, which would have been a dead giveaway that I was lying. It was hard enough to keep a secret from my dad as it was. "I was just snooping around. You know me."

"Yes, I know you," Dad answered. "If you're not investigating the murder, then you must be doing some other kind of research, perhaps for your blog, Goddess Anon?"

CHAPTER FOUR

I nearly swallowed my tongue. "Goddess Anon?"

"You might want to make sure you close all your tabs before you leave the office, Athena."

Oh, dear God. The last thing I needed was for my big Greek family to find out I was poking fun at them. "You haven't told anyone, have you?"

He put his hands on my shoulders. "Not a word to anyone."

I sighed in relief. "Thanks, Pops."

"Your blog has a lot of followers," he said, walking around the desk to take a seat in one of the chairs opposite me. "I'm one of them, by the way."

"Really?"

"You bet. And I never would have guessed it was you if I hadn't noticed that extra tab open on the computer. You've got quite a talent for humor, by the way."

"I have quite the family to provide it."

"True." He crossed his ankle over his knee and folded his hands in his lap, suddenly serious. "What's the story with Selene?"

I caught myself about to twist a lock of hair again, so I slid my hand under my leg instead. "You'll have to ask Selene."

"I did, and she said she's already explained what happened. But I can tell when one of my daughters is hiding something, so now I'm asking you to be frank with me."

"Pops, she made me swear not to tell anyone."

He narrowed his eyes at me. "Am I *anyone*?"

"No, you're a loving, protective father, and I love you, but I also keep promises."

"Athena Demetra Spencer," he said with a glare, "tell me right now. I know how to keep promises, too."

All four of us sisters had the same middle name. When he used it, I knew I was in trouble. Nevertheless . . .

"I can't, Pops."

"Okay, then." He reached for the newspaper on my desk, opened it, and began to read, giving me a chance to escape.

I stood up and moved quietly around the desk toward the door. But as my hand hit the doorknob, Dad said, "Tell me what happened with Selene, or I'll tell the family your secret."

I swiveled around. "You said you wouldn't tell anyone."

Without taking his eyes from the paper he said, "Correction. I *haven't* told anyone. I never said I wouldn't."

And I hadn't asked him to promise. With a frustrated sigh, I returned to the desk and sat down, waiting until he lowered the paper. A moment later, he looked over the page at me, clearly not reading. He knew he had me.

"Okay, here it is. But this time, you have to promise not to tell Selene that you know. It's her story to tell."

"I promise, Athena. The only way I would ever break a promise is if someone would be in jeopardy because of it. Understand?"

"I get it."

"So spill, daughter of mine."

He made me smile for the first time that morning. "Okay, this is it. Mandy Black told the police that Selene was having an affair with Brady, and that when Brady wouldn't call off his wedding, Selene stabbed him."

My dad didn't seem shocked by the news. He simply folded the newspaper, set it back on the desk, and steepled his fingers under his chin. "I have a hard time believing any of that is true."

"It doesn't matter what you believe, as long as the police believe Mandy. And they're going to zero in on Selene unless I do something about it."

Delphi rapped on the door then peered in. "Here you are. Why was the door shut?"

"I shut it by habit," Dad said. "Come on in."

She floated in wearing a long, multi-colored skirt, yellow knit top, and her ever-present green flip-flops. Dropping into the chair next to Dad, she said, "So what are we discussing?"

"Don't we have customers out there?" I asked.

"You bet," she said calmly. "Yet here you two sit while I'm out there running in circles, which is so not good for my chakras. But it's nice and quiet in here. Oh, and Mrs. Bird just walked in, by the way."

Dad stood up and stretched his back. "Okay, okay. I'm coming."

"We could use your help out there too, Thenie," Delphi added.

"She's got a lot of work to do here," my dad said. "I can handle old Mrs. Bird." As they left, Dad paused to glance back at me, mouthing, "You owe me."

I gave him a thumbs-up and returned to my research. But after an hour of total frustration, I decided that I needed to tap Case's expertise.

I glanced at my watch. Another half hour until time to leave for our lunch date . . . Make that lunch. Just lunch. No date.

Muttering that to myself, I closed all the tabs on the computer and went up front to take a turn behind the cash register.

The late May weather was pleasant, so I walked the short distance to Central Plaza. I spotted Case standing in line at the pizza truck, and my heart immediately sped up. He was dressed in a short-sleeved, navy-and-white plaid shirt, dark blue jeans, and navy boat shoes. Since I'd last seen him, he'd regrown the closely cropped beard that had been part of his Greek fisherman disguise, a beard that he'd once claimed to hate. His dark hair was no longer parted on the side and combed off his forehead but was back to the wavier look I'd fashioned for him to make him fit in with the Greek crowd.

"Hey, stranger," I said, trying to act nonchalant. "Long time no see. Did you get swallowed by a whale or what?"

"Just busy with a new business venture. I'll tell you about it over lunch."

"I notice that you went back to the Grecian look."

"Yep." He rubbed his beard. "Women seem to like it."

There was the reason why I didn't want to open my heart. Women found Case very attractive, and he didn't seem to mind at all. A little green imp called jealousy wanted to ask him *which* women, specifically, he was referring to; then I gave myself a mental slap. *None of your business, Athena. He's a free agent.*

Then why was I starting to sweat? The temperature had barely made it to seventy degrees. I fanned my face, hoping to keep it from turning red. "Must be the sun," I muttered.

"Are you talking about that big golden orb in the sky?" Case asked, holding his hand over his eyes as he gazed upward. "I'd say it must be the sun, too."

Had I said that out loud? Now I *was* blushing.

"How's Niko?" Case asked.

Thank goodness. A change of subject. "He's fine. Enjoying school but eager to be done for the summer. School is officially out on Thursday . . . Your new business venture wouldn't be babysitting, would it?"

Case let out a laugh, then stepped aside while I ordered my feta cheese and spinach pie.

"How's your family?" he asked as we picked up our iced teas.

"Still crazy."

"Ah."

"What's even crazier"—I paused as he pointed out an empty picnic table—"is that Selene has been accused of murder."

Case nearly spilled his tea. He set it on the table and wiped his hand with a napkin. "I did *not* see *that* coming."

CHAPTER FIVE

"Do you want to talk about it?" Case asked.

"You go first. Tell me about your business venture."

"After you dropped a bomb like that in my lap? Not on your life. What happened?"

I gave him a rundown of everything I had learned about Brady Rogers, including why Selene had quit the gym; rumors of her affair with Brady; Mandy's ridiculous accusation of murder; and Selene's police interrogation. Then I sat back while he digested the information. Our names were called, so Case went up to the truck to pick up our orders. When he returned, we each took a slice of our pie and began to eat.

"What I don't understand," I said between bites, "is how Mandy could accuse Selene, since they've been friends since high school. In fact, Mandy even asked Selene to fill in for an ailing bridesmaid just a week before the murder. You'd think if she suspected Brady and Selene of having an affair, she wouldn't have wanted my sister anywhere near him, especially at her wedding.

"What's worse is that Selene didn't tell the police that Mandy and her bridesmaids were in the hair salon an hour before Selene's scissors went missing. It would have been the perfect opportunity for Mandy to take them."

"Or one of her bridesmaids," Case said.

"But they weren't about to marry Brady." I took a sip of tea. "I know Selene is going to be the police's prime suspect. She had the means—her scissors. She had a motive—the bad blood between her and Brady. She also had the opportunity, because in accordance with police thinking, she has no alibi. She was alone at her apartment when Brady was murdered. That reminds me. I need to find out the official time of death."

I remembered the business card in my purse and began to dig for it. "And I know just how to get it. Bob Maguire gave me his phone number and told me to call if I had any questions. And here it is." I held up the card for Case to see.

"So you've decided to conduct your own investigation?"

"You bet I have."

"Why does this sound familiar?"

Ignoring his reference to our first case, I said, "I started researching Brady's and Mandy's background, but I got frustrated when I couldn't find anything useful. I know you have the expertise, so I was wondering . . ." I let my sentence drift off and gave him a hopeful glance.

"This also sounds familiar." Case put down his slice and wiped his fingers on a napkin. "So the Goddess of

Greene Street is back in action. Tell you what. I'll do the research for you and help you with the investigation on one condition."

"And that is?"

He took another bite and carefully wiped his mouth, letting me wait for it. Then he leaned forward to look me in the eyes. "You have to convince your *pappoús* to sell me his boat."

I blinked twice, my mouth open in total shock. "You still want to buy the *Páme*?"

"Buy it, refurbish it, and live in it," he said with a smile, "with your help, of course. I've also been doing a lot of research on my new business venture, and I want your input. Do we have a deal?"

I couldn't help but smile back. Case had been given permission to stay on the boat after he'd helped solve our investigation and secured my *pappoús* as the rightful owner of the statue, but I didn't realize he'd actually want to live there. I was happy at the thought "We have a deal."

He rubbed his hands together. "Where and when do we start?"

"That's the hard part. What I really want to do is have a little chat with Mandy Black. She seemed all too eager to pronounce Brady dead, even before the police did, but I doubt she'll want to speak with me. So I went through her social media profile, but all I can tell is that she has very expensive tastes. Brady's social media looked pretty clean, too. That's where you come in."

"Text me their full names, and I'll see what I can find," he said as he wiped his mouth and pulled out his phone. "Then what?"

"Then we need to start interviewing people, but the

problem is, I don't want anyone to know that I'm Selene's sister when—"

"—everyone thinks Selene is the murderer," Case finished.

"Exactly."

"We could always change your appearance. You could
get a tan, grow a beard, wear really uncomfortable
shoes."

I gave a friendly, mocking laugh in response. When I'd
met him, he was wanted by the police and had his picture
plastered all over town. I'd thought the disguise was a
great idea. "It worked, didn't it?"

Case flashed his bold, charming smile, creasing his
eyes and dimpling his cheeks ever so lightly. He touched
my wrist and goose bumps ran up my arm. "I'm a free
man, thanks to you. So, yes, it did work."

Yes, he was a free man, I reminded myself. I pulled my
hand away gently to retrieve my pizza and continued
after a small bite. "I figure we should start with the people who knew Brady and Mandy very well—bridesmaids,
groomsmen, friends, coworkers, that sort of thing."

"Let's start slowly," he suggested. "Start with the
second-tier people, like you said, coworkers. Where does
Mandy and did Brady work?"

"I found out that Brady worked at a gym. I don't know
what Mandy does."

"I'll see what I can find out," he said. "In the meantime, we start with the people who worked with Brady to
see what they can tell us. Then we interview the groomsmen and see if the stories match. What do you think?"

"I like it. Tomorrow is Sunday, the gym is open, and
I'm free all afternoon."

"That's fine by me. Do you want me to contact the groomsmen?"

"And say what?"

"That we've been hired to investigate Brady's death."

"Hired by whom?"

"I'm sorry, miss," he said in a deep professional tone, "I'm not allowed to give out that information."

"That works," I said.

"Text me their names, and I'll get on it today."

"Even better, give me your phone, and I'll type in their names."

As he handed it to me, I said, "Just one caveat. When we interview Brady's coworkers, I'll go by the name Karras, my mother's maiden name."

"Even if you change your name, won't they recognize you?"

"Not Brady's coworkers. They've never seen me. As for everyone else, I guess we'll have to cross that bridge when we come to it. I'm not good at undercover work."

"I've noticed," he said. "You're a terrible liar."

I slapped him playfully and said, "I'm getting better. Here, listen. You are a very handsome man, and I enjoy spending time with you. How was that?"

Case took my hand and smiled as only he could. "You know, I'm really excited to be working with you again." I was about to melt when he added, "How was that?"

Once again, I pulled my hand away and lifted my drink to my lips. "Didn't buy it for a second."

"Right. And just to be clear, what's the deal with us? What are we calling our relationship?"

I froze mid-sip. The iced tea began to trickle down the side of my mouth. I swallowed quickly and responded, "Relationship?"

"You and me. Are we partners now, or am I still your cousin from Tarpon Springs?"

My shoulders eased, and my mind flashed back to our first murder investigation. Not only had I been charged with finding a convincing disguise for Case Donnelly, but I'd also had to come up with a reason for him being in town. "We don't have to pretend to be related, but we can pretend to be partners."

"Why do we have to pretend?" he asked, his eyebrows pulling together.

I opened my mouth, but I didn't have an answer. The word *partner* seemed to stick in my throat, and I found myself pondering the double meaning and why that felt threatening.

Case chewed his last bite and cocked an eyebrow, waiting for my reply.

"Okay, partner," I said, "I'll talk to my grandfather about the boat the next time I see him."

He smiled and took a drink. "You know, if I buy your grandfather's boat, I might actually have to meet your family."

I finished typing the names of Brady, Mandy, and the groomsmen into Case's phone and handed it back to him. "It's not like I'm afraid to introduce you to them. They're just . . . a lot to handle. Plus, you've been MIA for weeks. No phone calls. No texts. What's that all about?"

"I'm sorry I haven't kept in touch. I had a lot to do. Uprooting my entire life to come to Sequoia hasn't been a piece of cake. Plus, I wanted to surprise you with my new business idea."

"Does that mean you're going to put roots down here?" I asked, feeling that tiny buzz of excitement fluttering in my stomach.

"More like an anchor if everything works out the way I hope."

"What do you mean?"

"I want to run a charter-boat fishing service, but I still need to figure out how to finance my business. Know any friendly bankers?"

"Yes, the banker who handles the garden center's business. He's at Sequoia Federal. I'll text you his info when I get back to work."

"Thanks." He finished his iced tea, wiped his mouth, and sighed. "Good pizza."

"I agree." I ate the last bite, balled up my napkin, and rose. "Speaking of work."

"What time do you want to meet up at the fitness club tomorrow?"

"How about two o'clock?" I pointed north. "It's called Fitness First, and it's about three blocks straight north of Spencer's on Greene Street. There's a marina right behind it."

"Got it."

Case rose, and we both reached for the paper plates, laughing awkwardly when our hands touched. "I'll take care of these," he said. "See you tomorrow, Goddess Athena."

I watched him gather up the plates and napkins and drop them into the recycling can before striding across the street. I stared after him for a moment, sighed, then caught myself and quickly headed toward Spencer's.

Sunday

I glanced at my watch, then looked down the sidewalk toward the marina. Two p.m. Where was Case? I checked my purse to make sure I'd brought my iPad, then cupped my hands around my eyes to peer through the large plate-glass window. I saw a row of people sitting on exercise bikes a few feet back from the window, cycling furiously. Case was seated near the end of the row, and he waved when he saw me.

I quickly pulled my hands away from the glass and walked toward the entrance. An overwhelming collection of smells greeted me. Body odor, deodorant, sweat, and a mixture of cleaning chemicals almost stopped me in my tracks, but I forced myself inside and took a quick look around. The front desk was unmanned. Motivational posters and signs hung on one wall, and the other was just one big mirror.

I saw the gym through a set of glass double doors: one main room filled with bikes, two rowing machines, four treadmills, and several weight machines. I wandered up the hallway to my left and found a room devoted to private workout sessions. To my right was a Pilates/yoga room. Beyond that were the showers and bathrooms, and then the manager's office.

I came back out to the front desk, and still no one greeted me. I looked into the gym and saw Case say something to an attractive blond woman seated next to him. Case saw me and waved, and then she waved, too, and my jaw dropped. It was Lila Talbot, Sequoia's richest resident, a new heiress who'd acquired the entire Talbot estate after her husband was found guilty of murder, thanks to Case and me.

Much to my dismay, she'd also acquired the hots for my partner when we'd helped put Sonny Talbot in prison. We'd had to interview Lila twice during our first investigation, and both times she had come on to him in a big way. Lila would have been behind bars if it weren't for our investigation, and at that moment, I wondered if that wouldn't have been so bad. Because there she was, seated right next to him. What a coincidence.

I tried to open the doors, but they were locked. Case said something to Lila as he got off the bike; then he strode toward me, wiping his forehead with a towel that hung around his neck. He exited the gym and came to open the doors for me, striding confidently in his navy tank top, displaying a well-developed torso, a pair of white workout shorts, and matching sneakers.

"Right on time," he said, glancing at his watch.

"And so is Lila," I muttered under my breath.

"I'm sorry. I didn't catch that."

"I said how long have you been here?"

"About half an hour."

"You just strolled in here and started using the equipment?" *Had I actually said that? Where was that jealousy coming from?*

"No," he said good-naturedly, "I strolled into the manager's office to join the club, *then* strolled over to the bikes."

"And took the seat next to Lila," I muttered under my breath.

"I caught that remark, and yes, I did, because it was the only one open."

How convenient for Lila.

Case wiped his face and hung the towel around his neck again "Ready to go to work?"

"Yep. Let's start by talking to the club—"

"Done."

"—manager." I narrowed my eyes at him. "Did you also talk to the workout trainers?"

"No, I waited for you." With a smile, he took my arm and steered me around the empty front desk.

"The workout room is back here," Case said. "Only two trainers are in today, but that should give us a start. One is named Tom, and the other is Terrence. The manager said that Brady was really going to be missed. Apparently, they were all pretty upset when they heard of his death, so tread lightly."

"Good to know," I said as I followed Case back through the glass doors. Instantly, I could feel Lila's gaze on me, but I ignored her. Still, I could feel heat rising up my neck as I asked, "Did you question the manager about Selene?"

"I did."

"And?" I asked, trying my hardest to focus my thoughts as we passed Lila.

"Selene did just as she told you. She filed a complaint against Brady and then ended her gym membership." He pulled out his phone. "I took a photo of the complaint as proof. He also told me that Selene's complaint wasn't the first one he'd received, and he'd also warned Brady that if there were any more, he'd be fired."

"That verifies Selene's statement. She'll be happy to hear that."

"I also contacted the groomsmen." Case stopped by a table to pick up his gym bag, put away his towel, and take a long drink of water from the water fountain nearby. "I set up a meeting with Patrick Dean and Trevor Kapellakis at twelve thirty Tuesday at the Blue Moon Café."

"Wow, that was fast. Did you learn anything about Mandy Black?"

"I sure did, and I found out that she has more than just expensive tastes." He nodded toward the two muscle-bound men on the other side of the gym. "Let's get this interview over with, and I'll tell you more about it."

One of the trainers was working with a client on a TRX machine, and the other was cleaning a set of weights with a sanitary wipe. We headed toward him, and as he threw the wipe in a wastebasket nearby, I said, "Hey, there. Are you busy?"

"Nope," he answered pleasantly. He wiped his brow with a large sweatband around his wrist, flashing his bulging biceps and forearms. He was wearing a white tank top with the gym's logo stretched across the chest.

"Great. Let me start with introductions. I'm Athena Karras, and this is Case Donnelly."

"Terrence Shaw," he said, shaking each of our hands in turn. "How can I help you?"

"We were wondering if you could give us some information about Brady Rogers."

His friendly manner changed to skepticism. "What's your connection to Brady?"

I had to pause for a moment to think so I didn't give away that I was Selene's sister. "I'm a friend of Brady's fiancée, Mandy Black. We're private investigators looking into Brady's death." All true. We *were* privately investigating it.

"Hold on." Terrence glanced over at the other trainer, saw that he was finished with his client, and motioned him over. He introduced us to Tom, explained our connection, and then crossed his arms as though he wasn't happy about our being there.

Tom sat down on a free-weight bench and asked brusquely, "What do you need to know?"

I took my iPad out of my purse and went to the file

marked QUESTIONS. "First of all, I'm sorry for your loss. I'm guessing you guys were close. We're trying to make certain that Brady's killer comes to justice, and we'd like your help."

They both nodded in appreciation but didn't say a word.

"Did Brady ever mention any problems between him and Mandy?" I asked.

Tom shook his head, and Terrence answered with a quick "No."

"Have you ever seen or heard anything to make you believe Brady was in any danger?"

Same wooden response.

I looked down at my notes and realized that there was no way to tread lightly with the questioning from that point on.

While I was trying to figure out the best strategy, Case asked bluntly, "Was Brady cheating on Mandy?"

I looked at him in shock.

The trainers exchanged glances but didn't reply.

"It's all right," Case said. "We'd already suspected that he was."

Tom scratched the back of his neck, saying hesitantly, "He might have mentioned there was another woman a time or two."

"Did he say who the woman was?" Case asked both men.

"Not to me." Terrence checked the time on his watch.

"Me neither," Tom said, standing up. "I've got another client due any minute, so Ter, I think you can take it from here."

"Thanks for your help, Tom," I called as the trainer returned to the TRX.

"Folks, I've got a client coming in, too"—Terrence directed our attention to the clock on the wall—"in five minutes."

I glanced down at my notes, then continued quickly, "When did Brady start mentioning this other woman?"

He paused to think. "Maybe a month ago."

"Did you ever see her?" I asked.

"If she was a member of the gym, then I may have seen her, but he never pointed anyone out to me."

"Did he ever say she was a member of the gym?" I asked.

Terrence inhaled deeply and let the breath out slowly, thinking carefully about his reply. "Not in so many words. Let's just say that Brady paid special attention to a lot of the women here. It's not a crime, but once in a while some of these women took his *interest*"—he used his fingers to make quote marks around the word interest—"seriously."

"Did it ever get to the point of causing a problem?" I asked.

"He was given several reprimands," Terrence said. "As far as I know, that was it."

"What about the women who took him seriously but *didn't* complain?" Case added. "Have you noticed any of these women hanging around lately?"

"Not lately, no," Terrence answered. "There was a woman Brady dated a while ago who would harass him from time to time, but I don't know her name and haven't seen her lately. Nothing has seemed out of the ordinary. Believe me, Brady's death came as a total shock to us."

I typed in his answer, then looked at Case. "Anything you want to add?"

"I think we've covered everything." Case reached out to shake his hand. "Thanks for your help."

"No problem," the trainer said. "Good luck."

As we left the gym and started toward the marina, I heard a woman call, "Case, wait up."

I turned to see Lila hurrying after us. She was wearing a low-cut, skin-tight gold top with snakeskin yoga pants, and gold sneakers. She pulled the ponytail holder out of her blond hair and shook it loose, which seemed an obvious ploy to get Case's attention.

"I'm glad I caught you before you left," she said, directing her comment to Case. "Hi, Athena. How are you?" She immediately turned back to Case. "I've been thinking about your charter-boat business."

He'd told Lila the details of his new venture?

"How do you plan to finance your boats?" she asked.

"I'm still trying to work that out," Case answered.

And I'd totally forgotten to grab the banker's number like I'd promised I would.

"I have an idea," she said. "Let me introduce you to a few friends of mine. I'm sure one of them will be able to help."

"I'd appreciate that," Case said. "Thanks."

"I'll give you a call as soon as I set something up." She opened up her tote bag and pulled out her phone. "What's your cell number?"

As Case dictated his number, leaning in to look at her screen, I crossed my arms and glanced away. Why was I jealous? I had no claim on Case.

"There," she said, then tucked the phone in her purse

as she gazed up at him with her big Barbie Doll eyes. She patted his arm and said in a sexy voice, "I'll be in touch soon."

As we walked toward the marina, Case gave me a hopeful smile. "My charter service may get off the ground faster than I thought."

That wasn't all that was getting off the ground. Obviously, he wasn't seeing what I was seeing—that Lila was up to her old tricks. Yet what could I say? What he did wasn't any of my business.

Or so I told myself.

CHAPTER SIX

"So what did we learn today?" Case asked.

As we walked toward my SUV I pushed Lila as far back in my mind as I possibly could and refocused on our investigation. "We learned that Brady had a girlfriend before Mandy, and that he was seeing someone while he was engaged to Mandy, which verifies what Selene overheard the bridesmaids saying. And that brings the question to my mind about how Mandy discovered that Brady was having an affair. Did she catch them? Did someone tell her? And the biggest question: did she take matters into her own hands and kill him?"

"How much do you know about Mandy Black?"

"Just that she comes from a wealthy family, and she and Selene were friends in high school."

"I did some research on Miss Mandy Black. Did you

know her father owns two hotels, one of them being the Waterfront Hotel right here in downtown Sequoia?"

"Wow. I didn't realize they had that much money. The Waterfront Hotel is a luxury hotel on the water. I've never seen the inside, but I've read about the lavish banquets they hold there. It's quite a wedding destination, too, so I wonder why they didn't have the rehearsal dinner there."

"We'll have to put it on the list of questions for her."

"Did you learn anything about her brother, Mitchell?"

"Not yet, why?"

"Because now that I think back, Mitchell was acting strangely at the dinner. He kept checking his watch, acting very put out. Maybe it was just because Brady was late. He was Brady's best man. At any rate, it struck me as odd."

"Then let's put the question on a list for him. I'll contact him after I get back to the boat."

My phone buzzed with an incoming text. It was from my mother: **Are you still at Spencer's?**

"I've got to go," I said. "My mother is looking for me, and I promised my dad I'd take a quick lunch. Spencer's has been crazy busy this week."

"What are you doing for dinner?"

"Our Karras family dinner is always on Sunday, with my entire family present, including my aunts and uncles. Talk about crazy."

As was the custom, our big Greek family gathered at my parents' house later that day for a traditional Sunday meal. The Spencer home wasn't a mansion by any means, but it suited our large family well, especially after my sister Delphi was born, when my dad and Pappoús knocked down the wall between the living and dining room and made one large gathering room.

We took our customary seats around a long, hand-crafted, olivewood dining table that had been handed down to my *yiayiá* from her mother, finding its way via a ship to its Michigan home. It was draped with an intricately cross-stitched cloth cover and filled with platters of lamb and rice, chicken cooked with roasted potatoes, moussaka, dandelion greens in lemon butter, tomato salad with feta cheese, and kalamata olives.

My father and grandfather had the place of honor at each end of the table, with my mother and grandmother on Dad's left, nearest to the kitchen. Next to them were Maia, Selene, and Delphi, who was seated directly across from me. To my father's right were my Aunt Talia and Uncle Konstantine, followed by Uncle Giannis, Aunt Rachel, and Nicholas and myself, with Pappoús at the foot.

On the plus side, I wasn't near Uncle Giannis, who had the most irritating habit of talking with his mouth full and slurping whenever he drank. What made it more annoying was Aunt Rachel's shrill harping every time she caught him doing it. On the minus side, I was so far away from my father that over all their chatter and Giannis's slurping, I couldn't hear a word he was saying.

"The article in the paper mentioned a pair of scissors, Selene," Uncle Giannis said between noisy sips, breaking into my thoughts.

I found myself gritting my teeth. Throughout our meal, every time Uncle Giannis brought up the murder, either Dad, Mama, Maia, or I would change the topic, only to have Giannis switch it back, making Selene so tense she could barely finish her dinner.

"You're doing it again, Giannis," Aunt Rachel said. "For heaven's sake, close your mouth."

Nicholas put his hand over *his* mouth, trying to hold back a laugh. I poked him gently and chomped down on my food, making him double over in silent hysterics.

"Time for dessert," my mother announced, scooting back her chair. As she and Yiayiá headed for the kitchen, my sister Maia kept the conversation moving by purposely bringing up a taboo subject, her decision to be a vegetarian, which always set off a heated debate.

"Don't think of lamb as a meat," Uncle Konstantine kept shouting, pounding the table with his fist.

"Then what is it? A member of the onion family?" my aunt Rachel argued back.

Finally, Mama brought out a platter heaped with the traditional Greek cookies called *kourabiedes* and wedges of baklava for dessert. Yiayiá followed behind, carrying two pitchers of sweet Greek coffee.

The table conversation slowed as the large quantities of food settled in our full bellies. Unfortunately, Giannis once again started in on the murder. I could tell Selene was struggling to keep her cool, so I glanced at Maia, who gave me a helpless shrug, letting me know she had run out of topics. I glanced at Delphi for help and noticed her swirling the grounds at the bottom of her coffee cup, so I nudged her ankle under the table. When she looked up, I gave her a slight tip of my head toward Giannis and picked up my own cup, hoping she'd understand.

She closed her eyes and began to hum the Yogi chant "ohm." Her second round of "ohms" drew everyone's attention. After her third chant, she opened her eyes and tilted her head as though listening to something no one else could hear. Then she held out her hand. "I need your cup, Uncle Giannis. Would you finish your coffee, please?"

I noticed Selene's shoulders relax. Delphi the Oracle was about to perform a miracle.

She swirled the soggy grounds for a few moments and then stopped, studying them intently. Her eyes opened wide, then she shook her head no and swirled again. And once again, after she'd stopped, her eyes opened wide. She turned to look at Giannis, blinking several times, and then gave a nod to someone unseen.

"What do you see?" Uncle Giannis asked, after clearing the lump in his throat.

"Do you take a D-Mannose supplement?" my sister asked.

"A D-Mannose supplement?" Giannis asked. "For what?"

Angrily, Delphi said, "Do you take a D-Mannose supplement or not? Yes or no!"

Giannis swallowed again. "No."

"I'm seeing a D and an M. Does that mean anything to you?"

"What the hell?" Giannis asked, glancing at his wife for backup.

"Focus, Uncle G," Delphi said. "I see a D and an M very clearly."

"Drew and Michael?" Giannis turned his head toward his wife, then swiveled in his chair toward Delphi. "Is something wrong with my boys? Are they in danger?"

Delphi pressed her lips tightly together, as though she had made a mistake. She shot me a quick glance, and I saw in her eyes that she had no idea what to say next.

And then I had a brilliant idea. "Giannis, I think I know what she means."

He turned to me, red in the face. "Tell me. What?"

"Your boys will be back from college soon, right? Would either of them be interested in a summer job at the garden center?"

His worry lines decreased in size as Aunt Rachel pulled the cloth napkin from her lap and wiped the sweat from his large brow. "I don't know," Giannis said. "I'd have to ask them."

"We could use some help ASAP, right, Pops? So let me know when you talk to them. The pay is good, and the hours are even better." I smiled at my own brilliance. In one fell swoop, I had helped switch the focus from Selene, saved the failed psychic attempt by Delphi, and possibly managed to find a new hire who was still within the family.

"Wait a minute. What was it about D-Mannose?" our very nervous uncle asked.

"Nothing," Delphi said. "Forget I said that . . . unless you're having trouble with your bladder."

Uncle Giannis thrust his chair back and stood up, suddenly in a hurry. "Rachel, it's getting late. We're going to have to say good-bye now."

Aunt Rachel rose obediently and followed him to the foyer. Mama hurried ahead to take their jackets from the coat closet. I saw Giannis whisper something to my mother, then head toward the bathroom up the front hallway.

I had to duck my head and bite my lower lip to keep from laughing. I glanced up at Delphi and saw her very calmly place Giannis's cup down and say, "What did I miss?"

* * *

After everyone had gone home, my sisters, Nicholas, and I helped Mama and Yiayiá clean up. As we washed and dried the dishes, Selene said, "Thanks for your help, Delph. I thought I was going to lose it."

"We could tell," Maia said, "but Athena was the one who came up with the best solution."

"That was a great idea, Thenie," Dad said as he brought in the coffeepots. He stopped next to Delphi. "What is D-Mannose for anyway?"

"For urinary tract infections," Maia said. "That was brilliant, Delph. Very funny."

Delphi tilted her head. "Thanks, but it wasn't my idea." She rolled her eyes heavenward.

No one said a word after that.

I was just about to head up the back staircase to read Nicholas a bedtime story when Mama called, "Athena, I have good news."

I had a sinking feeling about where this was going.

"I found the perfect man for you," she said, coming toward me. "His name is Thomas Gabris, he's forty years old, and he's a plastic surgeon making very good money. He would like to pick you up at six thirty tomorrow for dinner."

"I don't think so," I answered quietly.

"But he's a plastic surgeon!" she said. "Imagine the work he could do."

"Are you saying I need a facelift?"

"Not you," Mama said, eyeing herself in the mirror next to the stairwell.

"Mama, you are and always will be beautiful."

"Thank you, sweetheart."

"And no more blind dates," I said, emphasizing each word.

"But you need to find a good Greek boy while you're still in your childbearing years. Think of little Niko. He needs a brother or sister. You can even wear your pretty green dress that sets off your fair hair."

Now she was even selecting my wardrobe. Even though her heart was in the right place, mine wasn't. There was no way I was about to endure another torturous blind date.

I knew there was only one way to put her off. "Let me sleep on it tonight and tell you my answer in the morning."

"Good." She gave me a kiss on the cheek and went into the living room to sit beside my father and watch TV.

I went upstairs to the bathroom and splashed water on my face. My mother had also coordinated the reintroduction of Kevin Coreopsis upon my arrival back in Sequoia, and what a huge mistake that had been.

Kevin and I had dated for a short while in high school, then had gone our separate ways—me to college to earn a degree in journalism and Kevin to law school, after which he spent a few miserable years in Manhattan being what he described as a high-powered New York attorney.

When he came back to town to, as he put it, "find his roots" and start up a new law career, Mama decided that Kevin would be the perfect match for me. Thus, I suffered through a few weeks of dating Kevin but, unfortunately for Mama, also found him to be a complete bore. Later, he betrayed me by accepting a job with Grayson Talbot Jr., who almost had me killed for investigating a murder.

While Kevin had ultimately come to my rescue, the animosity between us was still palpable. That was why I didn't even want to think about going on another blind date. Somehow, I had to come up with an excuse to cancel the date.

With that in mind, I went to Nicholas's room to read him another chapter of *Harry Potter and the Sorcerer's Stone.*

Monday

Mondays were always slow at Spencer's, even during the summer months, which was perfectly fine with me because I was on edge as I waited to hear about Selene's early meeting with Kevin. The weather couldn't have been more perfect for the tourists who were coming back after a long, cold winter. The sun was peeking out from behind fluffy white clouds. The westerly wind brought with it the smell of the lake and the miles of sand along the lake front. And the temperature hovered around seventy degrees.

I'd worn a light navy swing coat over my red-and-white print shirt and navy slacks, but I probably wouldn't need the coat by lunchtime. Rounding out my outfit were my butter-soft navy leather loafers and my bargain-basement designer purse, also in navy. If my years in Chicago had taught me anything, it was how to put together a chic outfit on a shoestring budget.

While waiting for Selene to report back after her call from Kevin, I spent the first hour placing orders for Spencer's, then took my laptop and a cup of coffee outside to the patio area in the back to design a landscape plan for a new client. I sat at a black wrought-iron table, opened the design app, and selected the shrubs for the front of the house: a large blue hydrangea on each side of the front door, followed by an American cranberry bush

viburnum, three white flowering cotoneasters, with a tall
leatherleaf viburnum at the outside corners of the house,
and large Grecian-style vases on the porch filled with
bright pink diplodenias, white petunias, a green spike in
the center, and sweet potato vines trailing down the sides.

Just as I was about to save the file, I caught sight of a
little black-masked face peering over the fence at me.

I glanced around to be sure there weren't any customers
in the area, then said, "Oscar, what are you up to?"

He climbed onto the top of the fence and leaped onto
the table, sniffing around to see if I had any food. I got
up, went to the outdoor storage cabinet, and opened a
plastic container filled with peanuts. I took a handful
back to the table and sat down, holding them out while he
fished each one daintily out of my hand, put it in his
mouth, chewed it up, then sniffed around for more.

"That's all, Oscar. You've had enough."

He tilted his head as though trying to understand, then
took a few hops to the table's edge, leaped off, and began
to check out the garden area for more treats.

I watched for a moment, then remembered I hadn't
phoned Bob Maguire yet. I put in a call, but it went to his
voicemail, so I left a message asking him to phone me
back.

"Thenie, your new client called," Delphi said, stepping out from the doorway. "She wants to meet with you
this afternoon, if you have time." She handed me the
message, then spotted Oscar, and her eyes lit up. Holding
out her hand, she walked toward him, her bright purple-
and-white skirt swirling around her. "Oscar," she called,
"come here."

Like a small puppy, Oscar hopped over to her and allowed her to pet him.

"Delph, would you call her back and tell her four o'clock is perfect?"

"Sure."

I gathered my computer and coffee mug and headed inside. My phone rang, and I fished it out of my pocket to see Bob Maguire's name on the screen.

"Thanks for returning my call, Bob," I said. "I was wondering if you could tell me what time Brady Rogers died."

"Any particular reason?"

As I was trying to come up with a believable lie, he said, "You know what? Let's just say you're curious, and leave it at that. Hold on for a moment while I see what I can find out."

I closed the office door and sat down at the desk. Bob came back a few minutes later to say, "The approximate time of death was between ten a.m. and noon."

I jotted it down. "Thanks, Bob. I really appreciate your help."

I was just ready to put my phone in my pocket when it rang again, and Selene's name popped up on the screen. "Good news, I hope?" I answered.

She started to cry, and my heart jumped to my throat.

CHAPTER SEVEN

"What happened?"

"Kevin," she said sniffling back tears, "said that the police found a bloody T-shirt stuffed in the dumpster behind the hair salon. I told him it couldn't have been me who did it because I wasn't at the salon the day of the murder."

"What did he say to that?"

"All Kevin would say was that it would be tested for DNA, and that should clear me. He also said I needed to find an alibi witness for Friday. The problem is that I stayed home to do a thorough cleaning of my apartment. I didn't see anyone until I arrived at the Parthenon for the rehearsal dinner."

Two strokes of bad luck. DNA test results *might* clear Selene, but they wouldn't be back for a month or more, giving the police plenty of time to make life miserable for her. On top of that, Selene had no verifiable alibi, giving the DA more ammo to build a case against her. The clock was ticking.

"But that's not all," she said. "The scissors used to kill Brady have my fingerprints on them." She began to cry again.

"Okay, take it easy, Selene. Case and I are going to figure this out."

She sniffled a few times, then took a shaky breath. "Are you coming to the Parthenon for lunch? Please?"

"Of course," I reassured her, "I'll be there."

"Thenie," she said in a little girl's voice, "I'm going to move back home. I don't want to be alone now."

"Good for you, Selene. There's power in numbers, remember that."

"Thanks."

I ended the call, then sat with my chin in my hand, trying to reason it out. My sister had been home alone during the time of the murder; her scissors were used to commit the murder; and now a bloody T-shirt had turned up in her beauty salon's dumpster. It seemed that someone was setting her up. But who? Mandy Black, a long-time friend, who might have seen Selene as an easy scapegoat? The unknown woman with whom Brady was having an affair? *Think, Athena. Besides Mandy, who could you talk to? Who would know Brady best?*

His groomsmen.

I sent Case a text message, letting him know what I'd learned and asking whether he'd heard from Mitchell Black.

Case: **No answer. I'll try to arrange a lunch meeting with him on Wednesday.**

Athena: **I'll make myself available. How's the re-search going?**

Case: **I was going to tell you tomorrow, but here's what I found so far. Brady had numerous complaints filed against him, resulting in him being fired from his last job. The only other thing I found was a restraining order he filed against a Nora Modelle. That's as far as I've gotten.**

Athena: **Good start. Maybe the groomsmen can tell us more about her. Have to go now. See you tomorrow at 12:30.**

Case: **One more thing. Lila arranged a meeting for me with one of her financial advisers at Clemente's at noon today. Will let you know how it goes.**

Clemente's? I stared at his text for a long moment trying to puzzle it out. Why would Lila set up a business meeting between two men at a dimly lit, cozy Italian pizzeria?

Delphi came into the office for a cup of coffee, shaking me out of my thoughts. I texted Case a thumbs-up as she plopped down onto the chair in front of the desk to tell me she'd sold the last water fountain to a nice young couple who she foresaw as having a baby in the future.

"You didn't tell them that, did you?" I asked, sliding my phone away.

She was suddenly extremely focused on plucking a piece of lint off her skirt. "Not straight out."

"You read their coffee grounds, didn't you?"

"No," she said, then pursed her lips and looked away.

After I stared at her intently, she finally confessed. "I may have read their palms, though. And I might have suggested I saw a baby in their near future, which, in hindsight, may have been a mistake. They weren't very excited to hear the news."

"You have to stop scaring away customers."

"But they did offer their palms when I asked. How was I to know they were siblings?"

"Oh my God, Delphi."

"I'm just going to take my coffee back to the cashier's counter," she said, and slipped away.

At 12:15, I headed down Greene Street to have lunch at the Parthenon. As I passed Clemente's, I couldn't help but glance in to see if I could spot Case with Lila's financial adviser. And then I wished I hadn't.

Case was sitting at a table *not* with a man in a business suit, but with a bottle blonde in a tight white blouse and short, red leather skirt. She had one hand on his arm and was gazing at him as though he were a hot fudge sundae. Lila Talbot in the flesh, albeit some of that flesh was spilling out of her blouse.

If I'd been a cartoon character, steam would've been coming out of my ears. I shook off the anger and continued on. I had to let it go because there was nothing I could, or even should, do about it. Case's private life was Case's private life. The end.

I turned to walk backward so I could gaze at Clemente's and say, "So take that, little green-eyed imp." And so saying, I spun around, grabbed hold of my purse strap, and sailed forward.

Sitting at the family booth across from Selene and Maia, with Mama next to me, I tried to focus on their conversation but couldn't stop visualizing Lila with her hand so possessively on Case's arm. I noticed Selene pushing her food around on her plate, looking about as down in the mouth as I'd ever seen her.

"Selene, tell us about your appointment with Kevin," Mama said.

My sister's gaze shifted to me, and I knew exactly what she wanted.

"Selene, go ahead and eat, and I'll tell them," I said. "My food hasn't arrived yet."

She gave me a faltering smile and picked up her fork.

I told Mama and Maia about the T-shirt in the dumpster and the DNA test that should prove Selene's innocence. I didn't tell them about the fingerprints, the lack of a solid alibi, or that it could take a month or more to get back the test results, which was a smart move, considering that I could almost see steam coming from my mother's ears. An inherited trait?

"Someone set my little girl up?" Mama asked angrily. "Who would stoop so low?"

Maia scowled. "Someone who's chicken shi—"

"Maia, watch your mouth," Mama said, slapping the table.

"Don't you agree?" Maia asked.

"Yes, but I can think of a more intelligent way of saying it. *Kítrino koiliakó skoun*, for one."

Selene, who had gone to Greek school every Saturday morning, translated. "A yellow-bellied skunk."

"Selene's coming back home, Mama, and everything's going to work out just fine." And, somehow, I was going to make that happen.

"Athena," Mama said, jerking me back to attention, "did you sleep on what we talked about yesterday?"

Yesterday . . . Yesterday. Yikes! The plastic surgeon.

I was about to tell her I'd decided against it, but then the vision of Lila's hand on Case's arm flashed through my mind.

Hmm. Maybe there was some way I could deal with my conflicted feelings.

"I'm going on the date tonight, Mama."

I ignored the raised eyebrows all around.

IT'S ALL GREEK TO ME
by Goddess Anon

Blind Dates: A Fate Worse than Death

Is there anything less appealing than going on a blind date with a man whose ego is so large that there felt like there were three of us at the table? A man who actually honked his car horn instead of coming to the door to escort me out? A man who talked for a solid hour about all of his accomplishments and never once asked what I did for a living? A man who was so cheap, he suggested we split the bill? And all the while, I sat there so tense that my back began to hurt, wishing I had the courage to say, "Hey, Bozo! Do I get a turn to talk?"

Needless to say, I made up an excuse to skip dessert so I could get home faster. I practically jumped out of the car when he pulled into our driveway, causing him to text me minutes later asking if he'd said something wrong. I answered that it was my child's bedtime and hit Send. He didn't text back, clearly put off by the idea of dating a woman with a child.

Note to self: Remember to mention said child right away next time.

Wait. Next time?

Not happening, self. I've sworn off men, at least until that white knight comes charging in.

For now, this is Goddess Anon saying, Speak your truth.

Tuesday

Tuesday morning dawned sunny and warm, a perfect day to be outdoors at the garden center trying to forget the horrors of my blind date. What was the word for a man with a giant ego and a tiny brain who couldn't stop talking about himself? A bore? A big dull dud?

At any rate, as I unlocked the big front doors, I pushed away all memories of the dinner from hell and focused instead on the upcoming meeting with Lila—make that the groomsmen.

Lila? Where had that come from?

Sun. I needed sun.

To clear my head, I made a cup of coffee and grabbed a fresh bag of peanuts for Oscar. I passed the statue of Athena on my way to the back exit and paused. It was a good daily reminder to stand tall and stay strong. A reminder that I often needed.

I pushed open the back doors, letting in a bright burst of warm morning sun, and whistled for our little pet. He was nowhere to be found, which wasn't unusual as raccoons tended to be nocturnal, but that was until I sat down at the black wrought-iron table and tore open the bag of peanuts. Then he scampered out from behind a row of Knock Out roses and stopped in front of me, sitting on his hind legs, gazing at me hopefully.

"Sit, Oscar. Sit."

He cocked his head to the side.

I reached out with a peanut between my fingers. "Sit, Oscar."

He sat back on his hind legs and reached out one clawed paw, gently retrieving the nut and wolfing it down.

"You're a smart boy, you know that? Good boy." As I sat there, feeding my furry friend, I realized that this was the kind of blind date I would've actually enjoyed. Oscar was friendly, polite, and charming.

I finished my coffee and watched Oscar scamper away with the rest of the bag. Inside, my dad was already busy stacking fertilizer, and Delphi was setting up the registers for our morning rush, so I headed for the office, needing something to do. Thirty minutes until the store opened. Why not try my hand at some simple sleuthing?

I went online and did a new search for Brady Rogers. I found his Instagram page, where he was promoting himself as a workout trainer. There were a few photos of Mandy and some of him with his groomsmen, but mostly he'd posted videos. I watched half a dozen and noticed that they were always of him training women. I played the last one again. For some reason, she looked familiar. But where would I have seen her?

Then a light bulb went on. I pulled up Brady's Facebook page again and saw exactly what I'd found there before—training videos. Except this time, I found one with the same woman in it. And beneath the video was a comment left several months ago by a Nora Modelle: *Best trainer I've ever worked with.* It was followed by—seriously? A *heart* icon?

I clicked on Nora's name, and it took me to her Facebook page. The only information she'd posted on her
home page was that she worked at the Sequoia Public Library. She also had listed herself as single. Then I
checked her photo album and found dozens of pictures of
Brady Rogers, to the point of obsession. I immediately
picked up my phone and texted Selene: **Is Nora Modelle
a customer at the beauty salon?**

Selene: **Not my customer. I'll ask around.**

She texted back in a few moments: **I found out that
Nora hasn't been here for several years but came in
just last week to make an appointment.**

Athena: **Did she keep her appointment?**

Selene: **Her appointment was with Amber, who's off
today. I'll ask Amber tomorrow.**

Athena: **Will you get Nora's phone number, too?**

Selene answered with a thumbs-up.

It was clear that Nora had been obsessed with Brady
Rogers, to the point that he'd had to file a restraining
order against her. She'd also been at the beauty salon
sometime before the murder. Motive and a possible
means of taking Selene's scissors were more than enough
to put her on my list of suspects.

I opened up the file marked SUSPECTS and listed her as
number one, followed by Mandy and Mitchell Black. I
looked through my notes and typed out a quick list of
questions for the groomsmen, including about Brady's relationship to Nora Modelle.

"Thenie, we need help out front," Delphi said from the
doorway. "Dad's helping a couple pick out shrubs out
back, and I've got a line at the cash register. Can you be
on the floor for a while?"

"I'll be right there."

. Sometime later, after the store had emptied out, I glanced at my watch and realized it was almost noon. "Pops, I've got to go. I'm working on Selene's case and have a meeting set up in thirty minutes."

"I've got you covered," he said. "Go."

I grabbed my sweater, purse, and iPad and bolted out the door.

The Blue Moon Café was located on Oak Street, halfway between the garden center and the block of shops and dining establishments known as Little Greece. The café had a big outdoor eating area and open-air bar along the left side, between buildings, and a dining room inside for the cool months. Their specialty in the spring, summer, and fall was freshly caught perch, one of my favorites.

When I arrived, Case was seated outside with Patrick Dean and Trevor Kapellakis, all of them sipping bottles of Sequoia Breweries Pale Ale. They were seated at the far end of the building, which I assumed Case had chosen for privacy, as there were no other diners nearby.

Case rose as I joined them, made introductions as he seated me, then waved over a waitress to take our orders. There was a pleasantness about the two men that Case seemed to bring out in people. Sometimes too much so, unfortunately, and instantly my mind went back to Lila. I wanted to smack myself in the forehead, but instead pushed her into the recesses of my mind once again.

Both men greeted me warmly, which was in stark contrast to some of the other witnesses Case and I had interviewed. Case smiled at me and eased back into his chair, giving me a pleasant feeling as well.

After I'd ordered my fish sandwich, Case said, "I've already explained why we wanted to meet, and they're ready and willing to help us find Brady's killer. And lunch is on me, by the way, guys."

"Thanks, Case," the two said jointly.

"Have the detectives interviewed you yet?" Case asked.

"Yes, but only to clear us," Trevor said. "They asked a series of questions but never got into any depth. Mostly they wanted to know about Brady's relationship with Selene, and Selene's relationship with Mandy."

"What did you tell them about Brady and Selene?" I asked.

"We told them what we knew," Patrick said, "Brady was training Selene, then she reported him for harassment and quit the gym."

"That seems straightforward," Case said. "What about Selene and Mandy?"

"Again, just what we knew," Patrick said, "that they'd been friends in high school and Selene was asked to fill in for a sick bridesmaid at the last minute."

"Then we were fingerprinted and let go," Trevor said. "That was it."

"Who was the lead detective?" I asked.

"Detective Walters is the only name I was given," Trevor said.

"Same here," Patrick said. "Walters and another man also talked to Mitchell, so he may know more."

"By the way, we invited Mitchell Black to this meeting," Case told them, "but he wasn't able to make it."

The two men glanced at each other. Trevor lifted an eyebrow at Patrick as though to say that didn't surprise him.

"Why don't you start?" Case asked me.

As he took a sip of his beer, I fired up my iPad, clicked on the Brady Rogers file, and began. "First of all, let's start with Mitchell Black. You don't seem surprised by his absence, Trevor, and I'm wondering why not."

"Mitchell keeps to himself," Trevor replied. "He's not a team player."

"What was Brady's relationship like with Mitchell?" I asked.

"Kind of hard to tell," Patrick said. "Brady seemed to like the guy, but he got along with most guys. He was a man's man."

But not always a woman's man, if my sister was any indication. "Did you sense any conflict between Mitchell and Brady?"

"Not really," Trevor said.

"I'm not so sure, Trev," Patrick said. "Why do you think Mitch was always around when we were out partying? He didn't come out to have fun. That's for sure."

"He didn't trust Brady," Trevor replied, "but I never saw any conflict between them."

"If he didn't trust Brady," I asked, "why was he the best man at his wedding?"

"That was Mandy's instruction," Trevor said. "I don't think either one of them was happy about it."

"Did you guys party a lot?" Case asked.

"Brady was a big party guy," said Patrick. "He worked hard and played harder. Trev and I couldn't keep up with him most of the time. But Mitch was always around when Mandy was with us, like a chaperone. I can understand why he was concerned. Brady had quite a reputation as a playboy."

"And that playboy status didn't bother Mandy?" I asked.

"Didn't seem like it," Trevor answered.

"How do you know about the trust issue Mitchell had with Brady?" Case asked.

"We all hung out together," Trevor said. "We'd be at a club with Brady and Mandy, then Mitchell would just show up out of nowhere. He didn't really talk to anyone, just kept his eye on things. It was strange."

"Joni and Paulette stopped coming out with us," Patrick added. "They didn't like Mitch at all."

"The other two bridesmaids?" I asked, writing their names down.

"Yes, Joni Waters and Paulette Cendrowski," Patrick explained.

"And Mandy didn't mind her brother watching over her?" I asked.

"She didn't act like it," Trevor said. "They're really close."

"Anything else we should know about Mitchell?" I asked.

"I don't know anything else about him," Trevor said. "He didn't talk to us much, probably because we were Brady's closest friends."

"I know Mitchell works for his dad at the Waterfront Hotel," Patrick said.

"Does Mandy work there?" I asked.

"Mandy does two things—sits by the pool and shops," Trevor said. "That's about it. Her family has enough money to support her, which is why we figured Brady was so intent on marrying her, if we're being honest."

"Then you believe Brady was after Mandy's money?" I asked.

"He liked living the high life," Trevor replied, "which he did when he was with Mandy. She even picked up our bar tabs when we all went out together. She's generous, pretty, and wealthy. I don't think it was just about the money for Brady, but it didn't hurt."

"Do you think he would've given up his playboy lifestyle after his marriage to Mandy?" Case asked.

The two glanced at each other and shrugged. "We don't know," Patrick said.

"Did you endorse Brady's lifestyle?" I asked, feeling a bit catty about it.

"If you mean whether we liked his womanizing, no," Patrick said. "But we liked him all the same."

"Do you know if Brady was seeing another woman while he was engaged to Mandy?"

Again, the two men sought each other's gaze before proceeding. "Don't know," Patrick finally said.

"What do you know about Brady's relationship with Nora Modelle?"

Patrick took a long sip of beer and considered his answer. "I think it was serious, at least on Nora's part," he said. "They were together for quite a while. She had money, too, by the way, but not as much as Mandy."

Trevor replied, "Honestly, Pat, I don't know how serious Brady was about her, especially once he figured out that Nora was nuts." He turned to look at Case and me. "When she got *really* nutty, and I mean *Fatal Attraction* nutty, he stopped seeing her."

"And that made Nora go freakin' crazy," Patrick said. "Or crazier, at least. How she managed to keep her job at the library is beyond me. The scary thing about her was that at first she came across as super sweet—then went super needy. It went downhill from there."

"After Brady broke up with her," Trevor said, "she began sending him text messages, ten, fifteen at a time, all day long. She also stalked him, waiting outside the gym for him to leave so she could beg him to take her back. She even followed him to work in her car. He finally called the police, and they told him to file a restraining order."

"Did that stop her?"

"For a while," Trevor said, "but we saw her at the club a few times. Brady pointed her out to us. She kept her distance, but it was still creepy."

"As recently as . . . ?" I asked.

Trevor glanced at Patrick as he said, "A month or so. Actually, it was right around the time Brady and Mandy announced their engagement." He rubbed his arms as though the thought gave him chills. "She looked different, but it was definitely her."

"What do you mean by different?"

"She had dyed her hair dark brown, and she looked like she'd gained some weight. She looked unhealthy," Trevor said.

"Was Brady cheating on Mandy with Nora?" I asked.

"No," Trevor said. "I don't think it was Nora."

"So he *was* seeing someone else while he was engaged to Mandy?" I said.

Instead of answering, Trevor grabbed his beer and finished it off.

"It's okay," I said. "We've already confirmed it. Did he ever mention a name?"

They shook their heads. Then Patrick said. "He was being very coy about it."

"But we kind of thought we knew," Trevor added.

Case waved over the waitress and ordered another round of beers. "Athena, are you good?" he asked.

"I have water."

"Would you share the woman's name with us?" Case asked.

"I don't think we should," Trevor said.

"All you're doing is giving us someone else to consider," I said. "Let's call her a person of interest."

"What the heck, Pat," Trevor said. "We've already talked to the detectives about her."

"Come on, guys. Who are we talking about?" Case asked.

As the two men looked at each other, I had a sudden image of the rehearsal dinner scene at the Parthenon that I had first come upon. The one thing that stuck out in my mind was the almost frantic phone conversation Tonya had been having. Then later, after it came out that Brady had been stabbed with scissors, the knowing look she had given the other bridesmaids. "I know who she is," I said. "Tonya Upton."

"Tonya?" Trevor seemed totally shocked. "That's not what we thought. Why would you suspect Tonya?"

"Something struck me as odd about her behavior at the rehearsal dinner, but it wasn't adding up until just now," I told him. "I'll bet she was the one who called the police and reported Selene as the murderer. I knew Mandy didn't have time to make a call, but Tonya was on the phone when I arrived."

"She could've been calling anyone," Case said.

"It's just a strong hunch, Case."

"Maybe that's why the police arrived right after us," Trevor said. "I wondered how they got there so quickly."

"See?" I poked Case's arm.

Ignoring my teasing, Case asked, "Who was the woman you were thinking of?"

Trevor glanced at Patrick, then said, "Selene Spencer."

CHAPTER EIGHT

I went cold all over. "Why do you think it was Selene?"

"We overheard Mandy and Brady arguing one evening," Trevor said. "She'd found out about his affair."

"And later he mentioned Selene," Patrick said. "He wouldn't tell us much more, but we put the pieces together. And after she was arrested, it all made sense." Patrick studied me for a moment, then said, "You're related to Selene, aren't you?"

"I'm her sister."

"I knew it!" Patrick said. "I saw you talking to Selene at the rehearsal dinner, and I knew there had to be a family connection."

"You sure don't look like the rest of your family," Trevor said.

I glanced at Case, who lifted one eyebrow as though to say, *And you thought you could fool people.*

"Anyway," I said, "my sister told me she overheard two of the bridesmaids talking at the hair salon the day before Brady was killed. They said that Mandy knew Brady was having an affair and, according to one of them, was so upset that she wanted to kill him."

"And then your sister's scissors went missing," Patrick said.

"Exactly," I said.

"So you think Mandy killed Brady?" Trevor asked.

"We don't know who killed Brady," I replied. "That's why we're investigating."

"Brady and Selene weren't having an affair?" Patrick asked.

"No, they definitely were not," I said.

"Well," Patrick said, "I guess the cat's out of the bag. We know he was seeing someone, but if it's not Selene, then I have no idea who it was."

Our food arrived then, so we halted until everyone had taken a few bites. I was eager to continue the interview, but didn't want to rush everyone through dinner.

I needn't have worried. Patrick and Trevor ravaged their meals as though they hadn't eaten in weeks. I looked at Case and opened my eyes wide. He glanced at the two men eating and then winked at me, as though he knew exactly what I was thinking. He picked up his beer, holding it up to me in salute.

"Let's get back to the subject at hand," Case said when they'd finished. "Athena, what else do you have to ask these gentlemen?"

I had to stifle a smile. It wasn't the first time that I'd been amazed by how smoothly we worked as a team. "I assume you're both familiar with Brady's apartment. Would you describe it for me?"

"Let's draw a diagram," Case said, flipping to a clean page in his notepad.

Patrick started. "Big entranceway that opens into the living room. Dining room straight behind it. Kitchen in the back. Bedrooms on either end of a hallway off the dining room. Pretty standard layout."

"We've been there many times," Trevor added. "It's a nice place."

"What was the first thing you noticed when you entered the apartment before the police arrived?" I asked.

"The door was unlocked," Patrick said. "Anyone could have walked in."

"Do you know who had a key?" I asked.

"Mandy is the only one I know of," Trevor said. "I don't know about Nora."

"How about Brady's parents?" I asked.

"Brady's parents," Trevor repeated. "How can I put this nicely. They weren't good people—junkies, I think—so he's been pretty much on his own."

How sad, I thought. As annoying as my family could be at times, I couldn't imagine life without them. "Would you describe the position he was in when you found him?"

"He was lying flat on his stomach on the carpet, and his right arm was outstretched as though he was trying to reach the hutch in his dining room."

"Was anything overturned?" I asked.

Patrick answered. "Everything was in place."

"That seems to indicate it wasn't a robbery," Case said.

"Had he been dragged?" I asked. "Any blood smears? Throw rugs scrunched up?"

"It looked to me like he fell and then reached out,

maybe trying to draw himself toward the hutch." Trevor glanced down as though it hurt to visualize the scene.

"I'm sorry if it's upsetting," I said.

Patrick blinked back tears. "It's painful to think about."

Trevor took a pull of his beer, gazing off into the distance. After a few moments, he said, "I'm curious about something. Why aren't we suspects?"

"You were," Case said. "You're not now."

Trevor and Patrick gave us fist bumps.

"Let's get back to the diagram," Case said. "Did you see anything on the hutch that Brady might have been trying to reach?"

"He usually kept his phone charging there," Trevor said. "It wasn't there, though."

"The killer could've taken it," Patrick said.

"Or it could've been in his back pocket," Case said, "in which case the detectives would have it. Did you try to call him?"

"We did before we went there," Trevor explained. "No answer, of course."

"It would have to ping somewhere," I said to Case as I made a note in my iPad. "I'll check with Bob Maguire."

Everyone was quiet as we paused to finish our drinks, and then I said, "I asked you this before, and now, as you're picturing the apartment in detail, did anything strike you as out of place?"

Both men thought for a moment, then Trevor said, "Honestly, I can't remember. My heart was racing so fast I couldn't focus on anything but Brady's condition and how Mandy was going to take it."

"Did you move the body?" Case asked.

They both shook their heads. "No," Trevor said. "I've watched enough crime shows on TV to know better."

"It was a sight I'll never forget but wish I could." Patrick added.

"Then nothing stood out as being out of place?" Case asked.

They shook their heads. Trevor said, "We were too concerned about calling for an ambulance. And suddenly the police were right there, coming in the door, telling us to put up our hands and back away."

"Wait a minute," Patrick said. "I just remembered something else about the hutch. Brady had a large framed photo of himself with Mandy and Mitch on it. But it wasn't there. Or at least I don't remember seeing it."

"You're right," Trevor said. "It was gone."

"Could Brady have moved the picture?" Case asked.

"I wouldn't think so," Patrick said. "He liked it too much. He wanted it front and center."

"And Pat should know because he took the photo." Trevor put his hand on his friend's shoulder. "He's an amateur photographer—good enough to be professional."

"Describe the photo, Pat," Case said.

"It's a nine-by-twelve, black-and-white photo of Brady, Mandy, and Mitchell in a gray marble frame. Brady's standing between Mandy and Mitchell with his arms around their shoulders, smiling proudly, almost as if he were already a part of the family. They were all dressed in white shirts and black jeans."

"Brady really liked it, too," Trevor said. "I think it was because he didn't feel like he had a family. Anyway, I remembered that the photo was gone because it took up most of the room on the hutch other than a big blue decorative glass bowl."

"Brady had art glass in his bachelor's apartment?" I asked.

"It was Mandy's idea," Trevor said. "She decorated the place."

"I think she was trying to put her stamp on it," Patrick said.

Who would have moved the photo? Would Mandy kill her own fiancé just before her wedding and then remove their framed photo? It seemed highly unlikely. Or could she have taken it after she found out about the other woman? Or had Brady just put it elsewhere?

I finished typing my thoughts just as Case asked, "What made you remember the photo, Pat?"

"When I thought back to the scene in the apartment, I wondered whether Brady was trying to reach the marble frame to defend himself." Patrick glanced at his watch again. "And I need to get going."

"I have just one other question," Case said. "Are you familiar with Brady's coworkers Tom and Terrence?"

"We've hung out with them a few times," Trevor said. "They seem like good guys."

"One of them mentioned that Brady had flirtatious relationships with women at the gym," Case explained. "Besides Selene, did Brady ever mention the names of anyone else he was training?"

Both men shrugged. "He trained lots of women," Trevor said, "but never mentioned any names to me."

"Not to me, either," Patrick said.

Case glanced at me. "Athena? Any more questions?"

I pulled up Brady's Facebook page and scrolled to the photo with Nora Modelle in it. "Do you know who the woman in this photo is?"

Trevor nodded. "That's Nora—except her hair is dark now, like Mandy's."

Like Mandy's. That was interesting. I also noted that

none of the photos Nora had posted showed her with dark hair. "Thanks. I just wanted to verify it."

As they finished the last of their beers, I handed each my business card from Spencer's. "If you think of anything else that might help us, please give me a call. It might even be something you think is insignificant. Whatever it is, write it down. We never know what tiny bit of information might lead us straight to the killer."

"Will do." Patrick said as he stuck the card in his shirt pocket.

Trevor put the card inside his wallet. "Thanks for lunch. It was a pleasure to meet you both. And please feel free to call us anytime. We want justice for Brady."

Case and I waited until they'd left the restaurant, and then, after ordering espressos, we moved closer to compare notes. "You go first," Case said.

"Okay, first of all, I keep hearing Nora Modelle's name, so I looked her up on Facebook and found out that she works at the public library. Maybe we can pay her a surprise visit and see what she has to say."

"I'm on board," Case said. "I'll do a little more digging into Nora and let you know if I find anything noteworthy."

"Good. Okay, second, both groomsmen mentioned that Mandy and Mitchell are very close. "

"Like, close enough to plan a murder together?" Case asked.

"Exactly. I'd like to find out just how close they are, so I want to be with you when you talk to Mitchell."

"No problem."

We paused as our espressos were delivered. I added cream and sugar to mine then said, "Some other factors to consider. The front door was unlocked, so Brady either let the killer inside or someone used a key. So we need to know who would have had a key to Brady's apartment. Obviously, Mandy, but she could've made a duplicate for Mitchell."

"Nora might have had a key at one time," Case suggested.

"Or how about Mandy being the lone killer? She had the means, motive, and opportunity and she seemed certain that Brady was dead as soon as the groomsmen reported back to the rehearsal dinner."

Case put down his coffee cup. "Let's go back to Nora and what you saw on Facebook."

"You'll have to check out her page. She filled her photo album with pictures of Brady, so I can only imagine how jealous she was when she found out about Mandy. Maybe jealous enough to stalk her. Maybe jealous enough to dye her hair like Mandy's. So imagine this. She follows Mandy to the beauty salon that Friday and after Mandy leaves and Selene is at lunch, she strolls in and picks up Selene's scissors, pretending to *be* Mandy."

Case stuck a stirrer in his mouth, thinking. "If you follow that logic, then you'd have to believe Nora set up Mandy for murder, not Selene."

"True."

"How close were Mandy and Selene?"

"They've been friends on and off since high school," I said.

"Rivals at any time?"

"I'll have to check with Selene."

"Maybe it's time we talk to your sister," Case said.

"How about tonight after dinner? Selene and I can meet you at the *Páme*."

"Are you sure that won't interfere with your next blind date?"

My mouth dropped open. "How did you . . . Where did you . . . ?"

"Your blog, Goddess Anon."

I'd forgotten that Case had been the first to learn of my anonymous identity. My blog was beginning to feel like the best-kept secret in town. I just had to pray that the news didn't get back to the Greek side of my family.

Chapter Nine

On my way back to the garden center, I phoned Bob Maguire again and left a voicemail message to call when it was convenient. By the time I got back to Spencer's, I had a plan formulated for what I would say to Maguire.

I made it back to Spencer's well ahead of an appointment I'd made with the new client. I had to make sure I was out of the center early enough to eat with Nicholas and still have time to take Selene to the boat.

Based on the intake information the client had filled out, she wanted decorative trees in the yard, with a hedge to separate their lot from a church lot. I spent an hour selecting a variety of ornamental trees and potential hedges, then suddenly a thought popped into my head about the murder. I set my plan aside and phoned Selene, who had to step away from a customer to talk.

"I'll make it quick," I said. "Is there a security camera inside the salon?"

"Yes, but it's active only at night," Selene said. "There's also a security camera right outside the shop at the intersection of Catherine and White Streets. That camera should show the front of the shop."

"Perfect! Okay, that's all I wanted. Oh, wait. Don't make any plans for after seven o'clock tonight. We're going to meet Case at the *Páme* to discuss our new information."

"Good news, I hope?"

"We think so."

"Great. I could use it. Detective Walters came here again today for more questioning. Do you know how embarrassing it is to be pulled away from my client? I know I'm getting an ulcer."

"He questioned you at the salon? That's got to stop. I'll go see the detective myself and tell him—"

"Don't you dare, Athena," my dad said, entering with his coffee mug in hand.

"Gotta go, Selene. Forget what I just said. See you back at the house."

I hung up and glanced sheepishly at my dad. "Sorry, but I get angry when I hear the things that detective does to intimidate his, quote, person of interest."

"Yes, my little warrior goddess, I know you do, but isn't it better that he questioned her there instead of taking her down to the police station? That would've disrupted her whole day."

"Why didn't he ask her to come by the police station during her lunch hour or after work?"

My dad filled his cup and took a sip. "Be that as it

may, just be mindful that any action on your part could come back to bite Selene in the butt, okay?"

"Fine."

"Just fine?"

"No, you're right. I'll be mindful."

My phone dinged, and I saw an incoming call from Bob Maguire. I glanced at the time. Three o'clock. Shift change at the police station. Where had the afternoon gone?

"I need to take this, Pops."

"I'm leaving now."

"Hey, Bob," I said, as my dad closed the office door. "Do you have a few minutes?"

"I'm about to get into my car. Hold on." I could hear him open and shut his door and then fasten his seat belt. "I suppose this is about Selene."

"I'm sorry to bother you, Bob. It's just that I have no one else on the force that I trust, and I don't know who else to bounce ideas off of."

"Bounce away. I'm doing this as a favor from one high school nerd to the other."

"I was the nerd. You were the jokester."

"Yeah, because I was such a nerd. Go ahead. I can't promise anything, as you know, but I'll do my best to help within my legal bounds."

"Because you don't think Selene is getting a fair shake either, right?"

"You didn't hear that from me."

"Okay, Bob, here's what I'd like to know. I spoke with two of the groomsmen today, Trevor and Patrick, and they asked about Brady's cell phone since they didn't see it in his apartment. Did he have it on his body?"

There was a long moment of silence. Was he weighing

whether or not to answer? Finally, hesitatingly, he said, "No. It was missing."

"Wouldn't it be pinging somewhere?"

"Yes, it would and did ping somewhere—in the dumpster behind Selene's apartment building. They found it this morning, wiped clean. No messages, no fingerprints. Nothing."

"Isn't it obvious that Selene has been set up?"

"That's not how Detective Walters is proceeding. At any rate, the phone's been sent to the state police lab in Lansing for processing."

"How long will that take?"

"With their backlog, anywhere from four weeks to two months. And don't sigh, Athena. I know that sucks."

"*Big*-time. And the bloody T-shirt?"

"Also sent downstate."

"Don't you think it's a little coincidental that the T-shirt was found in the garbage bin behind Selene's shop and the cell phone in the dumpster behind her apartment building? Would a murderer really be that careless?"

"No, and yes, I do think it's coincidental, but it's not up to me. As I've told you before, detectives present their evidence to the DA, and he decides whether there's enough to make a case. That's the way it is, unfortunately, and there's nothing either one of us can do about it except for you to keep doing what you're doing."

"Okay, here's something else I need to ask. Can you take a look at the traffic camera video from the intersection of Catherine and White Streets? I'd like to see who entered the Over the Top hair salon on White Street the day before Brady was murdered. As you probably remember, that's when Selene's scissors went missing."

"I'll have to call in a favor, but I can get it done. In

fact, I'll do that tomorrow before my shift starts. No one will ask any questions then."

"Who would ask questions?"

"It's best if I don't name names."

I knew he was talking about Walters. I hadn't liked him when we'd investigated the Talbot murder cases, and I didn't like him any more now.

"I know I'm already asking a lot of you, Bob, but I have one more question."

"Go ahead."

"Have you seen the autopsy report?"

"No, I haven't. Why?"

"I want to know if Brady had any blunt-force trauma to the head," I explained. "A marble picture frame is missing from his apartment, and I'd like to know if that could be a potential piece of evidence."

"Wow, you are really deep into this investigation," he said. "I'll see what I can find out and call you tomorrow."

"I really appreciate your help, Bob. If there's ever anything I can do . . ."

"Let's just say if I were to assist in solving this case, it would earn some major brownie points."

"Brownie points?" I asked. "With whom?"

He paused. "What I mean to say is it would bring me one step closer to making detective."

"Good. Then we're helping each other."

"If all goes well. I just need to keep this under my hat. So no word to anyone else about what I'm doing for you, okay?"

"Just one other person—my partner, Case Donnelly."

"You have a partner?"

"Let's just say he's my partner in crime."

Bob laughed. "I've got to go. I have a date tonight."

"You have a date?"

"You sound shocked."

"I'm sorry. That was rude."

"Even nerds go on dates, Athena."

"Been there, done that, and happy to be single again."

"Time will tell, won't it?"

Smiling, I hung up and immediately called Case to tell him about my conversation. It was only afterward that it dawned on me. Case hadn't yet told me about his conversation with Lila.

After dinner with the family, I spent some quality time with Nicholas, helping him practice for a spelling test. I loved our evenings together. He was such a bright, happy boy that I couldn't help but give him warm hugs, which he claimed made him feel like a baby. And yet when I got home every evening, he was quick to give me a hug first. This evening, however, Nicholas ushered me rapidly through the study guide so he could spend time on Greek lessons with his grandmother. It worked out well, since I had made plans to take Selene down to the Páme.

We told Mama we were going out to take in the warm, evening air, deciding against telling her our true intentions so that Selene didn't have to endure questioning afterward. We also purposely didn't tell Delphi, as she was terrible at keeping secrets.

As we started toward the door, Delphi floated down the stairs wearing a pastel pink-and-white dress with short heels.

"Be back in a little while," Delphi said as she spun past us, swiping her keys from the console by the door.

"Where are you going, Delphi, *agapitós*?" Sweetheart. Mama asked.

Delphi gave me a quick, desperate glance. Judging by her outfit, I was guessing she was going on a date and didn't want my mother to know. So I decided to step in and help out. "She's coming on a walk with us," I said.

"In those heels?" Mama asked.

"Good exercise for your calves." I looped my arm through Delphi's, and we walked toward the door together.

Selene followed, calling back to Mama, "We won't be out late."

We left Delphi across the street from the marina, agreeing to meet back at the house at ten o'clock. She still had not revealed who her date was, preferring to keep him a secret.

At the *Páme*, Case greeted Selene and me as he helped us climb aboard. "Here you go, ladies. Life jackets all around."

"Life jackets?" I asked. "Are we in danger of sinking?"

"Not if I can help it." Case climbed up to the captain's seat and started the engine. "We're going to take a little ride up the eastern side of the lake and back."

"I didn't know the *Páme* still ran," Selene said, settling down into one of the swivel chairs positioned behind the captain's chair. "Pappoús hasn't taken her out in ages."

"I had a mechanic take a look," Case said, "and after a little cleaning, the engine purrs like a kitten. By the way, Athena, there's some champagne in the cooler."

"Aren't you going to join us?"

"Not when I'm piloting the boat. It's the law."

I opened the cooler built into a cabinet under the bench in the stern and took out the chilled bottle and two glasses. As Case started the motor and untied the moorings, I popped the cork and filled our glasses. Once he'd backed the boat out of its slip and headed toward the open waters, I carried my glass up front and stood near Case. Selene and I recounted some of our adventures as children on the *Páme*. It couldn't have been a more pleasant evening. As we chatted and sipped bubbly, the evening breeze lifted our hair and cooled our warm skin.

"Case, you're a natural sailor," Selene said.

Case smiled. "I've found a new passion. I love living on the water."

"Guess who wants to buy the boat from Pappoús?" I asked Selene.

"Seriously? I hope Pappoús goes for it. What a shame that the boat just sits here unused."

"I'd like to operate a charter-boat fishing service," Case told her, "as soon as I get the financing to buy a few boats."

"You're going to charter this boat?" Selene asked.

"No, it'll be for my personal use only."

"I'll help you work on Pappoús, Thenie," Selene said. "Then we can get the great big Karras and Spencer families on board for Sunday afternoon outings again. That is, if Case can handle our crazy family."

Case turned around to see if she was serious. When she winked, he smiled in relief. I reached out to clink glasses with her, then downed the rest of my bubbly.

"I'm hoping to get Athena's help decorating the inside," Case said over the sound of a passing boat. "It's pretty bare bones right now, and I've heard good things about her decorating expertise."

"I don't know," Selene said as she finished her last sip. "You should see her bedroom. It's like a hurricane swept through and she nailed the remnants to the walls."

Case laughed, and I playfully slapped Selene's shoulder. "What can I say? I like abstract art."

"So do I," Case said, giving me an appraising glance. "Maybe you can help me pick out some art for the walls. What do you think about that?"

He was flirting with me. "I think I like that idea," I said in a playful voice.

"I think I do, too." He smiled and I smiled back.

"I think it's time for more champagne," Selene said.

CHAPTER TEN

"What do you say we get started?" Case asked, pulling a third chair over to the small table in the middle of the room. He had artfully maneuvered the *Páme* back into the slip just as the sun set. The breeze from the water was growing chilly, so we'd come inside to warm up. "Can I get you ladies anything?"

Sitting across from Selene at the small kitchen table, I said with her, "Champagne." And then we both laughed the same laugh and high-fived each other like schoolgirls. I caught myself smiling like a schoolgirl as well. It seemed as though the bubbly was making us bubbly. Small sips, I kept telling myself.

I took out my notepad as Case poured fresh glasses of the sparkling wine for us.

"Athena, why don't you start?" Case said.

"Okay," I said. "Selene, tell us everything you remember about last Thursday, starting from when you arrived at the salon."

"I got in about eight a.m., as usual, and prepped my station for my first customer, who was coming in for a cut and color. When I finished her at ten o'clock, Mandy, Tonya, Joni, and Paulette had just come in and were in the waiting area."

"Mandy was the only one who used a different stylist, right?" I asked, making sure Case noted it.

"Right. Mandy wanted the works—haircut, color, facial, and mani-pedi. So Tonya took charge and asked my coworker Lori to work on Mandy. Apparently, Tonya had planned everything, even bringing sparkling wine and chocolates. The girls all seemed to be having a good time, too. Tonya let all the bridesmaids go before her, then she got into the seat next to Mandy, and they had mani-pedis together while the bridesmaids finished their wine and desserts."

"I'm surprised they came in on Thursday when the wedding was on Saturday," I said.

"Me too," Selene said. "Usually the bridal party comes in the day before the wedding or the day of to get their hair and nails done. But apparently that's what Mandy wanted, so that's what they did."

"Were any of the bridal party still there when you noticed your scissors missing?" I asked.

"No. They'd all left by then."

"Did any of the other stylists notice anyone hanging around your station while you were at lunch?" I asked.

"No one noticed anything unusual. Then again, we're always so focused on our customers that we don't pay much attention to what's going on around us. It's hard enough to hear our clients over the hair dryers as it is."

"How long have you known Mandy?" Case asked.

"Since high school."

"Have you ever had any fights, arguments, or any other reason to believe Mandy would want to do you harm?" he asked.

"I'd say just a normal amount of arguments. We weren't best friends, but we ran in the same circles. We dated the same guy in high school. I guess that was our only true fight, but that was years ago."

"And you married him," I said.

"I did, and we both know how that turned out."

Case raised his hand. "Fill me in."

"He was a jock, all hell-bent on a college football scholarship, which he got. Those were his glory days, and it was downhill after that. He got fat and mean, and I got out."

I put my arm around my sister. "That seems to be a common trait, among two of us sisters at least."

"Let's hope it ends with us," Selene said. "Sometimes I get the feeling Maia and Delphi are afraid of marriage because of our experiences."

"I hope not," I said.

"Do you think Mandy held a grudge about you marrying the guy she liked?" Case asked.

"As far as I know, that was all settled in high school," Selene said. "Water under the bridge, especially given how he turned out."

"Where's your ex now?" Case asked.

"Forgotten," Selene said. "Quickly." We snickered together.

"One thing has me puzzled, though," Selene said. "Mandy normally comes to the salon every two weeks to have her hair done, but for some reason she stopped coming. No call, no explanation, nothing until she made the appointment for last Thursday, and then she acted as though nothing had happened. I didn't ask her why, but it certainly puzzled me then, and even more so now."

"Selene, how long ago did you report Brady?" I asked.

She stopped to think. "Several weeks ago." She paused. "And shortly afterward Mandy stopped coming in."

"Several weeks ago," I repeated, looking at Case as the puzzle pieces started to fall into place. "That was about when Mandy learned that Brady was seeing another woman."

Selene's eyes widened. "She actually thought Brady and I were having an affair?"

"That's what the groomsmen seem to think," Case said. "We haven't confirmed it with Mandy yet, but—"

"Then why didn't she just confront me about it?" Selene took a deep breath to calm down and then continued, "She certainly didn't act like she was angry at the salon last Thursday, and I highly doubt she would have asked me to be her bridesmaid if she thought I was having an affair with her fiancé."

"Selene is right," I said to Case. "Mandy must have figured out that it wasn't her who was having an affair with Brady. Maybe she'd simply decided it was time to take action before she made the mistake of marrying him."

"I don't believe she's that diabolical," Selene said. "And Mandy wouldn't frame me. She wasn't like that—at least not the Mandy I remember. She'd have just called off the wedding and been done with Brady."

"After talking to the groomsmen today," I said, "and learning more about Brady, I can't help wondering why Mandy was so intent on marrying him in the first place."

"You know I wasn't a fan of his," Selene said. "I don't have a clue what she saw in him."

Case checked his watch. "Let's get this wrapped up so you two can get home. Is there anything else you remember about Thursday, Selene?"

"Just that the rest of it was frustrating," she answered. "I had to borrow a pair of scissors and then I had to buy a brand-new pair, and they're not cheap. They cost upwards of one hundred dollars."

"For a pair of scissors?" I said.

"For professional scissors," Selene said.

"Athena," Case said, "anything to add to that?"

"Just one thing." I held my wineglass up. "Here's to closing this case."

"Hear, hear," Case said, and we toasted.

On our walk home, Selene nudged me. "You two make a cute couple."

"Yep, just a couple who like to solve puzzles," I said, trying to brush off what she was implying.

"You know what I mean, Thenie. There's more to it than a love of solving puzzles."

"Okay. We both hate injustice, and that's what we've got here."

"Would you stop it?"

"Selene, trust me. I'm not looking for any long-term relationships right now."

"We'll see."

When we got back home shortly after ten, we could hear Delphi in the kitchen, being questioned about where we had gone.

"Why did Delphi come inside before we got here?" Selene whispered. "That wasn't the plan."

"I don't know but we'd better go rescue her," I whispered back.

Selene grabbed my arm. "What are we going to tell Mama? You know how she excels at interrogations."

"Don't worry. I *excel* at telling stories."

"You're not the only one," Selene said.

"We learned from the master," we both whispered, then giggled as we gazed at the swinging door.

Delphi eyes lit up when we walked into the kitchen, still giggling.

"What's so funny?" Mama asked, leaning on her elbows on the other side of the island.

"I think we're a tiddle bit lipsy," Selene said, and we both laughed again.

"A tiddle?" Mama asked.

"A little bit tipsy," Delphi translated, looking disgruntled as she sipped her tea.

"I thought you were just going for a walk," Mama said.

"We did," I said, "and then we found a bar."

"A floating bar," Selene said and laughed harder, sending me into a fit of laughter, too.

"A floating bar?" Mama asked.

"No, I said a float *at* a bar." Selene tried to compose herself but ended up laughing harder as she said, "An ice cream float at a bar."

"They're drunk, Mama," Delphi said, giving us a glare for effect. "That's why I left early."

"Drunk?" Mama narrowed her eyes as she studied us. "Are you two girls intoxicated?"

"We are not," I said.

"We are, too, not," Selene said, at which point Delphi slid off the stool and made a quick exit.

"What's the story, girls?" Mama asked, not smiling at all.

"Once upon a time there were two sisters who found a floating bar," I began, at which point Mama threw up her hands and stormed off.

"And that's how to tell a story," I said, brushing my hands together.

Selene put her arm around my shoulders, and we walked out of the kitchen smiling.

Wednesday

A pounding on the front door before dawn the next morning had me jumping out of bed in alarm. I grabbed my robe and put it on as I dashed into the hallway and headed for the staircase at the front of the house. As I started down, Selene, Maia, and Delphi also came out of their rooms, followed by Nicholas, who called, "Mom, what's going on?"

My mother and father were already at the door, opening it, as Mama tied the sash of her blue robe around her waist. Two police officers entered, looked up the staircase at me, and asked, "Selene Spencer?"

"What do you want?" I answered, then turned and said to Nicholas, "Honey, stay back. It's going to be okay. Maia, take him back to his room, and please close the door." I said it all with a rapidly beating heart, because I knew what was happening. They had come to arrest my sister.

My mind spun back to the previous Friday, when Selene had made her first trip to the police station. *"What if the police come to the salon to arrest me?"*

"Listen to me, Selene. No one is going to charge you with murder as long as I'm able to draw a breath."

I realized I had stopped breathing. I drew in a deep, shuddering breath and gave thanks that at least it had happened at home before any of the neighbors were up and about.

"Selene?" one of the officers said, snapping me to attention.

Before Selene could utter a word, I asked again, "What do you want?"

"You need to come down to the police station with us."

"Why?" I asked.

Still looking at me, one of the officers said, "You're under arrest for the murder of Brady Rogers."

I heard a muffled cry and then spun around as Selene collapsed onto the floor. I was so angry I wanted to punch someone. Instead, I said, "Delphi, help her get dressed."

My mom added in Greek, *"Viasteite, prin tin pároun ópos eínai."* Hurry, before they take her as she is.

"This is my daughter Athena," my dad said to the officers. "I'll bring Selene down."

"Sir, you're going to have to step back," one of the officers said, and the two started up the staircase until I stepped in their way.

"Miss, stand back, or we'll take you in, too."

"That's fine with me," I replied, folding my arms.

"Mom, no!" Nicholas cried from behind me. I turned to look and saw him standing behind Maia in his bedroom doorway dressed in only a blue striped T-shirt and his underwear, his blue jeans in his hand. His frightened, vulnerable little face gazed at me in fear, forcing me to rethink my decision.

Reluctantly, I pressed my back against the wall and let them pass, then watched with a sinking feeling as they reached the top of the stairs. And then Nicholas, my brave little Niko, stood squarely in front of them and said in a bold voice, "You can't take my aunt to jail. I won't let you."

One of the officers bent down to say to him, "Son, you need to let us do our job. We're just going to drive her to the station to ask her some questions, okay?"

"Liar," Maia said, her hands resting on Nicholas's small shoulders.

"Then at least let her get dressed, please," my son said sweetly.

"Let us through," one of the officers said.

"Nicholas," I said calmly. "Do as they say."

Nicholas stepped aside, and they filed into the long upstairs hallway, knocked on the first door, and called, "Selene Spencer?"

When no one answered, they checked the next room, after which Delphi opened her door and blocked their entrance. One of the officers asked, "Are you Selene Spencer?"

Delphi tilted her head as though curious and studied their faces. "Your auras are dark. Very negative. Are you aware of that?"

"Is this Selene's room?" one of them asked.

"It isn't right now."

The officers glanced at each other as though trying to decipher Delphi's cryptic reply. "Step aside, please," one of the men said, his patience obviously waning.

She moved out of their way, and we all crowded into

the hallway to watch them search Delphi's room. Delphi walked in behind them and said, "Do you know what an oracle is?"

"Miss, we don't have time to—"

"It's someone who predicts futures, and I'm predicting that this is all a big mistake and you're going to be apologizing to Selene shortly."

"That's fine," one of the men said. "Where is Selene, and no more games."

"We're not taking this as a game," my dad said from downstairs. "Athena, get Selene, please."

I stood face-to-face with the two officers, not knowing what to do. Maia, Nicholas, and Delphi were staring at me, silently pleading with me not to interfere. Did I stand my ground and get arrested myself or did I give up? I glanced at Nicholas's frightened face and realized I had no options. I stepped aside.

At the far end of the hallway, we heard a creaking door slowly open, then my oldest sister stepped out of her room, ashen and shaking. She was wearing jeans and a Grecian blue shirt that I knew was her good luck charm. The officers confronted her, asked her to put her hands behind her back, cuffed her, and escorted her quietly down the stairs.

Mama stood at the bottom of the stairs, blocking the officers from moving any farther. She took off her thick gold bracelet and snapped it on Selene's wrist. "Keep this on."

"Ma'am," one of the officers said, "she won't be allowed to keep it."

"Then she can wear it until she gets there."

"I'm going with her," I said, right on their heels.

"*I'm* going, too," Maia said.

"You can't take them," Nicholas said. With a cry, he ran down the steps and wrapped his arms around my waist. "I won't let them take you, Mom. I'll go with you."

"Mr. Spencer, if you can't control your family, we'll arrest all of you."

"*Mr.* Spencer?" Mama asked, stationing herself in front of the door as she stared daggers at the officer. "Girls, get ready. We're all going to jail."

I could hear my dad's palm smack his forehead.

"Can I get arrested, too, Yiayiá?" Nicholas asked her.

"No, sweetheart, you can't," I said.

"What better way to learn about our justice system than to experience it?" my mother replied. "John, call our lawyer."

"I'll call Kevin," I said. "He knows Selene's story. Niko, finish getting dressed and grab your schoolbag. We're going on a field trip."

CHAPTER ELEVEN

The two officers had to wait for the police van to come get us, then Selene had to ride with them in their squad car, with my dad insisting on accompanying her. While we waited for the van, I called Kevin first, then Maguire, and left detailed voice messages, asking them to meet us at the jail as soon as possible. Then I phoned Yiayiá and Pappoús to explain that the prosecutor had decided to file charges against Selene and to tell them not to worry, that we had everything under control.

My son and I sat in the waiting room while our family was booked and everyone except Selene placed in the same holding cell. I could hear Mama banging her gold bracelet on the bars to create noise. "I'm protesting unfair treatment," she announced loudly. "My daughter was arrested before dawn this morning before she even had a chance to dress or eat breakfast."

"We didn't eat either," Maia reminded her.

"I brought your protein bars," Mama said. "I have them in my pockets." At which point, I could imagine her pulling the bars out of the pockets of her voluminous skirt. How she'd smuggled them in was a mystery.

Within the hour, most of the family was released on a bail bond that our grandparents posted and given a date for their initial court appearance. Selene, however, wasn't so lucky. She was made to dress in an orange jumpsuit and black flip-flops and was put in a cell with another woman.

Kevin had met us at the station and was already filing petitions on Selene's behalf to get her released on her own recognizance and to have a speedy initial hearing date set. He reported that the first petition would probably be denied. The second one was pending the judge's ruling.

"We'll visit every day," Mama promised, as we crowded around her cell. "We'll make them sit up and take notice. Don't you worry, my baby."

Selene gazed at her with sad eyes. "Thanks, Mama."

Mama shook her fist at the heavy door we had come through and cried in a raspy voice, "*Elpízo óti ta dáchtylá sas tha svísoun, kýrie Eisangeléa, opóte péftete sto prósopo sas sto dikastírio.*" Roughly translated, it meant, "I hope your toes rot off, Mr. Prosecutor, so you fall flat on your face in court."

"I agree," I called, and Selene began to giggle through her tears, which started Maia, Delphi, and even Mama laughing. I had a hunch it would be the last time we'd laugh for quite a while.

Maguire showed up as we were leaving the station, and I gave him a rundown on what had happened.

"I wish I'd known," he said. "I would've come to the house to pick Selene up myself."

"That's so kind of you, Bob," Delphi said with a sweet smile.

"No problem," he said, returning the smile as he gazed into her eyes.

For a moment it was as if they'd forgotten anyone else was around, and then my mother said from behind, "At a decent hour, I would hope. None of this pre-dawn non-sense. It's done only to intimidate, isn't it, Officer Maguire?"

"Come on, Hera," my dad said. "I've got to open the garden center. Let these two talk."

"You wouldn't have arrested Selene, would you, Bob?" Delphi asked.

"Unfortunately, we take our orders from the captain, who takes his orders from the prosecutor's office. I could've minimized the damage, however." Maguire knelt down so he could talk to Nicholas. "Are you okay, Niko? Do you understand that this is just a formality? I'll personally check on your aunt every day to make sure she's doing fine, all right?"

"Hey, you called me Niko!" he said, beaming.

"That's what I hear you like to be called," he said. "How about if I give you a ride back home in my squad car. You can turn on the lights for me."

"Awesome! Is it okay, Mom?"

"Not back home," I said, ruffling my son's hair. "You need to go to school, sweetie. Today's your last day. How about if this kind officer drops you off there?"

"Even better," Nicholas said. "The other kids will be so jealous."

Maguire motioned for me to meet him away from my

family. He kept his voice low and his words short. "No info yet on the traffic cams, but I did take another look at the autopsy report. No blunt-force trauma to the head. The only wounds he suffered were to the back. Seven stab wounds total."

"Seven," I exclaimed. "My God."

"Indicates a very emotional attack," Bob added. "Brutal."

"Okay, thanks again."

"Bob," I heard Delphi say as she joined our huddle, "will you take us home?"

Bob turned to see the Karras clan watching him hopefully. "There won't be room for all of you in the car," he said. "Niko, how about if your mom and Aunt Delphi come with you, and another officer takes the others back in a van?"

"Cool. Let's do it, Mom." Nicholas took Delphi's hand. "Come on, Theia Delphi," he said, using the Greek word for aunt. "Let's roll."

And with a blush, Delphi let Nicholas take her hand as Maguire took Nicholas's other hand. I tailed the three of them down the hallway, wondering whether Delphi was aware that Bob Maguire had been flirting with her.

As soon as I'd showered and dressed again, I called Case to fill him in on our morning. I let him know that my theory about Brady being bludgeoned with a heavy picture frame was no good. I also informed him of the brutal stabbing attack. He agreed that we needed to step up our investigation, so, after getting the okay from my dad, I arranged with Case to meet me at the library at ten o'clock to interview Nora.

On my way across town, I remembered, too, that Selene was supposed to hear whether Nora had been in the hair salon last Thursday, so I did a quick about-face and headed back to White Street, two blocks east of Greene. At Over the Top, I asked for Amber, who stuck her head out of a back room and motioned for me to join her.

Amber was a beautiful, twenty-something dark brunette, with long locks that she'd lightly waved and highlighted with a medium-blond color. She was also a fitness buff, with arm muscles to envy and a tattoo of a heart on her right bicep.

As we sat down at a big folding table, where Amber was having a cup of hot tea, she asked, "Is Selene doing okay?"

I leaned forward to say quietly, "Not really. She was taken to jail this morning on murder charges."

Amber's big brown eyes widened. "She was *what*? *Our* Selene? No way!"

"That's what I said. No way could she ever hurt anyone."

"Did she know the police suspected her?"

"We knew they had marked her as a person of interest."

"Is that why she was asking about Nora?"

"Actually, it was me who asked her to find out."

Amber gazed at me quizzically. "Am I watching the Goddess of Greene Street in action?"

I had to smile. "You could say that, yes."

Amber took a sip of tea, thinking for a moment. "After Selene asked about her, I checked the appointment book. Nora was here last Monday to have her hair colored."

I counted forward. It would have been three days before the bridal party came in.

She picked up a lock of her long hair. "I asked her if she wanted it like mine but without the highlights, and she asked if I knew Mandy Black. She said she was a friend of Mandy's and wanted her hair the same color because she liked it so much."

I wrote down: *Nora asked to have Mandy's hair color.* "At any point, did Nora go near Selene's station?"

"Selene's station is to the left of mine, so anyone coming to sit in my chair would pass by her station. So, yes, she was near it. She also came back to the salon on Thursday to pick up her credit card."

"She waited until Thursday to get her credit card?"

"I know. It sounds odd, doesn't it? But she said she wouldn't be able to stop by for it until then and asked if I could keep it safe for her. I told her I'd leave her card in my top drawer in an envelope with her name on it since I wouldn't be there on Thursday."

"Who gave it to her when she came back?"

"She got the okay from Lori to get it herself."

And there was Nora's opportunity. While Selene was at the diner with the family and Amber was off, Nora was walking right past Selene's empty station, and no one was paying any attention.

Time to interview Ms. Nora Modelle.

The library was so quiet the proverbial dropped pin would have echoed loudly if it had hit the dark wood floor. Case hadn't arrived yet, so I decided to do some preliminary investigation by locating Nora. The tall bookcases muffled the sound of my footsteps as I walked through the library, heading for the information counter, where I was directed to the ancestry department on the second floor. There, through a glass window in a door, I saw two women sitting at desks, one an older woman working with a young couple, the other a woman around my age reading something on a computer screen through a pair of old-fashioned oval spectacles perched halfway down her nose.

My phone dinged. I checked it and found a text from Case: **I'm running ten minutes behind. Where should I meet you?**

Athena: **Second floor of the library, ancestry department.**

I entered the wide, musty room and eyed the long rows of tall bookshelves filled with large, white binders. Several smaller bookshelves were lined up perpendicular to the far wall, and nearer to me were a group of individual cubicles with computer monitors.

I thought I had found a nice quiet corner in which to sit and wait for Case when I heard from behind, "May I help you?"

I turned around. "I'm looking for Nora."

"I'm Nora," she said with a friendly smile. "What can I help you with?"

I stared at the woman I had come to investigate, at a loss for words. This was Brady Rogers's former lover? This bloated, blotchy, red-complexioned woman with conspicuously dyed dark hair the texture of straw? Even her outfit—a gray cotton-knit dress stretched too tight over exaggeratedly large curves—spoke volumes about her.

After Nora repeated her question, I snapped to attention and realized I had nothing prepared. Why hadn't I waited for Case?

"I'd like to research my mother's side of the family," I stammered, deciding belatedly that the truth would've probably been a better choice.

Nora led me across the room to a long table filled with three computers and stacks of notepaper. "Why don't you fill out this form, and then I can help you get started?"

She slid a sheet of paper in front of me, handed me a ballpoint pen, and left. I glanced around for Case, then sat down, hung my purse over the back of the chair, and clicked the pen as I stared at the questions. When the older librarian turned her head to give me a look, I realized I was still clicking and put my pen to the paper, only to remember that I didn't want to give away my identity.

"Are you having a problem?"

I gave a start at the voice coming from behind me. Nora pulled out a chair adjacent to mine at the head of the table and scooted in. "What can I help you with?"

For starters, where was Case?

"Can I ask you some questions?" I said.

"Of course."

The door opened, and I heard, "There you are. Sorry I'm late, honey. Traffic was a nightmare coming in from Chicago. Hi, I'm Case Donnelly."

I turned to see Case striding toward us, extending his hand. He was dressed in a tan button-down shirt, dark blue jeans, with a brown belt and brown boat shoes. His short beard was filling in nicely, giving him a slightly dangerous look. With that and his curly dark hair, I thought he looked particularly attractive. Apparently, so did Nora.

She rose and shook back her hair as though she were a

beauty queen getting ready to walk the runway. "Nora Modelle," she said, gazing seductively at him from beneath heavily coated black eyelashes.

I rose, too, following his lead on our new identity as a couple. "I apologize for not introducing myself before, Nora. I'm Thenie Karras, Case's fiancée."

CHAPTER TWELVE

"It's a pleasure to meet you both," Nora said, gazing only at Case, a kittenish smile on her puffy, burgundy-colored lips. Case, I noticed, was trying to hide his surprise at her appearance. Or was it the news of our sudden engagement that had his eyebrows quirked?

"Please, sit down," Case said, holding Nora's chair for her.

"Thenie?" he said, almost as if he were trying out my new name as he held the chair for me. I sat down, and he took a seat across from me. "Let's get started," he said, folding his hands on the table.

Nora also folded her hands on the table and rested her bosom on top of them, making sure he noticed, as she said with a fey smile, "What would you like to know?"

"Actually," Case said, looking at me. "I think my wife—"

"Fiancée," I corrected.

"My fiancée has a few questions for you."

"We're investigating Brady Rogers's death," I said, loving the flash of shock in her eyes as she turned to stare at me.

Still smiling, Case said, "We thought you might be able to help us fill in the details of his personal life. We understand you and he dated."

Nora sat back in her chair and placed her hand across her heart as though she had just been exposed, like we had uncovered too much truth. Her already blotchy skin took on an even redder shade, and instead of flirting with Case, she suddenly looked like she was flirting with the idea of charging the exit.

Case put his hand on the table, his demeanor calm and relaxing. "It's okay," he said. "You can talk to us. Whatever you say here is confidential."

She touched a perfectly groomed fingernail against her eyebrow, then tossed her hair again as she regained her composure. "Actually, we were engaged." She turned to me and said in a skeptical voice, "Why the ruse about your ancestors?"

Case quirked his head, as though to say, *Yes, Athena, why the ruse?*

"I–thought I would learn a little about my ancestry while I waited for my husband."

"Fiancé," Case corrected.

"That's what I meant."

"You're just so eager, my sweet," Case said. "Remember, we haven't even told your family yet."

"I remember," I said, flashing him a quick glare. I took my iPad out of my purse and opened it to a Word file marked Nora. "When were you engaged to Brady?"

"Until he dumped me three months ago." Nora turned toward Case and said sweetly, "I tried to warn him about Mandy, but he refused to listen to me."

"Warn him in what respect?" Case asked.

"When I found out he was seeing her I tried to tell him that she was no good for him, that her family was no good. I knew she would hurt him in the end. I just didn't think she would kill him."

"What was Brady's response to your concerns?" Case asked.

"Anger. Outrage that I would sully the name of little Miss Amanda Black."

There was venom in her tone when she spoke Mandy's name.

"Lo and behold," she continued in the same tone, "soon afterward, he became engaged to Amanda. It became apparent that he was after somebody with money."

"Would you mind explaining how you reached that conclusion?" Case asked.

"Because he'd hardly had a chance to get to know her when he proposed to her. And suddenly they had a wedding date. You can't tell me he wasn't after her money, she with the silver Porsche and diamond-encrusted watch. He was blinded by her money. I knew he still loved me. He just couldn't see me because of the glare of her gold."

Not that Nora was jealous or anything. Still, I had no trouble imagining how hard it must have been for her when she'd learned about Mandy. I could almost hear the sound of her heart slamming shut.

"So you believe Mandy killed Brady," I said.

"Absolutely."

"Do you believe he saw you as a meal ticket, too?" I asked.

Nora paused, as though she hadn't considered it before. "Looking back, I'd have to say yes, although it didn't seem that way at first. We had chemistry, passion. We were in love, even after I learned about his . . . *proclivities*."

"And by his proclivities you mean?"

"His wandering eye." She shook her head, looking deeply offended. "The way he stared at every woman, it was as though he was assessing her, and not just her body but also her net worth. It was embarrassing."

Given what I'd learned about Brady, Nora was completely believable.

She took a breath, rearranged her hair, and said, "Anyway, you said you're investigating his death. At whose request?"

"We're not at liberty to say," I said.

Obviously not happy with my answer she said coldly, "I thought the police had a suspect. Selene Spencer. At least that's what was in the newspaper."

"That's the police's theory," I retorted.

Case sat back in his chair. "We're open to any other possibilities, though."

"I'm unsure as to why your client feels the need to conduct his own investigation," Nora said. "It seems a fairly open-and-shut case to me. Selene had an affair with Brady. She was incensed when she found out he was going to marry sweet little Amanda"—once again Nora said Mandy's name with great venom—"and to get even, she killed him with her scissors."

I was about to defend my sister when I felt Case nudge my foot under the table. "It doesn't seem likely that there was an affair," he said. "Did you know Miss Spencer had filed a complaint against Brady with Fitness First?"

"She complained about Brady?" Nora asked. "What for?"

"We can't give out that information," I said, "but based on what you told us about him, I'm sure you can figure it out."

"Not necessarily," Nora said with a glare. "Maybe Selene filed that complaint out of jealousy. And then she killed him for the same reason. You never know what people are capable of."

"I thought you believed Mandy killed him," I said.

Nora's eyes narrowed, became crafty. "You're trying to trip me up."

"You stated"—I read from my notes—"'I knew she would hurt him in the end. I just didn't think she would kill him.'"

"She could have," Nora said, lifting her chin. "Either one of them could have."

"I understand Brady took out a restraining order on you," I said.

She folded her hands on the table and glared at me. "Only because I filed one on him first."

I made a note in the iPad to look it up at the courthouse. "Is it true that after you'd broken up with him, you followed him to the gym in the mornings and to his apartment after work?"

Nora looked around at her coworker very casually. "Why don't we get a cup of coffee next door?"

I thought she was talking about Pie in the Sky Bakery, but she led us out of the ancestry department to a room next to it that had a snack machine, a K-cup machine, two round Formica tables, and white plastic chairs.

After she'd made herself and Case a cup—I'd passed—

she took out her phone and placed it on the table. To Case she said, "I'm expecting a call from the front desk about some materials I ordered. I have a couple coming in to pick them up at ten thirty, so I won't be able to talk much longer."

"We don't have much more to ask," Case said, "and we appreciate any time you can give us."

She smiled at him so sweetly I could almost hear her heart creaking open. If Case wasn't careful, he was going to have a fan club.

"Going back to my question," I said, "is it true that you followed Brady to the—"

"Yes," she said, cutting me off. "But I did that only once or twice and that was because I was upset and was trying to talk to him. But he'd clearly moved on, so I stopped."

"Then it wasn't due to the restraining order?" I asked.

Her tone was curt. "The restraining order was unnecessary. As I said, he filed it because I filed one against him."

"Why did you file a restraining order?" I asked, puzzled. "Was he following *you?*"

"He was making threatening remarks." With a wounded look she added, "He frightened me."

Nora was so unbelievable I wanted to laugh. She must have seen it in my expression because she folded her arms across her chest and looked away.

Case gave her a sympathetic smile. "It must have come as quite a shock when you heard that Brady and Mandy were engaged."

"I gave him my everything," she said, sniffling back invisible tears, "and all I got were phony promises of marriage and a broken heart."

Her *poor me* attitude was getting under my skin. "You've dyed your hair," I said.

Nora's face flushed bright red. "Yes, I did. I needed a change. When the heart is broken, sometimes a change helps."

"It's Mandy's color, isn't it?" I asked.

She fingered a lock of dry hair, gazing at me with hostility. "Is it?"

Case gave me a warning glance and changed the subject. "When was the last time you saw Brady?"

"I'll have to think." Her phone dinged, and she glanced at the screen. "That's the front desk. I'm going to have to run downstairs in a minute. And to answer your question, I don't remember the last time I saw Brady. It must've been weeks ago."

I asked, "Do you have a key to his apartment?"

She turned her head to glare at me again. "I gave it back when he broke off our engagement."

The older woman stuck her head in. "The Steins are here, Nora."

"I'll be right there." To Case she said sweetly, "Are we about finished?"

"I have just a few more quick questions," he said.

She rose. "I'll run down and pick up their material so they can start reading it, then I'll come back and we can finish."

"Please," Case said with a smile.

With a coquettish tilt of her head, she said playfully, "If you insist."

After she'd left I said, "Could you be any more flirtatious?"

"It works, doesn't it?" Case pulled her phone closer to him. "And look what Nora left."

"A lasting impression?"

"She certainly got under your skin, *Thenie*. And next time give me a heads up about an engagement."

"Sorry. I needed an excuse. It seemed like a good idea at the time."

Case pushed a button on her phone, opened up her contact list, and scrolled through it. "Look who we have in here—Brady . . . and Mandy. How about that?"

"Interesting. How about finding Nora's phone number for me?"

Case took out his phone, snapped a photo of the screen, then went into her settings, read off her cell phone number, and slid the phone back in its place. "Done."

I glanced at my watch. "I'm ready to wrap this up."

"One more thing," he said. "When Nora returns, don't be so confrontational. It isn't professional."

"Professional? There's nothing professional about flirting either."

"It gets the job done."

"In that case, I guess you could say that Lila is being extremely professional with you."

Case studied me with a little grin. "Are you jealous of Lila?"

"I'm not jealous. She just irritates me, that's all."

Nora came back at that moment, apparently in a rush to get to the couple in the other room. "I really have to leave," she said directly to Case.

"We'll make it quick then," I jumped in to say. "Would you tell us where you were last Friday morning?"

Narrowing her eyes at me, she said with barely concealed scorn, "I was here at my desk, doing my job as usual."

With as much grace as I could muster, I thanked her, then typed her answer into my notes.

Case held out his hand to shake hers. "Nora, we appreciate your help. Thank you for taking time out of your busy day."

"You're very welcome," she said with a genuine smile, then turned her back on me and sashayed out of the room.

Downstairs at the information desk, Case smiled at the young woman with an auburn pixie cut. "Can you tell me who was working last Friday in the ancestry department?"

"You'd have to talk to the head librarian," she said.

"And where would we find her?"

"She's a him, and he's not here today. He's at a conference in Grand Rapids."

Case leaned an elbow on the counter and smiled at her as only he could. "Is there any way you can check last Friday's schedule for us?"

She raised an eyebrow, completely unaffected by Case's charm. "There are several ways I can check last Friday's schedule. Is this regarding the death of Brady Rogers?"

"In fact, it is," he replied. "We're investigating—"

"That's all you had to say." She tapped a few keys and, without looking up from her monitor, replied, "Nora called in sick last Friday. Now, if you'll excuse me."

As soon as she'd stepped into a back room, Case glanced over at me and gave me a shrug. I shook my head sadly. "Should have been more professional."

As we started walking north up White Street, Case said, "So Nora called in sick last Friday. Interesting."

"She probably didn't think you would question her story after she batted those long eyelashes at you."

Ignoring my jab, he said, "What else did we learn about Nora Modelle?"

"We know she hates Mandy, that's for certain. She couldn't speak her name without her upper lip curling. We know she thinks Mandy could have killed Brady, although she seemed perfectly willing to let Selene take the rap for it. We know she stalled when I asked about her hair color but was quick to answer that she didn't have a key, which I'm not sure I believe. And we know she feels mighty sorry for herself, an emotion you egged on, by the way."

"See what charm can get you?"

We waited for a car to pass, then crossed the street and headed up to Greene. "I forgot to ask before," Case said, "but what is our wedding date, Thenie? I need to start planning my bachelor party."

"After you called me honey, that was all I could come up with. And you can go back to calling me Athena now."

"Well, then, Athena," he said, "would you like to discuss your Lila comment? Or are you more comfortable with the passive-aggressive approach?"

"I'm neither passive nor aggressive. My comment stands."

After an awkward pause during which neither of us knew what to say, I said, "So, the next thing on my list is to go to the courthouse records department to see if it's true that Nora filed a restraining order against Brady. I'll do that tomorrow before work."

"Let's interview Mandy Black next," Case said. "I'm eager to talk to the woman at the center of it."

"Have you heard from her brother?"

"On it." Case took out his phone and texted Mitchell, reading out loud as he typed: **Are you free to talk this evening?**

His phone dinged a few seconds later. He let me read the text with him.

Mitchell: **Not available this evening**.

Case: **Tomorrow evening?**

Mitchell: **You spoke with the other groomsmen. Why do you need me?**

Case: **To get a brother's viewpoint. Let's meet at Bar None at 7 p.m.**

There was no reply.

We continued north on Greene Street, and as we passed by the block of Greek shops known locally as Little Greece, Case checked his phone. "Still no reply." He slid his phone into his back pocket and said, "We may have to drop by the Waterfront Hotel and catch Mitchell there. What do you want to do about interviewing Mandy?"

"Until we get a better feel for the situation, let's not set anything up. In fact, let's try the element of surprise. She doesn't work, and according to what the groomsmen said, she likes to shop, so we might be able to catch her at home tomorrow morning before the shops open at ten. If we miss her, we can set up a formal meeting."

"No problem getting away in the morning?"

"When it's for Selene, don't worry. My dad would be the first to give me a push out the door."

As we approached Oak Street, where he would turn off to head for the marina, I took a deep breath and asked, "When do you hear about financing for your charter fishing boat operation?"

"I'm waiting for an answer from Lila's finance manager on how we're going to structure it."

His phone dinged, and he said, "Maybe that's her now."

Speak of the devil.

He pulled out his phone and read the text then showed me.

Mitchell: **Bar None at 7 tonight. See you then.**

Case replied with a thumbs-up icon. He started to put his phone away when it dinged again. He read it and smiled. Instead of showing me the text message, he slipped the phone into his pocket. "I think my financing went through. Lila wants me to meet her at the bank at three p.m. today."

"That's good news. I'm happy for you."

Then why wasn't I smiling inside?

Chapter Thirteen

Lunch at the diner was a sad affair. Maia and Mama had gone to the jail to visit Selene before noon, and now, as they sat in the booth across from Delphi and me, discussing Selene's mood and living conditions, no one felt much like eating. Knowing my stomach wouldn't let me take a pass, I ordered a Greek salad loaded with kalamata olives and feta cheese and supplemented it with piping-hot bread dipped in olive oil, hoping that would keep me fueled until dinner.

"I'm going to see Selene at three o'clock today," I said.

"Then I'll go this evening," Delphi said. "We can spread it out, so she's not so alone."

"You might want to go before five," I said. "I don't think there are visiting hours in the evening."

Delphi sighed, then immediately brightened. "I know.

I'll ask Bob Maguire to take me to see her. He said if there was anything he could ever do . . ."

"Any Greek blood in the Maguire family?" Mama asked.

"I'm not sure," Delphi said, glancing at me for help.

"Isn't there a little Greek in everyone?" I asked Mama with a teasing smile.

"Wait. I'm getting a message," Delphi said, and closed her eyes. She rested her hands palm side up on the table and pressed her lips together for a few moments, then said, "In ancient times, Irish monks traveled to Greece to teach, leaving behind Irish genes and taking some Greek genes home." Then she opened her eyes.

"You just now heard that message?" Mama asked, cocking an eyebrow suspiciously.

Maia laughed. "You didn't just hear it. We learned that at Greek school."

"I just now *remembered* it," Delphi said, "with a little help from my friends." She glanced heavenward.

Mama propped her chin on her palm. "So what you're saying is that there's a little Irish in everyone, too."

"Basically, yes," Delphi said, and sipped her tea, looking pleased with herself. "Anyway, it doesn't matter. Bob and I are just friends."

"Go see your sister this evening," Mama said. "I don't care how you get in, just do it. In fact, why don't you take Pappoús with you? He hasn't been to see her yet."

Looking not quite so pleased, Delphi put down her teacup and said, "I guess I can take Pappoús."

"I'm sure Bob will love it," I said, and got a pinch under the table.

*   *   *

Delphi and I returned to Spencer's at one o'clock and found Dad checking out a line of customers. I asked Delphi to take over and give Dad a break. While she took her position behind the cash register, I did a walk-around, checking in with several tourists in the barn and a few more serious shoppers in the outdoor part of the center.

"Thank goodness Drew agreed to help out this summer," I whispered to Delphi as she finished up with the line.

"Let's hope his chakras line up with the store's energy," Delphi said.

"At this point, I don't think it matters," I said. "We need help badly."

"Here's another idea," Dad said, joining us. "Instead of sending Niko to day camp, why don't you have him come here? You know he'd enjoy it, and it would teach him a lot."

"Good idea, Pops. Today is his last day of school. He can start tomorrow."

Since it was just my first year back in Sequoia, I was still working out our living arrangements. One day I hoped to have my own place, but that would have to wait until Nicholas was older and I had paid down my debts. For now, living with my parents worked well for all of us.

By three o'clock, the afternoon rush had died down, my father was relaxing with a cup of coffee in the office, and Delphi was rearranging a display of violets she'd placed around the statue of Athena. I promised I wouldn't be long and used my break time to dash over to the jail.

After depositing my purse with the matron and going through an X-ray machine, I walked down the long hallway and through a security door, where I saw two guards eating baklava on paper plates.

Mama?

When Selene shuffled into the visitor's room, her ankles in shackles, and sat in the cubicle across the glass divider from me, I wanted to cry. We picked up the phones, and she did cry.

"I can't take this, Thenie. I hate it here. It's hot, it stinks, the food's lousy, and my roommate whines all day."

"I'm doing everything I can, Selene. We talked to the groomsmen yesterday. We interviewed Nora this morning. I talked to Amber this morning, too, and Case and I are going to meet with Mitchell at seven o'clock this evening. Tomorrow we're going to see Mandy, and after that, we have Tonya and the other bridesmaids to interview. I can jam only so many things into a day. You're not being mistreated, are you?"

"Not mistreated, but then there are these." She jangled her ankle cuffs. "I'm doing nothing but reading, and I can barely focus on that." She pulled a tissue out of a box nearby and blotted her eyes. She looked like a ghost without her makeup, and the orange jumpsuit made her complexion look sallow. I wanted to hug her, but, of course, I wasn't allowed.

"Mama and Maia came before lunch," Selene said with a trembling sigh. "Mama brought food."

"That was nice of her."

"For the jailers."

"I knew it! That was *Yiayiá's* baklava I saw the guards eating. I'm sorry."

"The guards weren't sorry. They love it. And Mama is under the impression that if she keeps bringing food, they'll treat me better."

"I'm assuming she's wrong."

"They treat everyone the same, Thenie. Not badly, just the same. Food doesn't matter. She won't believe it, though."

"Then let her do it. She thinks she's helping."

"I guess." She heaved another sigh, wiped away the last bit of moisture from her eyes, and asked, "Have you found out anything more?"

I ran through everything we'd garnered, omitting only Nora's mention of Selene being the killer. "So, several big revelations. Nora had a reason to be at the salon Thursday when your scissors were stolen. She dyed her hair to look like Mandy's. She stalked Brady after they'd broken up. She claims to have filed a restraining order on Brady. And she doesn't have an alibi for the time of the murder."

"That's a lot of evidence," Selene said.

"Exactly."

"Was she trying to *become* Mandy to convince Brady to take her back?"

"Possibly."

"Do you have any proof that Nora was at the salon on Thursday?" Selene asked, her red-rimmed eyes hopeful. "Any proof that will clear me?"

I hesitated, trying to formulate an acceptable answer. "Not yet, Selene, but we're still searching." My heart felt like it was breaking in two as I watched the hope slowly fade from her gaze.

She let the phone slip as her head dropped into her folded arms. I sat across from her, watching in despair as my oldest sister sobbed behind the glass. "I will get you out of here, Selene," I said loud enough for her to hear through the glass. "Don't give up."

* * *

Fifteen minutes later, I left the jail and crossed the street to the courthouse. Situated on White Street almost directly behind Little Greece, the big, limestone building housed four courtrooms, and numerous offices, including the district attorney's office, the tax assessor's office, the treasurer's office, and the records department.

In Sequoia's records department, I found that Nora had indeed filed a restraining order against Brady just two weeks prior to his death, well after the date I was fairly certain Brady had filed his. To be sure, I asked for Brady Rogers's records to compare dates, only to learn that they had been pulled. I noted it as another matter for Maguire to handle.

On my way back to Spencer's, I phoned Maguire and left a message for him to call me. I remembered that Case was meeting with Lila and made sure to detour around the bank to get back to the garden center. I didn't want to see her through a window again. I had a bad feeling about Lila that wouldn't go away.

Shortly before seven that evening, with the sun still glowing brightly an hour from sunset, I entered Bar None, a modern bar decorated in black and white, with touches of bright green. Tourists, hungry from a long day of sightseeing, sat at black high-top tables chatting and laughing, while locals filled the seats around the bar.

I spotted Case sitting at a high-top near a window and started toward him. Case stood as I approached and held a stool for me. After I was seated, he sat down across from me and handed me the bar menu.

"I'll have a cabernet," I told the waitress, then glanced

around for signs of our guest. "Do you think Mitchell will show?"

"We can flip a coin on that call," Case answered.

"How did your bank meeting go?"

"I misspoke earlier. The financing hasn't come through yet. The banker wants some prices on boats, rental fees, salaries for employees, that kind of thing. I'll do my research tomorrow morning."

"Is Lila being helpful?"

He took a sip of beer and put it down. "Very."

My wine came, so Case picked up his beer and clinked it to my wineglass. "Here's to Mitchell showing up."

"And to getting your financing," I said, and took a drink of wine. "By the way, I've been so busy I haven't had a chance to talk to Pappoús about the boat, but hopefully, I'll get to that tomorrow."

"I'd appreciate it." Case's phone dinged. He glanced at it and said, "Mitchell's here, but he doesn't know who to look for. I'll go get him."

He got off his stool and walked toward Mitchell, who was standing inside the door, gazing around. Case brought him to our table and introduced me as his partner. I'd decided not to hide behind a fake name this time because I knew Mitchell would remember me from the rehearsal dinner.

A clean-shaven man in his mid-thirties, Mitchell had the same dark brown hair his twin sister had and the slender physique of a store mannequin, which complimented his crisply ironed, blue-striped, button-down shirt with navy pants and expensive leather loafers. A light-yellow paisley tie hung from his collar, his sophisticated style in sharp contrast to the casual lakeside setting. He had a blunt, yet still polite manner as he shook my hand

and penetrating blue eyes that studied me as though I were a lab specimen.

"Thanks for meeting with us," I said. "We had a very fruitful meeting with Patrick and Trevor. We hope this one will be as helpful to our investigation."

"I'll do my best." Sitting, he asked, "What do you need to know?"

As I readied my iPad, Case said, "We're trying to get a more complete picture of Brady. We understand you spent quite a bit of time with him."

"Not because I enjoyed his company," Mitchell said, then immediately grew red in the face. "That didn't come out right. Please don't write that down. What I meant to say was that I felt it necessary to be around Brady whenever he was with my sister."

He paused to give the waitress his bar order, then started again, "What I mean is that Brady had a reputation, and I wasn't happy about my sister being with him, so whenever the group went out, I did, too. In that regard, yes, I spent quite a bit of time with him."

That was the long way around a simple yes. "Do you believe Brady loved your sister?" I asked.

Looking unsettled by the question, Mitchell replied, "Perhaps in his own way."

"Meaning?" I asked.

"Brady was quite a partier, very outgoing and effusive, so it was difficult to discern whether he was truly in love with my sister or if that was just his way with all women. My suspicion was that it was the latter."

"What was your parents' opinion of Brady?" Case asked.

"They didn't know Brady at all. We all went out to dinner a few times, and each time Brady turned on the charm. I seemed to be the only one who could see through him."

"Had you heard that Brady was seeing someone other than Mandy before his death?" Case asked.

"It was rumored."

"By whom?"

Mitchell paused to thank the waitress, then took a sip of his iced tea. He was not at all forthcoming with information. "I believe my sister told me."

"She must have been furious," I said.

"Upset," Mitchell quickly corrected, "and rightly so. She cried as though her heart was broken."

"Why didn't she call off the wedding?" I asked.

His lips thinned in anger. "Is that question truly necessary?"

"Your answer might be helpful," Case replied.

He brushed a crumb off the table to show his impatience. "She didn't call off the wedding because they worked it out. Brady admitted to having an affair and said it was a mistake that would never happen again. Mandy forgave him, and then they went forward."

"When did that happen?" Case asked.

"Two weeks before the rehearsal dinner."

"Did Mandy know who he had the affair with?" Case asked.

Mitchell darted a glance at me before replying, "Yes. He told her it was with Selene Spencer. And yes, I understand that Selene is your sister, and I suppose you're outraged by the accusation of murder. Nevertheless, I do believe Selene is responsible for Brady's murder."

The temperature in the room seemed to rise rapidly as my face flushed with heat. "You're basing that on what

Brady told your sister? How could Mandy know for sure that Brady was telling the truth?"

He looked at me with indifference. "I suppose she trusted him."

"After he cheated on her?"

Mitchell sipped his tea.

"Does it stand to reason that Selene would have confessed to Mandy about the affair on the eve of her marriage?" I asked.

He tapped his fingers on the table, clearly annoyed. "I suppose not."

"Isn't it possible Brady lied about who he was having an affair with?"

Mitchell set his glass down, positioning it perfectly over the condensation mark left on the napkin. "It's possible, yes. But to what end?"

"Possibly to protect the woman he'd actually been seeing, especially if it was someone close to Mandy."

"Like Selene?" Mitchell asked pointedly.

I leaned in closer and said quietly, "My sister is innocent, Mitchell. She didn't have an affair with Brady. In fact, she filed a complaint against Brady for misconduct and quit going to the gym because she didn't like him. That was it."

I leaned back in my chair. "If you think about it, how stupid would she have to be to use her own scissors to kill him, leave them at the scene of the murder, and stuff a blood-soaked T-shirt in the garbage bin behind her own place of employment?"

Mitchell traced a drip down the side of his glass. "I suppose it doesn't make sense."

"Thank you," I said.

"What did you do when you heard that Mandy was going to proceed with the wedding?" Case asked.

Mitchell picked up his glass and swirled the ice, his expression stony. "I wished her good luck."

"So you were okay with her decision?" Case asked.

"Her life. Her call." Mitchell glanced at his watch and then looked around at the door, as though expecting someone. His gesture reminded me of a similar move I'd seen him make before.

"On the night of the rehearsal dinner," I said, "were you alarmed when Brady failed to show?"

"Not at first. Brady always took his time. He wasn't at all concerned with punctuality."

"I saw you checking your watch at that dinner," I told him. "You seemed agitated."

"Wouldn't you be?" he snapped. "Of course I was agitated, especially when Mandy, and then Trevor, couldn't reach him by phone."

"Do you have any idea why your sister's first thought was that Brady was dead?" I asked.

"How would I know that?" He shoved his glass away. "Where is this line of questioning going? Are you trying to get me to say that Mandy is responsible for Brady's death?"

"That's not our intent," Case said evenly. "We're trying to put together a cohesive picture of Brady."

"Do you believe Brady truly loved Mandy?" I asked.

He took a deep breath and blew it out as though trying to calm himself. "I hope so."

"Is it possible he saw your sister as a meal ticket?"

Mitchell flinched as though I'd struck a nerve. "Why do you think I kept an eye on him?" His fingers closed hard around his glass as he picked it up and took a drink.

"Do you know Nora Modelle?" I asked.

"I know who she was to Brady."

"Nora believes that Brady was looking for a meal ticket and found Mandy."

Mitchell drained his glass and set it on the table with a hard *thunk*, "I hope that wasn't the case."

"Your family is wealthy," Case said. "That would've been a big meal."

"As Mandy's brother," I said, "what would you have done if it were?"

His jaw muscle ticked furiously. "What do you want me to say? That I killed Brady on the *assumption* that was his reason?" He pushed the glass aside. "This meeting is over."

"Mitchell, here you are!"

I looked around, and there stood Mandy.

CHAPTER FOURTEEN

Mitchell jumped off his stool as though he'd been poked by a pin. "Mandy, what are you doing here?"

"Mother and Father are waiting outside. We have dinner plans tonight, remember?"

Dinner out so soon after Brady's death? That was quite a short mourning period.

Looking nothing like I would've expected a grieving fiancée to look, Amanda Black gazed around her with blank eyes, as though she was on some kind of drug. Her dark brown hair was pulled up in a loose knot, and her lips were coated in a nude lipstick. She had on a tailored beige linen jacket with a brown blouse, brown slacks, and brown leather flats. Over her shoulder she carried a beige bag with a gold D & G logo on it. *Dolce & Gabbana.* I could see how someone like Nora would feel threatened by Mandy.

"Hello, Athena. How are you?" She pronounced each word as though it was an effort to get it out. She turned to Case and said in that same flat voice, "Case, isn't it? You're investigating Brady's death."

Case shook her hand. "Case Donnelly."

"Where are you having dinner?" I asked.

Mandy stared at me as though she didn't have a clue.

"At Sage, just up the block, isn't it?" Mitchell prompted.

"I saw Trevor this afternoon, Athena," she said. "I'm sorry to hear that Selene's still in jail. I wouldn't have believed she could ever do such a"—she paused as though searching for the right words—"thing, but . . ." She paused again, and didn't seem to know how to end the sentence.

"But the evidence is mounting," her twin finished. "However, it's best if we don't get into this now. My sister has a long way to go before she recovers." He put his hand on Mandy's back and said with a forced smile, "Shall we?"

As he escorted her to the door she looked back and said, "I'm sorry about your sister."

And with that, the two of them walked out.

I looked back at Case. "That was good timing on Mandy's part."

"What did you think of Mitchell?"

"He struck me as an angry man. And he made it very clear that he didn't like our questions."

Case picked up his beer. "He played it close to the vest, very deliberate in his word choices, especially when it came to his feelings toward Brady. He also seemed surprised when Mandy walked in."

"I don't think it was genuine."

"You think he faked it?"

"She got him off the hook, didn't she? She had to have known about our meeting."

Case finished his beer and laid thirty dollars on the table. "Let's find out if she was telling the truth about that dinner."

I left my half-finished drink, grabbed my purse and sweater, and followed him out of the bar. We scanned the sidewalks but saw only some window-shoppers and a family sitting outside an ice cream parlor a few shops down. We walked half a block down to Sage and Case went inside.

"I saw no sign of them anywhere," he told me when he came out. "Let's go back to the bar. I want to try something else."

Case slipped back inside the bar and came out a few minutes later. "The customers at the table by that window"—he pointed—"saw a dark-haired young woman arrive in a silver Porsche."

"That has to be Mandy's car," I said.

"She was alone, Athena. No one was with her."

"I wonder why she lied."

"To make her excuse more believable."

As we headed north on Greene Street, Case said, "After we talk to Mandy I'm going to interview Mitchell again, but alone this time."

"Why?"

"There's something about him . . . Just a sense that there's an undercurrent he didn't want us to see."

"Did you notice him clenching his glass?"

"That's what I mean about an undercurrent. I think you got it right when you called him an angry man."

"Are we still going to Mandy's parents' house tomorrow?"

"Yes, I'll pick you up at nine-forty in the morning. And after that I'm going boat shopping."

"You're going to pick *me* up? Don't you need a car to do that?"

He glanced at me sideways. "I have one."

"A rental?"

"Nope, I bought one."

I stared at him in surprise. "When were you going to tell me?"

He poked my shoulder playfully. "I just told you."

"What kind of car did you buy?"

When we paused at the light he gave me a little smile and put his arm around me. "You'll have to wait and see."

"Talk about keeping things close to the vest."

As we crossed the street I said, "I think I'll use my lunch hour to talk to the bridesmaids. I'll see if I can set something up with them now."

I pulled out my phone and called Joni but was directed to her voicemail. I left a detailed message and asked her to get back to me ASAP. I checked my messages but there was no word from Maguire.

Case walked me all the way home, pausing on my porch to say good night. It was a lovely evening, and although it had been a very long day, I almost wished I lived alone so I could invite him in for coffee or an after-dinner drink. But I needn't have worried about that. Before he could move, the door swung open, and Mama appeared in the doorway.

"Please," she said, "come in for some coffee."

Case smiled at her. "I'll have to take a rain check, but thanks, anyway."

Delphi and Maia appeared in the doorway on each side

of her, and then Nicholas snuck past and came out to take Case's arm. "Come on, Case. Yiayiá says my aunt Delphi can read your coffee grounds."

I grabbed Case's other arm. "No coffee after eight o'clock. Isn't that your rule, Case?"

"For heaven's sake, make it decaf then," Mama said in exasperation. "I'll go get it started." And off she went toward the kitchen.

Twenty minutes later, we were sitting in the living room around a coffee table littered with empty plates of baklava and coffee cups, four women and one tired boy eagerly listening as Case and I discussed our investigation with them. And finally, Mama got to the reason she'd invited Case inside.

"So you're part Greek, eh?" Mama asked. "How much of a part?"

"We went over this already, Mama," I said firmly. "His great-grandfather had a museum in Crete, remember?"

"People can live in Greece and not be Greek, Athena," she said.

"Nicholas—Niko—time for bed," I said.

"But Yiayiá said I could stay up an extra fifteen minutes because today was my last day of school."

"He's a smart boy, Thenie," Mama said. "Just like his *pappoús*."

"And Yiayiá," Nicholas added, smiling at his grandmother.

"See what I mean?" Mama asked.

"He's not going to be smart tomorrow if he doesn't get enough sleep tonight," I countered. "Upstairs, young man. You need to be well rested for your first day at Spencer's. I'll be up shortly to tuck you in."

"And I need to get going," Case told him.

Reluctantly, Nicholas said good night and trudged up the stairs.

Case finished his triangle of baklava and had barely downed his last sip of coffee when Delphi whisked the cup away from him and settled cross-legged on the sofa. "I'm going to do a reading for you, Case."

She wore purple-print harem pants and a white top, her hair tied up on top of her head like a genie with a purple elastic donut. She swirled the last few drips of coffee through the grounds, closed her eyes, and hummed the yogi's chant, "ohm," three times. Then she opened her eyes and gazed at the pattern the grounds had made.

I'd seen her do it hundreds of times, but never had I felt such trepidation. What was going to come out of her mouth this time? I glanced at my mother and saw her check her watch.

"I'm seeing the letter M," Delphi said, then glanced up to see if it registered with Case.

He gave me a quizzical look. I shrugged.

"Do you see anything else?" I asked.

Delphi closed her eyes and tilted her head as though listening to something. Then she opened her eyes and said, "It's the answer to a question you're asking."

"A question I'm asking?" Case repeated, darting me another quizzical glance.

"Who killed Brady!" Nicholas cried from the top of the stairs. "Is that it, Theia Delphi?" he said. "Mom, does that help?"

"Maybe," I said. "Now say good night, Nicholas."

"Night," he said in a pout, and finished trudging off to his room.

"M for Mitchell?" Case asked. "Or Mandy?" He looked

thoroughly confused. I'd warned him about my oracle sister, but this was the first time he'd witnessed her in action.

"Delph," I said, "are you sure it's an M? Could it be an N?"

"Possibly." She studied the grounds again. Mama tapped her foot impatiently.

"On the other hand," Delphi said, "maybe it doesn't have anything to do with Mitchell or Mandy. It could be an M for marriage, or for—"

"More coffee?" Mama asked, rising.

"Might have to take a rain check," Case said, and also rose. "Thank you for the refreshments, Mrs. Spencer. Ladies, it's been a pleasure."

"I was only going to say murder," Delphi said.

IT'S ALL GREEK TO ME
by Goddess Anon

Dial M for Marriage

Marriage is a sensitive subject, at least it is in my big family. Some of us are all for it, as in the idea that everyone needs to get married. Some of us are against it, saying they'd feel trapped, confined. Then there are those who are uncommitted, who can't decide if they'd feel complete with a loving partner or completely shackled. It's like the Mae West quote: "Marriage is a great institution, but I'm not ready for an institution yet."

The ancient Greek philosopher Euripides said, "Never say that marriage has more of joy than pain." I can't say he's wrong, because my marriage was a disaster, and I'm happily free of it. But then I can't let my experience sour me for the future either. I'm of the opinion that when you find the right person, the person who actually does make you feel like a part of you had been missing, then marriage is the way to go. It's like insurance. You feel better with it, and you're protected in the future, even though you might never need that protection.

I'd like to do an unofficial poll, so please write in and tell me what your opinion on marriage is. Are you for or against? I'll let you know the results next week.

For now, this is Goddess Anon bidding you adío.

Thursday

I woke up bright and early after a well-deserved eight hours of deep sleep. Niko was exhausted after his exciting last day of school, so I'd had no trouble tucking him in and writing my blog before bed. My head was propped up on a few pillows as I quickly edited the previous night's post, and I had just hit the SUBMIT button when I heard my phone ding and saw that a message had come in from Maguire.

Before I could read the text, my mother popped into my room and made herself comfortable leaning against the door frame and crossing her arms, her oversized bangle reflecting the morning sun gleaming in through my open blinds. She wore her Ionian blue work shirt and black slacks with comfy black shoes.

"What are you working on so early?" Mama asked.

I shielded my eyes and blinked away the bright spot lingering in my field of vision. "Just answering some emails," I said.

"So, Case Donnelly is a nice boy. Don't you think?"

And there it was, the real question. I closed my laptop, relieved that Mama wasn't on to my little secret, and answered, "Yes, Mama. Case is a very nice *man*."

"I was speaking with Petronia yesterday at the diner, and her son is a professor at Michigan State. He'll be home for a few months during summer break, and I was wondering . . ."

She paused at the exact moment I normally interrupted her, but I sat in bed, waiting. Mama was smart. She knew I wouldn't give up any information about Case if I were truly interested in him. She knew her girls very well. So instead, she was trying to blackmail me with the threat of another date.

"But I won't go to the trouble," Mama continued, "if you're already seeing someone."

I let out a loud sigh. "Mama, I'm not seeing anyone, and I don't need another date."

"You're a vibrant young woman. You shouldn't be alone. If nothing else, do this for me, *agapitós*." Dear.

"I've got Niko."

"Niko, ha!" she exclaimed. "He's just a boy. You need a man in your life."

"I'm not going to debate you, Mama."

"Then it's settled."

"You bet it is." My phone beeped again, reminding me of Maguire's text. "I have to answer this."

"Okay then, I'm off to the diner," she said. "I'll let Petronia know you're available." And then she was gone.

Maguire: **RE: your questions. Brady Rogers filed a RO against Nora Modelle 2 months *before death*.**

I texted him a thank-you then immediately texted Case the news.

Athena: **Brady filed a restraining order 2 months before his death, well before Nora ever filed hers.**

Case: **Nora waited until 2 wks before his murder to file hers. Reason?**

Athena: **Plotting murder? Alibi reason?**

For a minute, there was no reply, then,

Case: **Sorry, busy with something. I'll see you later this morning**.

Athena: **I'll be ready.**

Case: **Kaliméra.**

Good day—he was learning Greek.

I reread his message and wondered whether he'd been busy with something—or some*one*. And there I went again bringing Lila into the mix. I heard footsteps barreling down the hallway and then Nicholas bounded into my bedroom and bounced on top of the bed. I hugged him tightly. "Good morning, sweetheart."

"I'm all ready for my first day of work," he exclaimed.

I gave him a big sloppy kiss on the cheek, and he recoiled with a "Yuck!" wiping his face with his sleeve.

"I'm nowhere near ready for work," I told him, "so go jump on Aunt Delphi's bed while I get ready."

He leaped off the bed, his backpack bouncing on his shoulders as he called out a warning to his aunt. "Here I come, Theia Delphi!"

Before heading to Spencer's that morning, we stopped at the Parthenon to talk to my *pappoús*. We arrived just after the diner opened, so most of the tables hadn't filled up yet. Mama was taking orders at a far table, and Yiayiá was behind the counter, pouring coffee for a couple of regular early birds. Maia was also there, helping out on her day off from the yoga studio. Nicholas gave my sister a high five on his way around the front counter to find his true target, his great-grandmother, to give her a hug.

I found Pappoús in the kitchen, as usual, making a skillet of scrambled eggs Greek-style—creamy and delicious with lots of whipped feta and butter.

"*Kaliméra*, Pappoús," I said. "How are you this morning?"

"I woke up," he said in his gravelly voice. "That's always a good thing. What do you have up your nose today?"

Charming. "Since you don't use your boat anymore, Case was wondering how much it would take to buy it from you."

His reply was immediate, as if he'd already thought it through. He enumerated on his thick fingers. "He pay me fifty thousand, plus what I already paid for yearly slip fee and insurance cost and he can have the *Páme*. *Endáksi*?"

Okay?

"Thanks, Pappoús. I'll pass it along."

"How's the boy?"

As if on cue, Nicholas burst through the swinging kitchen doors and enveloped Pappoús in a fierce hug. "Good morning, Pappoús."

"Spunky as ever," I said.

"Niko," Pappoús said. "Skinny boy. I fix you *omelétta*."

"Come, Niko," my *yiayiá* called through the order window. "Come sit, and I make you chocolate milk."

Nicholas left the kitchen and joined my grandmother at the front counter.

"Niko is good boy, Athena. You do fine job raising him."

"*Efharisto*, Pappoús." Thank you. Praise wasn't easy to come by from the older Greeks.

"Two orders *omelétta*, coming right up. Go. Sit."

"Thanks." I'd already had a protein bar, and that was usually enough to get me through to lunch, but the overwhelming smell of feta cheese, eggs, and pepper made my stomach growl. I was always up for my *pappoús*'s scrambled eggs.

While we ate, I pulled out my iPad and began a list of questions for the bridesmaids. I checked my phone, but still no response from either Joni or Paulette.

Mama took a seat next to us. She and Nicholas chatted in broken Greek as I did a mental review of some of the interviews Case and I had already conducted. After I jotted down a few notes, one question kept bugging me. Why was Selene the scapegoat?

As I typed in the question, my cell phone dinged, and I read the text from Joni saying they were available at noon and wanted to meet at the Hot Spot Bar and Grill. I texted back a thumbs-up and then immediately texted Case to let him know.

At Spencer's a bit later, Delphi and Niko were out back playing with Oscar, while I prepared the register and Dad enjoyed his morning cup of coffee in the office. When I'd finished, he called me in for a chat.

"Couple of things," he started. "How's the investigation going?"

I relayed the information Case and I had uncovered, and Dad stopped me with the same question I'd been asking myself. "Why Selene?"

"Brady was Selene's workout coach," I said. "She filed a complaint against him because he made advances. That's the only connection I can find."

"It's very thin," my dad observed. "The scissors, the

shirt in the garbage behind the hair salon, the cell phone in the dumpster behind her apartment. It doesn't take a detective to see that Selene's been set up."

"That's the problem, Pops. The detectives think they have an open-and-shut case. They won't look any further until the DNA evidence from the T-shirt comes back."

"And how long will that take?"

"About two months," I answered. "In the meantime, there's a killer on the loose."

"And my poor daughter's in the Sequoia slammer."

"Especially that," I said. "Selene broke down yesterday when I couldn't give her any good news. I feel so bad for her." I checked the time on the wall clock. "Case is picking me up soon for an interview with Mandy. Fingers crossed we get something useful."

"Take as much time as you need."

"What's your second thing?"

"How about some coffee first?" My dad held up his empty cup, knowing full well that he shouldn't be drinking so much caffeine.

"Okay, but just one more."

I made us both a fresh cup as he continued. "Your cousin Drew is starting work today. I don't think it will take him long to the learn the ropes, but I'd appreciate some help training him, and"—he looked out the windows as Delphi ran past, holding a bag of peanuts, squealing as Oscar chased her around a table—"I think we can cross off Delphi."

"Call me when Drew arrives," I said. "I'll come back as soon as I can. And thank you for suggesting that Nicholas help out here. He'll love it."

"Niko will be in good hands," my dad said. "I'll let him dust shelves and unload some of the smaller boxes."

"Please do," I said. "Let him wear off some of that energy so I can get him to sleep at night."

My phone rang, and I excused myself. It was Case.

"I'm outside," he said. "Ready?"

I glanced at the clock and hopped up. "I lost track of time. I'll be right out."

He met me by the front door. "Ready for a spin in my new Jeep?"

"You have a Jeep?"

He led me to the parking lot on the north side of the garden center, where I came to an abrupt stop at the sight of his brand-new, army-green Jeep Wrangler. And it wasn't the model of the car that stopped me.

"Case, where are the doors?"

"I removed them."

"We're going to ride around town in a car with no doors? This isn't the beach."

He kept walking. "Come on. It'll be fun."

"Fun? On the highway with no doors? I'll be thrown out."

"That's what seat belts are for."

"That's comforting. What happens in the winter?"

He put an arm around my shoulders. "I'll put the doors back on."

"If I had known I was going to be riding in a car with no doors," I muttered, "I would've tied my hair back."

"Oh, now I see," he said with a teasing smile. "You're not worried about your safety. You're worried about your hair." He pulled a pair of sunglasses down over his eyes and gazed at his brand-new purchase. "Just wait. You're going to love it."

"Love being blown to bits before a meeting with fashionista Mandy Black?" And suddenly I felt like my mother, griping about my hair. I pressed my lips together and vowed not to complain again.

"You'll look fine. You always look fine." He gave me a hand to climb up into the Jeep then went around to the driver's side, climbed in, and started the motor. He eased out of the parking spot, left the lot, and headed north to the exclusive lakefront neighborhood of Hampton Hills.

At first, I held my hair down, but as I began to point out some of the more expensive homes along the lake, I forgot about my appearance and instead began to enjoy the ride. The air rushing in through the open Jeep was warm and exhilarating. By the time we'd located the Black mansion at the back of a long cul-de-sac, I was wishing our ride could go on forever, windblown hair or not.

"You survived," he said as he pulled up in front of the sprawling, two-story pink brick home.

"You were right," I admitted. "That was fun."

Case just smiled and shook his head, as if to say, *I told you so.*

The enormous two-story home had a multitude of windows and roof peaks with chimneys in at least three places. In the long, curving driveway, in front of a three-car garage, sat a silver Porsche.

The door was answered by a middle-aged woman wearing a white blouse and black slacks. She asked us our names, then said, "I'll get Miss Black," and had us wait outside.

As we waited, I nudged Case. "Let's see if you can get through this interview without charming your answers out of Mandy."

"Oh, ye of little faith. Let's see how far you get without letting your emotions take over," he said and nudged me back.

When Mandy opened the door, she had the vacant stare I'd seen the day before. "Oh, it's you," she said in a bored voice. "I suppose you're here to ask me the same questions you asked Mitchell."

"Not exactly the same," I said.

"I'm sorry, but I don't know why this is necessary. We all know Selene did it."

I felt my temper rise. "Selene is innocent, Mandy, and you know it in your gut. You know she couldn't have done anything like that."

"Sorry, Athena. My gut tells me a different story."

Before I could retort, Case casually placed his arm around my shoulders and gave her his dimpled smile. "Athena is just trying to help her sister. Isn't that what you'd do for your brother?"

She studied her nails. "I suppose so."

"And I'm sure there isn't anything Mitchell wouldn't do for his beautiful twin sister, is there?" he said.

She sighed. "I suppose not."

"We just want to ask a few questions. Five minutes max." He smiled at her again.

With that she softened. "I suppose you can come in then."

Charm wins the day again.

"Tea or coffee?" the same woman who answered the door asked as Mandy lounged on one of a pair of sofas upholstered in white silk. I declined, but Case took the woman up on her offer. "I'll have tea, with honey, if you have it."

Case and I sat down on a sofa across from Mandy. The sofas faced each other over a beautiful burled-walnut coffee table. At one end were twin chairs, also in white. The furniture sat on a Persian rug in front of a fireplace fronted in black marble. Above the mantel hung a huge oil painting of the Black family—Mandy and Mitchell and their parents.

"And for you, Miss Black?" the woman asked, handing Case his cup.

"Thanks, Connie, but I'll get my own." Mandy got up and walked over to a serving station, where she poured tea from a ceramic teapot that had a black rose on it, stirred in honey, and picked up the matching china cup and saucer. She came back and sat delicately on the sofa, holding the cup as though she were British royalty. "Go ahead," she said irritably. "I don't have all morning."

I glanced at my list of questions and realized I'd written them without taking into consideration that Mandy had just lost her husband-to-be.

"What's the problem?" Mandy asked, gazing from me to Case with a puzzled expression.

As though sensing my unease, Case said, "Let me just say, for the two of us, how sorry we are for your loss."

"Thank you," she said in a sincere voice. "And can I just say that I'm truly sorry Selene got herself mixed up in this?"

"Selene didn't do this to herself, Mandy," I said. "You asked her to be a bridesmaid because you trusted her, and then you accused her of killing Brady. Does that make any sense at all?"

"The detectives told me the evidence will prove that

Selene is guilty." She shrugged. "I didn't want to believe it, just as I didn't want to believe that Selene and Brady had an affair, but then there's the evidence."

"The evidence is a pair of scissors, a bloody T-shirt, and a cell phone," I said. "Anyone who wanted the scissors could've taken them when Selene was away from her station, and the same person could've easily stuffed the T-shirt in that dumpster and the cell phone in the trash can at Selene's apartment building. All the evidence proves is that someone wants Selene to look guilty."

"Maybe so," Mandy said, "but that's three solid pieces of evidence pointing to Selene."

"And I'll ask you the same thing I asked your brother," I said. "How stupid would Selene have to be to use her own scissors, leave them at the scene, and throw away a blood-soaked T-shirt and Brady's cell phone behind where she works and lives?"

Mandy blinked rapidly as she thought it over.

"Forget your gut," I said. "What is your heart telling you? You've known Selene since you were in school together. Is she the type to kill someone? Or, for that matter, to have an affair with a good friend's fiancé?"

"I didn't think so. But the evidence . . ."

"Was planted," I said in growing frustration. "Someone stole Selene's scissors the day you and your bridesmaids were in the salon. All the stylists will verify that. And Brady's boss can verify that Selene filed a harassment complaint weeks before his death. And why would Selene take Brady's bloody T-shirt and dispose of it where it was likely to be found by detectives?"

"It wasn't Brady's T-shirt, Athena. It was a woman's white T-shirt, size medium. Isn't that the size Selene wears?"

CHAPTER FIFTEEN

I sat there, stunned, barely hearing Mandy's next words. Was there any way Selene's DNA could be on that T-shirt? Could it possibly be hers?

"Do you see my situation, Athena?" Mandy asked. "On one hand, I know what a sweet person Selene can be. But if she went to Brady's apartment to ask him to call off our wedding, you can figure out for yourself how she might have ended up with blood on her T-shirt."

I gazed at her skeptically. "Do you actually think Selene stabbed Brady because he wouldn't call off your wedding?"

"Yes, Athena. That's what I think."

"Mandy, Selene didn't have an affair with Brady. I'm sorry to say this, but she didn't like him. And she wouldn't have asked him to call off the wedding. She was happy for you. Please believe that."

"That was the conclusion I'd reached before we had the rehearsal dinner, but then . . ." She sat back. "Truthfully, I don't know what to think now."

I had to count to ten in my head so I wouldn't get angrier. Case used the opportunity to ask a very important question, one that I hadn't even thought to ask.

"Do you know who placed the phone call to the police?" When Mandy didn't immediately respond, he rephrased it. "The groomsmen said the police showed up at Brady's apartment right after they did. Do you know who called them?"

"I don't know. It was all such a blur."

"Mandy," I said, "you've known Selene for a very long time. Just think back to everything you remember about my sister. I promise you won't find anything in her background that would ever make you believe she could kill anyone."

Mandy studied her nails again, clearly unconvinced.

Case picked up the questioning. "What do you remember about leaving the hair salon last Thursday?"

She paused to think, her eyes closing as though it helped her remember. "I was the last to finish," she said. "Selene had already gone to lunch, so I didn't say goodbye to her. I left the salon and went down the street to have lunch with my bridesmaids."

"Did you see anyone go near Selene's station while Selene was gone?" Case asked. "That would include any of your bridesmaids, a stranger, one of the other stylists . . ."

"No, and I wasn't that far away. I think I would've noticed someone holding her scissors."

"Was your vision ever blocked while you were getting your pedicure?" he asked.

"Well"—she paused to think—"there are always people passing by. And sometimes my nail tech was right in front of me."

"So your answer is yes," Case said.

Mandy gave a reluctant nod.

"Do you know who Nora Modelle is?" he asked.

Mandy's nose wrinkled with distaste as she set her teacup down in the saucer with a sharp clink. "Don't repeat that name. I hate her." She stood up and walked to the serving station, poured herself another cup of tea, and sat back down again.

"Did you see her that day in the nail salon?" Case asked.

Mandy crossed one leg over the other and swung her foot angrily. "No, and it's a good thing because I might've slapped her. She made Brady's life a living hell after he broke up with her." Mandy paused. "Was she in the salon Thursday, too?"

"She came in to retrieve a credit card she'd left behind," Case said.

Wide-eyed, Mandy said, "Maybe *she* stole Selene's scissors. I wouldn't put anything past her."

I took the next question. "How did you find out Brady was having an affair?"

"About a month after we got engaged, he started making excuses about why he couldn't see me. When he wouldn't answer my texts late at night, I knew he was up to something. When I confronted him, he told me that he'd made a big mistake, but it was over. He was truly contrite, and I believed him."

"What made you believe his affair was with Selene?"

"I found a gym pass in his apartment," she answered. "It must have slipped out of her bag. I found it under his bed."

"And he said it was Selene's?" I asked.

"Not at first," she said. "He said I was crazy for accusing him of having an affair. But when I told him I was going to the gym to find out whose pass it was, he told me it was Selene's."

"He actually said it was Selene's gym pass?" I asked.

"Yes."

"Did it have her name on it?" I asked.

"No, just the gym logo."

"Where is that pass now?" Case asked. "That could be important evidence."

"I'm pretty sure I threw it away. I was really furious with Brady."

"Will you look for it?" I asked. At her hesitation, I said, "Would you do it for Selene?"

She finally nodded.

"Did you confront Selene about the pass?" Case asked.

"I couldn't bring myself to do it. I just stopped going to her for my haircuts."

"Then why did you ask Selene to be a bridesmaid?" I asked.

"Because I thought it would be a good test."

"You didn't want to accuse Selene," I said, "but you asked her to be a bridesmaid to *test* her?"

"I wasn't testing *her*."

"Then I'm confused," I said.

"I wanted to test *Brady*. I didn't know if he was telling the truth about Selene, so Tonya and I figured that the only way to really know if they had had an affair was by inviting Selene to be a bridesmaid. Can I tell you how relieved I was when she said yes? So then I had a talk with Brady and told him that if he wanted to marry me, he couldn't think about even flirting with another woman. I also told him I didn't want to know about anything else in his past, recent or otherwise." She reached for her teacup.

I had to stop to process the logic behind Mandy's convoluted idea, but it just wasn't making sense to me. While Mandy sipped her tea, I glanced over at Case with eyebrows raised. Had Mandy been a starry-eyed fiancée or a calculating killer?

"Whose idea was it to ask Selene to be a bridesmaid?" Case asked.

Mandy took a sip of tea, then set the cup down. "Tonya suggested it. She was in charge of the bridesmaids, so I took her advice. And like I said, I thought it was a good test."

I wrote down the information then redirected my line of questioning, "At the dinner, you stated that you were sure Brady was dead, even before the police came. Why were you so certain that the news was going to be the worst possible?"

"Expect the worst and you won't be disappointed, someone once told me. So that's what I did. I was hoping it wasn't true, but of course"—her voice cracked with emotion, and she stopped, gazing toward the window as her eyes filled with tears—"it was."

I gave her a moment to compose herself, then said, "I was told that you redecorated Brady's apartment. Is that true?"

Her face wrinkled in disgust. "Oh my God, yes. You should have seen it before."

"Did you place a framed photo of you, your brother, and Brady on the hutch in the dining room?" Case asked.

"No," she answered, "that wasn't me. I bugged Brady about it for weeks. I spent a lot of time and money to make over his apartment, and he refused to get rid of that hideous gray frame. It didn't match anything."

"Are you aware that the photo is not on the hutch now?" Case said.

"Maybe he finally decided to take it down," she said.

"When was the last time you were in his apartment?" I asked.

"Wednesday evening."

"Was the photo on the hutch then?"

She nodded.

"So sometime between Wednesday evening and Friday evening, the photo was removed from the hutch," Case said to clarify.

Mandy shrugged. "Maybe Brady put it inside the hutch so his cleaning lady wouldn't tip it over. Why are you so interested in the photo?"

"It was a detail the groomsmen noticed," Case said. "They thought it was odd that it was gone."

"I'm sure it's around somewhere. Brady loved that photo."

"Which is why they found it odd that he moved it," I said.

She shrugged again and sipped her tea.

"Who do you think might have held a grudge against Brady?" Case asked.

Mandy's expression hardened. "The stalker, of course."

"Nora?" I asked.

"Please never say her name to me again."

"Miss Black, excuse me," Connie said, coming from the hallway. "Your brother is on the phone. He said it's important."

"I need to take this," she said and, replacing her teacup, rose daintily and left.

While she was gone, Case glanced at me and raised an eyebrow. "Want to bet she's going to have some reason that she has to leave now?"

"And I was just about to ask what she was doing the morning of the murder."

Case started to speak, but then stopped when Connie returned.

"I'm sorry, but Miss Black had to leave. Her brother needed her help at the hotel."

Sure he did.

"Comments?" Case asked as we drove home.

"I love this car," I said with a smile, leaning back in the sun.

"Thanks, but it's a Jeep, and I meant about Mandy."

I ran my fingers through my hair and let it fly out behind me, enjoying the freedom as the air whipped around me. "I'd have to say that if she's the killer, she puts up a good front. She came across as fragile, grieving, and angry—everything you'd expect from a woman who'd just lost her future life partner."

"Did you follow her elaborate scheme to test Brady about the affair?" Case asked.

"It was elaborate, all right. Why go to all that trouble?"

"I can think of one possibility," Case said.

"She set up Selene for the murder."

"That sums it up. So is she still low on your suspect list, Sherlock?"

"I'm undecided. She seemed pretty sincere. But she had the means, motive, and opportunity to kill Brady, so I'm putting her even with her brother at number two."

"Nora is still number one, I'm assuming. Who's number three?"

"Tonya Upton. She had her hand in a lot of Mandy's decisions."

"I caught that, too." He flipped the turn indicator and turned off onto the lakeshore road that wound around the tourist beach near the edge of town. The sun was starting to warm the sand, and the beach was filling up quickly. "Tonya seems to have a lot of influence over Mandy. Maybe it's time we had a chat with her."

"I'll see what I can learn from the other two bridesmaids first, and then get in touch with suspect number three."

"Sounds good, partner."

Case dropped me off and headed for Holland, Michigan, to price fishing boats. I was about to ask if Lila was going with him, but decided that would be tempting fate and said nothing. Meanwhile, I had a few hours before my meeting with the bridesmaids, so I put them to good use at the garden center, showing our new employee the ropes.

Lunchtime rolled around before I had a chance to train Drew on the register, so I promised my dad I'd do it later. I hurried out to my SUV and punched the address for the new Hot Spot Bar and Grill into my GPS. As I followed the route, I noticed that I was heading in the opposite direction from all the local restaurants, and when instructed to turn onto Sandy Beach Road, I suddenly realized where I was headed.

The Hot Spot was not a restaurant. It was a beach bar,

decorated with fishing nets, beach balls, and blue high-top tables and stools set right in the sand. Behind it was the two-story Beach Club Hotel, with balconies that looked out over the water.

I got out of the car and held my hand over my eyes to look toward the beach, where people were swimming and sunbathing and gulls were flying overhead. I glanced down at my long-sleeved white shirt, beige slacks, and leather flats with a sigh. I was going to boil.

Joni and Paulette were already there, sitting under an umbrella at a high-top near the bar area. They waved when they saw me.

"How is everyone today?" I asked, sliding onto a bright blue wooden stool. The beach bar was only partially shaded, and my seat happened to be right in the sun.

"We're fine," Joni replied, and Paulette nodded. Both women had shady seats.

Joni was short in stature, with medium-length blond hair and very tanned arms. She wore a sleeveless sundress in a pink-and-yellow print that showed off a sturdy frame and her bright, cheery smile. Paulette was her exact opposite, with short dark hair, a pale complexion, and a tall, thin frame sporting a pale green sundress. She, too, was smiling, but her smile seemed more hesitant, not quite as trusting, as though she was wary of me.

"We spoke with Mandy a little while ago," Joni started off. "She said you were convinced Selene is innocent."

Right to the point. I was okay with that. "Once you hear the evidence, I think you'll agree with me."

"She told us what you said about your sister's situation," Paulette said, "and I see where you're coming from. Selene seems like a genuinely nice person. But don't you think, in the heat of the moment, she could've lost her head and then run off and left her scissors behind?"

The heat of the moment was sending rivulets of sweat down between my breasts. I opened my iPad, and answered as calmly as possible, "Let me explain something about Selene. She filed a complaint against Brady for making advances and quit the gym out of her dislike for him. She never had another thought about him until Mandy asked her to fill in for a bridesmaid."

"We heard about the complaint," Paulette said. "We were told it was a revenge move."

"Revenge for him hitting on her?"

"No, for dumping her," Joni answered lightly.

"Dumping her would imply that they'd had an intimate relationship," I said, "which is as far from the truth as you can get." I was trying my hardest not to sound combative, but neither of the women seemed to have thought the situation through. The sun on my back wasn't doing anything for my mood either.

"Are you thirsty?" Joni asked. "We've already ordered." She lifted her finger and the waitress made her way through the sand to take my drink order.

"Water, please." I said. "With lots of ice." I directed my next question to Paulette. She seemed to be the more serious of the two. "Why would Mandy have asked Selene to be a bridesmaid if she didn't trust her?"

"She told us it was a test for Brady," Paulette said.

I typed it into my notes. "But think about it. If she was truly doubting Brady, would she have taken a chance on Selene being a bridesmaid? After all, once she asked her, it was too late to take it back."

Both of them were quiet, as though they were letting that settle in.

The waitress stopped tableside to bring their tall drinks rimmed with sugar and packed with fruit. She then set down in front of me a small glass of water with one lone ice cube that was quickly melting. I took a long drink, hoping it would help cool me off.

When the waitress had gone I asked, "When did you hear that Brady was seeing someone else while he was engaged to Mandy?"

"We'd heard rumors about it a few weeks ago," Joni said, glancing at Paulette, "when we were out at a club. We weren't sure whether it was true until Mandy said that Brady had confessed."

"And when you heard it was Selene," I asked, "did you believe it?"

"We didn't know Selene then," Paulette said, "so, for all we knew, it was true."

"I have to admit I was surprised when I met her," Joni said. "She didn't fit the image of the person I'd concocted in my mind."

That was good to hear. "Do you know Nora Modelle?"

"We do," they said together, both wrinkling their noses.

"Did you ever hear Brady talk about her?"

"Only in the most negative way," Paulette said. "He rarely brought her up, but Mandy did. She had a hard time getting over their relationship. She hates Nora to this day."

"Did she feel threatened by Nora?"

"I don't think so," Paulette answered, glancing at Joni for confirmation.

"Then why does she hate her so much?" I asked.

"She was a stalker," Joni said. "That's what we called her. The stalker."

"Did Mandy ever confront Nora?"

"Not that I know of," Joni said, and Paulette shook her head no in confirmation. "Nora would even show up at the club in wigs and stuff to spy on us. It was super creepy."

"Had you noticed Nora hanging around the clubs recently?" I asked.

"We can't answer that," Paulette said. "We stopped going out to clubs with Mandy because it was getting too weird."

"Weird in what way?" I asked.

"Mitchell Black started showing up all the time," Joni answered. "Just standing there, watching us." She shuddered. "We didn't feel comfortable around him."

I typed it into my notes. "Mitchell seems quite protective of his sister."

"A bit too protective, if you ask me," Paulette said. "Everywhere Mandy goes, so goes Mitchell." She rolled her eyes. "Mandy isn't helpless, believe me, but he treats her that way."

"Did Mitchell seem concerned about his sister marrying Brady?"

Paulette glanced at Joni, then paused to take a sip of her drink. "I'd say so," she said. "He never took his eyes off of them when they were together. If I were Mandy, I'd have found that annoying."

"But she's the same way with him," Joni said to Paulette. "Remember when that waitress came on to Mitchell, and Mandy practically had her in tears over it?"

"So she can be tough?" I asked, popping a straw into my water.

"More like critical," Joni said. "I don't know if anyone is good enough to date Mitchell."

"Is he okay with that?"

"He's tight with his twin," Paulette said. "But he didn't become so overprotective until Brady came into the picture."

My understanding of Mandy and Mitchell was growing. They protected each other.

"We used to go out all the time, just us girls," Joni said. "Mitchell hardly ever came out back then."

"Who are the other girls?" I asked.

Joni answered on her fingers. "Me, Paulette, Mandy, Jill, and Tonya."

I could feel the sweat beading between my shoulder blades and dripping down my back. I stopped the waitress and asked for more ice, then said, "Tell me about Tonya."

"Tonya," Paulette said, twirling her straw in her drink, "is complex. She's very organized, a super planner, but very aggressive about it. Everything has to go according to plan, or she gets really upset. She was on top of everything for the wedding, though. I don't think Mandy could've done it without her."

"Tonya was amazing," Joni said. "She was at Mandy's beck and call. Anything Mandy wanted, Tonya was on it. She found the new rehearsal dinner space, signed up a new bridesmaid, and planned our visit to the salon. She kept Mandy calm and made sure everything ran smoothly." As though confiding a secret, Joni leaned closer and said, "Mandy has a tendency to overreact."

I typed in her statement then said, "Like when she was sure Brady was dead even before the police confirmed it?"

They nodded, and I continued, "And like when she said that Selene killed Brady?"

"She didn't have to tell us," Joni said. "We figured that out right away."

I had to bite my lip. The waitress brought me another water, but there wasn't any amount of ice that would cool me off at that point. Every single person I'd talked to had said the same thing. They were all certain it was Selene.

CHAPTER SIXTEEN

I took a long, cooling sip of water and tried to collect my thoughts. "Don't you think it's possible that Selene was set up? That it was a little too convenient that she was suddenly asked to be a bridesmaid?"

"Of course," Joni said. "It *was* a setup. Mandy wanted to keep a close eye on Selene and Brady, and Tonya made it happen."

"But it didn't play out that way, did it?" I said. "Mandy put together this intricate plot to test Brady, and my sister ended up being charged with murder."

Paulette took a moment to think. "Then who killed Brady?"

"That's what I'm trying to find out," I said. "Think about it. As you said, all of the evidence points to a setup, and you just admitted that they set Selene up as bridesmaid for a reason. Doesn't that suggest something to you?"

Paulette and Joni glanced at each other. "What do you mean?" Joni asked.

"For example," I said, "why did the two women get Selene to be a replacement at the last minute? What happened to the other bridesmaid?"

"That was Jill Carlson," Joni said. "She caught the flu about a week before the rehearsal dinner. Thank goodness, the seamstress had enough time to let out the dress for Selene." Joni flushed red. "I'm sorry. That sounded rude."

"That's okay. I'm surprised Jill got sick so late in May. The flu went around in January and February."

"She caught it right out of the blue," Joni said. "It was strange."

Paulette set down her glass, nearly sloshing the liquid in her rush to talk. "Joni, do you remember what we were doing the evening before she got sick?"

Joni shook her head.

"Bridal shower at the Waterfront Hotel," Paulette reminded her. "How can you forget? Crazy stuff went down that night."

"What happened?" I asked.

"There was a fight," Paulette said. "Brady showed up drunk and demanded to talk to Mitchell. I didn't even know Mitchell was there, but thinking back, of course he was. He was always around Mandy somewhere."

"Do you know what the fight was about?" I asked.

"No idea," Joni said.

"Brady was belligerent," Paulette explained. "Mitchell had to restrain him and drag him out of the room. There was shouting and glass smashing, and then Mandy ran out to stop them. When she came back, she was in tears. She wouldn't tell us what had happened, but Jill and Mandy left for a while. Eventually things got back to normal, but not long after that Jill started complaining that she didn't feel well."

I typed notes as quickly as I could, and then refocused the questioning. "Is it possible Jill got food poisoning that night?"

"We didn't get sick," Paulette said. "We ate the same food Jill did."

"Could someone have tampered with her food?" I asked.

"For what reason?" Paulette asked.

I knew I was reaching, but I had to put it out there. "To make sure there was an open slot for Selene as a bridesmaid."

"So you're saying Mandy tampered with Jill's food?" Paulette shook her head. "Not possible at all. Mandy and Jill were inseparable."

"Until Mandy caught Jill making eyes at Mitchell," Joni said, "and then not so much after that."

"But I can totally see Tonya doing that," Joni added. "She seems friendly and helpful, but she has a jealous side."

"Jealous of Jill?" I asked.

"Tonya wanted to be Mandy's best friend," Joni said. "That's why she made herself indispensable."

"You're wrong," Paulette said. "First of all, Tonya didn't poison anyone. She was very upset when Jill got sick. She had everything planned out to a T, and that wasn't part of her plan. Second, would she even have known how to poison food? I sure don't know how. And for that same reason, Mandy couldn't have poisoned her food either."

Joni shrugged. "They could've Googled it."

"Just so Selene could be a bridesmaid?" Paulette asked. "Someone would have to be pretty desperate to do that."

"Do you have Tonya's phone number?" I asked.

Paulette reached for her purse and pulled out her phone. She read off Tonya's number, but added, "She works a lot. You might have better luck if you go visit her at Furri-Paws."

"The dog-grooming place on Elm?"

"Yep," Joni answered. "She's very in demand there."

I typed it into my notes, then said, "And what about Jill? Have you heard from her recently?"

"We invited her out today," Joni said, "but she said she still wasn't feeling well."

I looked over my notes. My picture of Tonya was filling in. She seemed to be the loyal helper, the dedicated friend, the strategic planner, but I didn't have a motive for Tonya unless it was to help Mandy carry out a murder.

"I think that's all I need for now. I appreciate your help."

"No problem," Joni said.

"Good luck," Paulette said.

I gave them a smile and hoofed it back to my air-conditioned Toyota.

After leaving the Hot Spot, literally the hottest spot I could've imagined, I did a search on my phone for Furri-Paws and called to find out when Tonya scheduled her lunch hour. But the woman I spoke with wouldn't reveal the information, and Tonya was working on a client, so I ended the call without leaving a name. Then I detoured over to the jail to see Selene.

She was even more dejected than she'd been the day before, and nothing I said cheered her up, not even making fun of Mama, who had again brought baklava for the guards.

"Next thing you know, she'll be bringing them a lamb roast," I said. But if I was hoping for a laugh, I didn't get it. Instead I got a heavy sigh and tears.

"She probably will. I'm already being laughed at for the dessert."

"I'll talk to Mama," I promised, and then wondered how I was ever going to convince our mother that she was hurting Selene by bringing a delicious dessert for the staff.

"Selene, do you still have your gym pass to Fitness First?"

"Yes, why?"

"I found out why Mandy thought you were the one having an affair with Brady."

Selene perked up, holding the phone with a tighter grip. "Why?"

"Mandy found a gym pass in Brady's apartment, and Brady told her it was yours."

"Why would he do that? He knew how I felt about him."

"I don't know, but if I can find your pass, I can prove to Mandy that it wasn't you, and maybe she can convince the detectives to keep digging."

"That would be wonderful," she said. "I think it's still in the gym bag in my closet."

"What does the pass look like?"

"It's white with the Fitness First logo on the front."

I high-fived her through the glass. "I'll go get it right now and try to get in touch with Mandy again."

This time, I left my sister with a smile on her face. I walked out of the jail with newfound confidence. I was finally on the right track.

Standing at Selene's apartment door, I flipped through the keys on my key ring: Spencer's, the Parthenon, house key, car fob, and, finally, Selene's apartment key. I entered and hastily rummaged through her messy closet. It looked like she'd been in a hurry to pack up and move back home, but I could definitely relate. I'd done that same thing when my life had fallen apart.

As I rummaged through the closet, Maguire called with a report on the traffic camera. According to the descriptions I'd given him, three of my suspects—Nora, Mandy, and Tonya—had gone into the hair salon on Thursday, with Nora being the last to arrive and leave. Mitchell was the only one who hadn't been to the hair salon that day. If he were the killer, someone else would've had to pick up the scissors for him. I could think of only one person.

I thanked Maguire and hung up the phone. As I did, I noticed a purple ripstop backpack in the back corner of Selene's closet. I zipped open the bag, and there it was, her Fitness First gym pass.

I called Case next. "I have good news. I found Selene's gym pass."

"That's great," he said.

"You bet it is. It's more proof she didn't kill Brady. How did your morning go?"

"Let's just say that only one of us has good news."

"What's wrong?"

"I never realized how expensive it would be to buy and maintain one fishing boat, let alone three. I highly doubt whether the bank will loan me the money."

"What's the bottom line?"

"Over a million and a quarter. That's for three used boats costing approximately three-hundred-fifty thousand each, an annual maintenance and repair cost of twenty-seven thousand each, and boat captain salaries equaling eighty-one thousand."

"Wow."

"That was exactly what I said when I figured it out. Wow."

"But Lila's on your side. She should be able to persuade the bank to lend you the money."

"We're supposed to have dinner with her personal banker this evening, so we'll see."

Was it me, or was Lila worming her way into Case's life more each day?

"How did your interview with the bridesmaids go?" he asked.

"It was interesting," I began. "You know how everyone we've spoken to who was involved in Mandy's wedding is convinced that Selene killed Brady until they're presented with the facts? That's how it was with Joni and Paulette.

"Now, after talking with them, I have two theories. The more complicated theory involves either Mandy and Mitchell, or Mandy and Tonya working together to frame Selene."

"Do they each have a motive?"

"That's the tricky part. I can conceive of a motive—for Mandy, jealousy, and for Mitchell, hatred—to see them working together, but the only motive I have for Tonya is weak. I won't know more until we talk to her. So on to my other, simpler theory.

"All of our interviews lead back to this alleged affair, this other woman everyone keeps mentioning, but there's no proof of who she is. Selene is an easy target. She worked out with Brady, filed a complaint against him . . . basically she was in the wrong place at the wrong time."

"Or in the killer's case," he said, "the right place at the right time."

"Exactly. My other theory is one we've discussed before, that this other woman, the woman who had an affair with Brady, killed him because he was marrying Mandy."

"You're talking about suspect numero uno," Case answered. "Nora Modelle."

"It all adds up," I said.

"We'll have to speak to Nora again."

"Maybe I should talk to her alone. She seems to like you a bit too much."

"That could work in our favor."

"I don't know, Case. I'd hate to play with this woman's emotions, especially if she's the killer."

"What about your number two suspect?"

"There's definitely something about Mitchell that makes me strongly suspicious of him. I learned from Joni and Paulette that Mitchell got into a fight with Brady at the bridal shower and threw him out of the restaurant. There was obviously bad blood between them well before the wedding, and when Mandy decided to go ahead with the marriage, that could've tripped Mitchell's wires."

"What was the fight about?"

"Neither woman could tell me, but hopefully Tonya will know more."

"I might be able to get it out of Mitchell, too."

"Have you gotten in touch with him?"

"No," Case answered. "He hasn't returned my calls or texted me back."

"Why am I not surprised?"

"So next up is an interview with Tonya," Case said.

"Correct, and it seems that she's a very busy person. I may have to make a grooming appointment to get us in to see her."

"And to think I just had my hair trimmed."

I laughed. "She's a dog groomer, you dork."

"I knew that. Why don't we drop by at closing time to talk to her?"

"That'll work. I'll need to call back and find out what time Furri-Paws closes."

"Hold on. I'll look it up." He came back on the line in a minute to say, "Furri-Paws closes at six o'clock."

"I can do six o'clock."

"Let's meet at Spencer's and walk there together."

"By the way," I said, "I spoke with my *pappoús* about the *Páme*. He said to tell you that you can have the boat for fifty thousand plus what he already paid for the annual slip fee and insurance costs. That adds up to about ninety thousand."

"Wow," Case said. "Is it sad that ninety thousand is the most reasonable price I've heard all day?"

"You'll get your financing," I said. "You just need to charm the right banker."

I could picture his sardonic smile. "I'll see what I can do. Any word from your police officer buddy?"

"As a matter of fact, Maguire called to say that three of our suspects showed up on the traffic camera outside the hair salon—Mandy, Nora, and Tonya—all between the hours of twelve and one o'clock, which means Nora had the opportunity to grab Selene's scissors. But the only way I can fit Mitchell into the mix is to speculate that if he were involved in the murder, he'd have had to have his sister take the scissors."

"That's a possibility," he said. "It fits with your first theory."

"Hopefully, Tonya can give us some helpful information. Next to Mitchell, she's the closest to Mandy." I paused to think. "Maybe you should handle Tonya's interview, Case. If she's stubbornly set on Selene being the killer, I may not be the best person to question her."

"Are you asking me to charm her?" Case asked.

"All I'm saying is that we need this dog groomer to give us some good information or we're out of options. So do whatever you need to do."

Chapter Seventeen

When I got back to Spencer's, I found Nicholas and Drew in the back of the big barn, dusting the furniture and patio décor. Nicholas ran up to hug me and immediately started tugging me toward the back door, saying, "Come with me, Mom."

"Where are you taking me?"

"It's a surprise." He pushed open the thick glass door, led me into the patio area and over to the outdoor cabinet, where he took out a small bag of peanuts.

"Watch what happens," he said, a big smile on his face. He shook the bag and then pointed to the fence. In a few moments, a little black-and-gray face peeped over the top, and then Oscar appeared. He hopped down onto a table and scampered over to us, sitting up on his hind feet with his front paws outstretched.

"Good boy, Oscar," Nicholas said, and gave him a

peanut. "See, Mom? He knows me now. Theia Delphi said he could be my pet."

"Of course he can," Delphi said, coming over to stand with us. "Oscar loves Niko."

Nicholas gazed up at me with his big brown eyes. "Is it okay, Mom?"

I ruffled his hair. "As long as you're careful. Don't make any sudden moves toward him or you'll scare him off."

"I won't. Theia Delphi taught me all about how to feed him. Watch."

"Niko, your mom has to come back inside and teach Drew how to work the cash register," Delphi said. "We've been so busy that your grandpa hasn't had a chance to show him."

"I'd be happy to help," I said. "Niko, you're doing a good job with Oscar. Just don't feed him too much or he'll get fat. He needs to find his own food, too, or he'll forget how to fend for himself."

I left Nicholas outside with Delphi and headed in to find Drew. There was a lull in customers, so I was able to take him up to the front counter to show him how to use the cash register. Drew was a good-looking young man, a little on the short side and a bit stocky like the rest of our Greek relatives, and he was quick-witted and tech-savvy. Fortunately, he'd worked at the campus bookstore and had learned on a register similar to ours, so it wasn't hard at all for him to grasp what he needed to learn. Within the hour, he was ringing up customers like a pro.

"Athena," my dad said, standing off to the side with me, "I have to thank you. Hiring Drew was a great idea. Now we've got the extra help we need, and it's still all in the family. And I can't forget Niko. He's a quick study, and an extra pair of hands is always welcome. I'll bet in two years he'll be ringing up customers, too."

"I'm glad it worked out, Pops."

"What's the latest on your investigation?"

I gave him a quick rundown on what I'd learned about Selene's gym pass and how that could help, but spared him the details from the bridesmaids' and Mandy's interviews.

"It sounds like you're making progress."

"It's slow going, Pops. I just hope we're moving faster than the DA is."

Ten minutes later my mother stopped by the garden center to check on Drew, who seemed to be a family project now that he'd been hired.

"Be prepared," Mama said to me. "Your uncle Giannis will undoubtedly be checking in to see how Drew is doing. And you know my brother. He'll be poking his nose into the garden center's affairs, too."

"Annoying, isn't it?" I asked her.

She cocked her head. "What are you getting at?"

"Why are you taking food to the guards, Mama?"

"I take food to Selene. The guards get only dessert."

"But it embarrasses Selene, and it doesn't get her any better treatment."

"My duty is to keep my daughter well fed, which that disgusting jail food isn't doing. How can I take food for Selene and not for anyone else?"

I lifted my hands in the air and walked away. I knew when to call it quits.

That afternoon, my father asked me to work up a landscaping plan for a customer who'd come in while I was out. After he gave me a schematic of the customer's house and an idea of the colors she wanted to see in her landscape, I took my iPad to the garden area outside and began to design. The house was a ranch-style home with a door off center and the majority of the house stretching out to the left. It had a large picture window on the right and a driveway on the right side of the house.

I started at the left outside corner with a tall Marie's *viburnum plicatum*, followed by three Ward's yews and two compact Lemoine deutzias for summer color. In the middle of the small front yard, I put in a Brandywine crabapple, a small, disease-resistant flowering tree, for spring color. In front of the picture window, I included a row of dwarf pink hydrangeas interspersed with pots of annuals for season-long color. At the far-right corner I decided on another of Marie's *viburnum plicatum*, following the rule of thumb that you should never have just one of any shrub.

I was finishing up when Delphi brought Maguire outside. He thanked her with a big smile, sending a blush from her neck up to her forehead, then sat down at the patio table across from me and took off his police hat. "How's your investigation going?"

"I've got an interview today with the maid of honor, and that's the last of the new interviews. I've spoken with the groomsmen, the other two bridesmaids, the bride, and her brother, and can come up with a motive for three of them so far—Nora, Mandy, and Mitchell. Three of them also had the opportunity to steal Selene's scissors the day before the murder—Nora, Mandy, and Tonya. I'm not sure whether Nora would've had access to Brady's apartment, but Mandy did."

"You've got one person who hits all three categories—means, motive, and opportunity."

"Mandy."

"That's what it looks like to me."

"There's also the possibility that she and her brother killed him. They're very close, and Mitchell was definitely not a fan of Brady's. The problem is, they are not really fans of mine, either, so we may have a problem getting any more information from them."

"All I can say is that you'd better hurry." Maguire glanced around, then said quietly, "I hate to be the bearer of bad news, but it appears that the DA has enough evidence to make a case against your sister. He knows Selene can't be held forever without just cause, so I wouldn't be surprised if he convenes a grand jury on Monday."

My stomach churned sickeningly. "That gives me just three days, Bob. We need more time."

"I wish I could give it to you, Athena."

"Was there anything the detectives found that might *help* Selene's case?"

"Not that I'm aware of."

"That isn't surprising considering that they've been focusing on her and no one else."

"They interviewed the groomsmen and the bridesmaids, the bride and her family, and all of them indicated that they believed Brady and Selene were having an affair. They have only Selene saying it never happened, and we have no eyewitnesses that can disprove it. Add that to the scissors, the bloody T-shirt, the cell phone, and the lack of an alibi witness, and you have a case."

Poor Selene. I looked down, blinking back tears. Somehow, someway, I had to clear my sister. But could I do it before the grand jury convened? "I have one interviewee left, Bob, and then I'll start over if I have to."

Maguire rose, adjusting his hat on his head. "I have to get back. I just wanted to drop by to give you a heads-up."

And possibly see Delphi as well? Slipping my phone into my back pocket, I rose. "I appreciate your help, Bob."

"I'll do whatever I can. And if I do help you prove who killed Brady, it'll benefit me, too."

"It won't make you too popular with the detectives, though."

"Maybe not, but I'll be a hero to your sis—your family."

"You bet you will," I said with a smile.

Shortly before six o'clock, I met Case outside the Furri-Paws dog grooming shop. The shop was one in a line of renovated old houses on Elm Street, each with their own unique business. Next to Furri-Paws was a bookstore, and tucked back between the dog groomers and a flower shop called Back to the Fuchsia, was an art shop called Water Lilies. It was a quaint section of downtown, full of the charm I loved about Sequoia.

I filled Case in on Maguire's visit and let him know that we had only three days to find our proof.

"Then let's get to it," he said. "I'll take the lead."

We stood at the reception counter in the parlor of the old, Victorian-style, blue-and-beige house and told the receptionist that we needed to talk to Tonya. She told us Tonya was just finishing up with a Maltese named Pepper and would be out shortly.

When Tonya came up to the reception desk, holding a small, neatly trimmed salt-and-pepper-colored dog, Case introduced us and asked if we could talk to her privately. She didn't act surprised to see us and took us into a waiting room that contained a beige-and-blue-print sofa and two blue wing chairs, where she was going to wait for Pepper's owner.

Tonya was wearing a blue bib apron, with the words FURRI FRIEND imprinted on it, over a white sleeveless top and blue jeans with white sneakers. Her tanned arms were toned and strong, and her long blond hair was pulled back in a bobbing ponytail. She indicated that we should sit on the chairs while she took the sofa. Pepper sat quietly in her lap, panting softly, gazing up at Tonya every so often and wagging her tail when Tonya stroked her silky fur.

"I was wondering when you'd get to me," she said with a smile. "I was starting to feel left out." She turned to Case. "And you are?"

Case introduced himself and then said, "Just so you know, we didn't go in any particular order."

She gave Pepper a hug and said with a laugh, "I was joking. Go ahead and ask your questions."

"Athena is going to take down your answers," Case said, as I readied the iPad.

Tonya gave him a nod.

"How long have you known Mandy?" he asked.

"A few years. We met at a pet-charity event that was held at Mandy's parents' hotel."

"And how about Brady?"

"I met Brady about four months ago when Mandy and I joined the gym. He was Mandy's personal trainer."

"What did you think of Brady's and Mandy's relationship?" Case asked.

Tonya leaned back to look out the window, then petted the dog as she said, "It had its ups and downs."

"How long were Brady and Mandy engaged?"

"I believe it was two months."

"That's not very long," Case remarked.

Tonya said with a sad smile, "The heart wants what the heart wants."

"True," he said. "And her heart wanted Brady no matter what. Is that right?"

"I'm not sure what you're asking."

"Mandy knew about Brady's reputation and even about his alleged affair," Case began, "and still went ahead with her wedding plans."

Tonya continued to pet the dog. "As I said, the heart wants what the heart wants. And Mandy gets what Mandy wants. But she's not a murderer, if that's what you're getting at."

"How well do you know Mitchell Black?" Case asked.

"Oh, boy," she said with a chuckle. "I know where this is going."

"Tell me," Case said.

"I'm guessing by now Mitchell is looking pretty guilty, and I understand why. And it doesn't help that he's been dodging you." She took long swipes down the dog's back until she curled up on Tonya's lap and closed her eyes.

"Why do you think Mitchell looks guilty?" Case asked.

"For one thing, he didn't like Brady," Tonya said. "I'd heard him plead with Mandy to leave Brady, begging her to let him go. And he was right. Brady was a playboy, and he was lying to Mandy. But she saw something in him that the rest of us didn't. He was like . . . well, like a puppy at the pound, always seeking attention but never finding a good home. I think Mandy wanted to give him that good home, so she overlooked his past. You said two months isn't a very long engagement, but it was enough for her because she wanted to get Brady to commit quickly. She truly loved him."

"Going back to Mitchell," Case said, "you commented that he looked guilty, but asking Mandy to leave Brady doesn't make him guilty of murder."

"There's more," she said. "I'm sure you've heard about the fight at the Waterfront Hotel by now."

"Can you tell us more about that?" Case asked.

"Brady had been out at his bachelor party," she explained. "I don't know why, but for some reason, he showed up at the Waterfront during Mandy's bridal shower completely wasted, yelling for Mitchell. It was confusing, because we thought Mitchell had gone to the bachelor party, too, but apparently he hadn't."

"Do you know what Brady wanted?"

"I can only assume he found out that Mitchell was trying to stop the wedding," she said. "It was sad. Brady was almost too drunk to stand. We couldn't even understand him."

"And that's when Mitchell took him out of the room?"

"Yes," Tonya answered, "and supposedly drove him home. Then Mitchell came back and told Mandy that he wasn't going to allow the rehearsal dinner or the reception to be held at the Waterfront. They had a big blowout and she claimed that Mitchell wanted to make sure the wedding never happened."

"If Mitchell felt so strongly about Brady," Case said, "why did he agree to be the best man in the wedding?"

"Because Mandy asked him to," Tonya explained. "And I think he followed through with it to keep his eye on Brady."

"What was your first thought when you learned Brady had been stabbed?"

She looked at me as if to apologize. "I hate to say it, but I thought immediately that Athena's sister had done it."

My first instinct was to react in Selene's defense, but I steadied myself and let Case handle it.

"You thought she was guilty because of the scissors?" Case asked.

"Not just that. Also because we had heard that Selene had been having an affair with Brady, and that when he tried to call it off, she had gotten so angry she filed a complaint against him to get revenge. To me that seemed like a motive for murder."

My Greek temper flared again, and before I could stop myself, I blurted, "Selene didn't have an affair with him, Tonya. And she didn't file that complaint to get revenge. Brady was practically molesting her at the gym. That's why she filed the complaint and then quit. She agreed to be a bridesmaid for Mandy's sake, that's all."

Case shifted position, gazing at me as though telling me to relax.

"Athena, you didn't let me finish," Tonya said kindly. "I don't believe Selene is guilty anymore. And I'm sorry I ever did."

Her demeanor seemed sincere, and her words were comforting, yet her story didn't add up. "Tonya, you were the one to ask Selene to be a bridesmaid. You were the one who orchestrated this whole thing supposedly to test Brady. If you truly don't believe Selene is guilty, why haven't you talked to Mandy about her? Or to Mitchell? Why haven't you done something to make it right?"

Tonya sighed heavily. "You're right. I should've done something."

"Then do something now."

"I can't."

"Why?"

She closed her eyes and pinched the bridge of her nose. "Because I planned the whole thing."

I stared at her in surprise. Was she confessing to murder?

CHAPTER EIGHTEEN

I had to pull on the mental breaks. That couldn't be what she meant. I glanced at Case to make sure he was taking notes, and he nodded as though encouraging me to proceed. This time, I had to try not to blow my fuse because I still had the feeling we were on to something big.

Pressing her palms together as though she was praying, Tonya continued, "Before you get upset, let me explain."

Too late, I wanted to say. "Explain away."

"First, Mandy came to me sobbing because she'd finally found out who Brady was having an affair with. She knew about his flirting with rich women at the gym and his previous relationships with them, but Selene is neither of those. She was Mandy's friend, and that really pissed Mandy off. I'm not trying to be rude or mean. I hope you understand."

"That's okay," I replied. "Selene would be the first person to admit it. And she would've told you the truth about her feelings for Brady if you'd asked."

"I know that now," Tonya said.

"What changed your mind?" I asked.

"Word spreads, Athena. I've talked to Joni, Paulette, and Mandy. And now we all feel terrible because you're right. Selene was framed. And I set the whole thing up." She shook her head slowly as though she was still in dismay over it. "Mandy was upset because she couldn't believe Brady would cheat on her with Selene, and we were desperate for a bridesmaid, so we came up with our little scheme."

"You still haven't explained why you're so sure Selene is innocent now."

"I asked Selene to be a bridesmaid, and she offered the use of your family restaurant for the rehearsal dinner. I saw her sincerity. I should've known right away that it wasn't her. I was just so wrapped up in the whole thing. But then with Brady's death, and all the evidence pointing to her . . ."

"All of the evidence still points to her," I said.

"Why didn't you tell the detectives any of this?" Case asked her.

"I knew they'd want proof, and unfortunately, I don't have any. And I also couldn't think of anyone else who would've wanted to kill Brady. That is, until Mandy told me about your interview, and then I was reminded of Nora."

"Tell me about Nora," I said.

"Nora Modelle," Tonya said. "Another sad notch in Brady's belt."

"I'm surprised you're allowed to speak her name," I said.

Tonya seemed to reflect a bit before answering. "The crowd I hang with," she paused to search for the words, "can be a bit of a mean girls' club. I'll be the first to admit it. When Mandy doesn't like someone, we don't either. First Nora, then Selene. It's easy to get caught up in the drama. But I can tell you that Nora does have a motive to hurt Brady, more motive than Mitchell and definitely more than Mandy."

"We know about Nora," I said. "We know she stalked Brady. We know about the restraining order and dying her hair and spying and all of that. Is there anything you can think of that would prove Nora was the woman Brady was having an affair with?"

She thought for a long moment before finally shaking her head.

"Tonya, a few more things need to be cleared up if you don't mind," I said.

"Go ahead," Tonya said.

I glanced over my notes. "It sounds as though Jill and Mandy were very close. Did that make you jealous?"

"Jealous of Jill?" Tonya laughed. "Joni and Paulette told you that, didn't they?"

Tonya was on top of her game.

"It's true I was upset with Mandy," she continued, "but not because she was close with Jill. I was upset because we were supposed to be planning a wedding, and Mandy wanted to spend all of her free time sunbathing on Jill's boat out on Lake Michigan."

"Do you know why Jill suddenly became sick at the bridal shower?"

"I don't," she said, "but that was a huge wrench in my plans."

"Seems like a pretty convenient way to get Selene involved," I said.

"Believe me," she said, "it was not in any respect convenient."

"You mentioned that Mitchell wouldn't allow the rehearsal dinner or reception to be held at the Waterfront, so you chose the Parthenon for the dinner. But what about the reception? Where was that to be held, if not at the Waterfront?"

"We went back and forth with Mitchell on that one. Selene offered up the Parthenon after being invited into the wedding party, but because of the large guest list, we had to have the reception at the hotel. There was no way around it. Finally, I got Mitchell's parents involved, and they made the final decision." Tonya smiled. "Mitchell is fierce, but he's no match for me."

"How well do you know Mitchell?" I asked.

"Just through Mandy."

"And Brady?"

"Through Mandy," she answered.

"You'd said you met Brady at the gym. Is that correct?"

"Yes, I'd met him there. He trained Mandy, and Terrence trained me."

Tonya was seemingly being very forthright, so I decided to hit her with everything I had. "Was Brady a punctual person?"

"Not really."

"Did you call the police from the rehearsal dinner?"

"I did," she answered.

"Why?"

Tonya looked down at the dog, stroking her soft fur, taking her time to answer. "If Brady was never on time, why did I call the police when he was late to the dinner? I'm guessing that's the real question."

"It is."

"Mandy was freaking out. She was sure something had happened to him. When the groomsmen left to check on him, Mandy kept getting more hysterical, so I called the police to help calm her down."

"What did you tell the police?" I asked.

"I don't remember."

"You seemed to be very descriptive in all of your other details, so think carefully," I cautioned.

"I'm sorry, but you'll have to check the police records. We were in a panic, and I truly don't remember. And please know that I've been open and honest with you. I've apologized for my actions, and I want you to know that if there's anything I can do to help Selene at this point, just tell me."

"There *is* something you can do," I said. "You, Mandy, and the other bridesmaids can go directly to the detectives and tell them everything you know. If you and the others don't do something right away, Selene is going to be tried for murder. So will you talk to the detectives?"

Tonya chewed her lip, looking suddenly unsure of herself. I could almost feel her tension, and I wondered about the reason for it. "Okay," she finally said, "I can do that. And I'll make sure the other two bridesmaids do, as well. Mandy will have to make up her own mind."

A door opened, and a young woman stuck her head out. "Tonya, would you come help me for a minute? I've got a dog who won't hold still for his eyebrow trimming, and his owner will be here shortly. I know he'll hold still for you."

"Sure." She scooped Pepper up in her arms and said, "I'll be right back."

I sat back in the chair and rolled my shoulders. Case gave me a moment before asking, "What are you thinking?"

"She's got an answer for everything. The only thing that tripped her up was when I asked about the phone call to the police."

"We'll have to check up on that. Do you have anything else you need to ask her?"

"I can't think of anything. My hope is that Tonya's telling the truth and they do go speak with the detectives. That might buy Selene some more time."

Tonya stepped back inside, apologizing as she crossed the room and sat down. "We're about to close," she said. "I don't want to rush you, but we should wrap things up."

I suddenly realized that we'd missed one very important detail. "I have just one other question," I said. "Where were you the morning of the murder?"

"I was with Mandy at the church, setting up for the rehearsal that evening," she answered. "When we left we took separate cars, because I wanted to head straight over to the Parthenon. You can check with your mom. She let me in early."

"Where did Mandy go?"

She blinked a few times as though trying to remember. "I don't know. She never told me."

"I think that's all then, Tonya," I said. "Thank you for your help."

Tonya rose and opened the door. "If there's anything else I can help you with, please let me know."

As we walked back down the sidewalk toward Spencer's, Case said, "Doesn't it seem odd that Tonya had an answer for everything except for Mandy's whereabouts during the murder? Wouldn't you think she would've asked Mandy about that?"

I thought about what Case was implying. "Either she truly didn't know, which makes Mandy look guiltier than ever, or Tonya just threw Mandy under the bus."

"What reason would she have to throw Mandy under the bus?" Case asked.

"To protect herself."

We came to a crosswalk across from where the *Páme* was docked and stopped. "What would be her motive?"

I was silent, thinking. "I'll work on that," I finally said.

"I think we should bump Mandy up on the suspect list," he said.

"I agree. I really want to hear what she has to say about Selene's gym pass."

"We also need to confirm Mandy's whereabouts on the morning of the murder," Case said. "In the meantime, we'll need to verify Tonya's report to the police. Do you want to call Maguire about that?"

"Sure."

"I've got a meeting scheduled with Mitchell for eleven tomorrow, so I'll find out what his fight with Brady was about."

"You actually convinced him to meet with you? I'm impressed."

"Yeah, well, I sort of bent the truth a little, so we'll see what happens."

"How about I take an early lunch and go with you?"

"Are you sure you want to come? We talked about this before, Athena. Mitchell's a wild card."

"Here's a thought. Why don't you see if you can convince Mitchell to bring his sister along? He wouldn't act up with her there."

Case rubbed his nose, thinking. "I can try. Where should we meet?"

"Blue Moon is very crowded. Pie in the Sky Bakery is too small. The Hot Spot is too hot. How about Jivin' Javas, the coffee shop just north of Little Greece? It's always busy there, but not too crowded."

"I'll call Mitchell and set it up," Case said. "I can pick you up at Spencer's around ten forty-five tomorrow morning."

"Perfect," I replied.

"Then it's a date."

"Speaking of which, let me know how your date goes with Lila."

"It's *not* a date. And her banker will be there."

It wasn't a date. *Yet.*

CHAPTER NINETEEN

"It's just a date, Athena, a single date for Saturday night. You're not marrying the man."

I was standing at the kitchen counter, paring potatoes for that evening's dinner, and I had to put down the knife. "Mama, I am not going on any more blind dates."

"It won't be blind if you meet him beforehand," she said, dredging a plate full of chicken breasts through bread crumbs. "Tomorrow at noon, go down to the grocery store, go to the fruit department, and ask for fresh dates. That's how I ended up talking to him today."

Maia snickered. She was sitting at the table, snapping the ends off of green beans.

"Don't laugh," I said. "You're next."

Mama ignored our banter. "I talk to Paul all the time. He's a very nice man, Athena. A little older than you, but at your age, you can't be too picky."

"At *my* age?"

"You've crossed over the thirty-yard line, my sweet *kóri*. You're not young anymore."

Being called a sweet daughter didn't stop her remark from stinging. "How old is this guy?"

"This guy has a name. As I said, it's Paul. Paul Stephanodis, and he's forty-three."

"You want me to go to dinner with a stranger you talk to once a week at the grocery store." I glanced over at Maia. "This can't be happening. I told her last time no more blind dates."

"Next time I see him, I'll let him know you're interested," Mama said. "Unless . . ." She opened the cupboard door, pretending to search for something. I let her search until she finally closed the door and turned to give me the eye. "Unless you're already seeing someone. A nice young man perhaps?"

"I'm seeing plenty of men," I retorted. "Tom, Terrence, Trevor, Patrick, Mitchell . . . In fact, I've met more men this week than I have in a long time. And I will continue seeing these men until I find out who killed Brady Rogers and get Selene out of jail. Wouldn't you rather have me working on her case instead of fending off strangers?"

Mama slapped a chicken breast into the crumbs, sending them flying in all directions "See? That's your problem. You see your job as one of fending off men instead of welcoming the opportunity to find someone to spend your life with."

"At the grocery store? Over the dates?"

"Just one date, Athena, that's all I ask. You won't be sleuthing on a Saturday night, will you?"

"It so happens I have a date Saturday night."

"With whom?"

"With Case." Why did I make that up?

"Aha!" Mama slapped the counter again, her bangle banging loudly. "I knew it."

"It's not actually a date," I backpedaled. "We're working together on Selene's case. So can we focus on her, please? She's miserable, and you're busy trying to fix me up with strangers."

"I will make sure Selene gets treated fairly," Mama said confidently. "I have a plan."

IT'S ALL GREEK TO ME
by Goddess Anon

The word stubborn *should be synonymous with the word* Greek. *Take Odysseus, for example. How persistent was he to travel for ten difficult years to get back home to his wife, Penelope? How many other men would have done the same, fighting off a cyclops, a witch-goddess, cannibals, a six-headed monster, sirens, a deadly whirlpool, and a line of suitors all vying to replace him? Talk about tenacious.*

That's what I mean. You get a Greek stuck on one idea, and you'll never change his mind. The only—and I mean ONLY—way to get a Greek to change is to make it his idea.

*Look at the Greek word for persistent—*epímonos—*which also means stubborn, insistent, tenacious, importunate, and persevering. If you break it down, you get two words:* epi—*meaning on, over, near, before, upon, or in other words, more than you bargained for. And combine it with the Greek word* mono, *which means single, one,*

alone—and you have an individual who is very mono-
thymía, *or single-minded. That would describe Odysseus,
for sure. And also my entire family, who seem to believe
that, by sheer persistence, they can get me to do whatever
they set their minds on.*

*Well, two can play at that game. If my family is
Odysseus, I will be Penelope, patiently—or perhaps per-
sistently—waiting for my day to come. In the meantime, I
will stay eponymous. That is to say, good-bye from
Goddess Anonymous.*

I finished my blog and looked at the clock. Was it too
late to call Case and ask about his meeting with Lila and
the bankers? I checked my phone, but no new notifica-
tions had come in. After I lay back on my bed and turned
off the light, my mind started to wander. As I thought
back on all of our interviews, it was clear that Selene was
unjustly targeted by a group of mean girls who wanted to
see her suffer. But did Mandy, Mitchell, or Tonya really
have a solid motive to murder Brady?

That reminded me. I texted Bob Maguire and asked if
he was busy. I got a return phone call immediately.

"What's up?"

"Thanks for calling, Bob. I know it's late, but could
you check the nine-one-one logs for the day of Brady's
murder? I want to know whether Tonya reported Brady's
murder before the police did."

"Let me call dispatch. I'm on duty right now, so I'll get
back to you when I can."

"You're the best."

I really wanted to believe that Tonya was sincere, that
she and the other women would confess to the detectives

what they'd done. Then I realized how ridiculous that sounded. Would they really confess to a scheme that could possibly implicate them in a murder plot?

We were running out of time. I felt suddenly sick to my stomach.

My phone rang again. "I have bad news," Case said.

"You didn't get the loan?"

"Not for the full amount. My financial health isn't what it used to be because I spent the last several years tracking down your statue of Athena, not worrying about my credit score."

My mind went skidding down the road. If Case couldn't get his business off the ground, would he still have a reason to stay in Sequoia? My heart ached at the thought of him leaving town, and then I was immediately angry at myself for getting so wrapped up in Case's life.

"The good news," Case said, "is that Lila said we could possibly work out a deal for a smaller loan. I would have to come up with the first fifty thousand, and Lila would have to be the guarantor. She's all for it but I told her I would have to think about it."

And then I was angry for a whole new reason.

"Can I assume by your silence that you're not thrilled with the idea?" he finally asked.

"I'm thinking it through," I said. "How involved will Lila be?"

"She'll have to sign a few documents."

"How about the day-to-day running of your business?"

"I doubt she'd be interested in a fishing business, Athena."

"When it comes to Lila, I wouldn't put anything past her."

"Do I detect a note of jealousy?"

Luckily, he could only detect a note because there was an entire symphony of jealousy playing in my mind. "Not a bit," I replied.

"Good. I'll pick you up tomorrow at the garden center at ten forty-five for our meeting with Mitchell."

"It's a"—I paused to consider what I'd been about to say—"deal."

"And on that note, I'll say *adío,* Athena."

Friday

"Do you see what I mean, darling? Where are the roses? I've got to have roses."

"Yes, Mrs. Petrakis, I understand. But do you know what roses like? They like great soil, nice black loam that lets the water in and doesn't dry as hard as a rock, like your clay soil does. Unfortunately, you have clay. And if the roses get weak from lack of water, they're more susceptible to black spot and Japanese beetles, which have been a problem in your area."

"Then put those hardy ones in, you know, the knock-overs."

"Knock Out roses, and yes, they are somewhat hardy, but they still prefer—"

"You don't look at all like the Karrases, do you, darling?"

"I take after the Spencer side." I drew her attention back to the landscape drawing I'd made. "Along here, I thought we'd put in flowering deutzias. They're summer-blooming, hardy, and very pretty."

"But they're not roses. Do you understand that I want roses?"

Stubborn didn't begin to cover Mrs. Petrakis. Willful, argumentative, disputatious . . . I could've gone on thinking up additional words to describe her, but that would have just send my blood pressure spiking, and I had more important things on my mind. Like Selene spending the rest of her life in jail, and Case going into business with a rich widow. "Roses it is."

Because it was such a beautiful morning, I'd taken Sophia Petrakis outside to the patio to sit at a table with a cup of Greek coffee, which she'd jumped on. I watched now as she picked up her cup and sipped noisily—was she related to Uncle Giannis?—while I went over the drawing once again.

At ten forty-five, Case came striding across the sales floor with a smile on his face. He was wearing a white, short-sleeved shirt, blue denims, and tan boat shoes, his dark hair thick and wavy now that he'd let it go natural. Surprisingly, he'd shaved off the beard he'd been growing, and as he approached, I could see the tan lines on his face.

"You shaved."

"Funny story. After we had dinner with the banker, Lila suggested I'd look more business-like with a clean-shaven face, so . . ."

The buzzing in my ears blocked the rest. He'd shaved for Lila? And that was *funny*?

"We should get going," I said. "I'll grab my purse and meet you by the door."

The buzzing continued as we walked to his Jeep. The coffee shop was just a block before the Parthenon, so the drive was short. On the way, while the wind whipped my hair around, Case described the boats he wanted to buy, the boat captains he'd researched, and, most importantly, that Lila wanted to be there when he interviewed the captains.

Why? I wanted to ask him, except that I already knew the answer. Lila wanted to be a part of his life. I wondered if Case realized it. Maybe he did, and he was fine with it, or maybe he felt conflicted, afraid she'd change her mind if he said no way. Whichever it was, I was too chicken to ask.

Suffer in silence then, *deilós*, I told myself. Amazing how the word for coward came tripping forth.

Case parked the Jeep in an empty spot along the curb. As I got out, I had a sudden feeling that we were being followed; I glanced around but didn't see anyone I recognized. As we continued down the sidewalk, I kept feeling eyes on me, but each time I looked around, I saw nothing unusual about the people surrounding us.

Jivin' Javas was jumping when we entered. The ultra-modern coffee bar, decorated with lots of glass and metal, had a line of people waiting to order, and all of the high-top tables were filled. I glanced around for a place to sit and saw a hand go up.

"There's Mitchell," I said to Case. I glanced around again, to be sure Lila wasn't there, then told myself to knock it off. Surely, she hadn't followed us. Had she?

Mitchell rose when we approached. He was wearing a light gray business suit with a white-collared shirt, unbuttoned, with no tie and gray leather loafers. He said stiffly, "Mandy couldn't make it, and I don't have much time. I'm needed back at the Waterfront immediately."

"Would you like some coffee?" Case asked. "I'm buying."

"I've already ordered," Mitchell said, a look of impatience on his face.

"I'll take a half-caf with a shot of vanilla," I told him.

"I'll be right back."

"Case said you had some important news," Mitchell said at once.

I blinked several times, trying to figure out what Case was referring to. "Let's wait until he gets back to go over it." I took out my iPad and opened the Brady file, scrolling down to my questions for Mitchell.

When Case returned, he had Mitchell's coffee with him.

"Thanks," Mitchell said, going for his wallet.

"Don't bother," Case said. "It's on me."

"I'd prefer you didn't." Mitchell took out a handful of singles, counted them out, and set them in a neat stack on the table. "No offense." He took a sip of coffee and set it down. "What's the important news?"

I folded my hands and waited for Case's answer.

"We've learned why Mandy thought Brady was having an affair with Selene," he said.

"In what way is this important to me?" Mitchell asked.

We hadn't prepared an answer for that. This time, Case was the one who blinked several times and, with a shift in his gaze, passed the torch on to me. I picked it up and ran.

"We thought you'd like to know that your sister found a gym pass in Brady's apartment. When she confronted Brady, he said it was Selene's, but look at this." I took the gym pass out of my purse and slapped it down on the table in front of him.

Case's name was called. He left to grab our drinks while Mitchell studied the pass. "What does that prove?" he asked guardedly.

"It proves the pass Mandy found wasn't Selene's," I said. "I found this one in Selene's gym bag."

"This," he said, putting a finger on Selene's pass, "doesn't prove anything. There are no markings, no way to verify whose pass that is. It could be a brand-new one."

"I'm sure the gym can verify that it's Selene's original pass by the bar code on the back."

"It still doesn't prove that Selene is innocent. It doesn't even prove that Selene wasn't having an affair with Brady."

"Mitchell," I said evenly, "we believe that Brady was having an affair, but not with my sister. We believe he was protecting someone when he told Mandy it was Selene's. Whoever left that gym pass in Brady's apartment could be the real killer."

"You know what?" He leaned toward me. "I don't care."

Case returned with our piping-hot drinks and placed them on the table. Ignoring his coffee, Mitchell checked his watch. "Is there anything else we need to address? I have a late appointment."

I glanced at Case for help, and he immediately jumped in. "We'd appreciate just a few more minutes of your time. I know it's a pain, but we're trying hard to clear Athena's sister. I'm sure you can understand that."

Mitchell picked up his coffee and blew on it. "Then ask your questions, because I'm leaving when I finish my coffee."

"No problem," Case said. "Did Brady start a fight with you on the night of the bridal shower?"

"Not a physical fight. He was drunk and making a fool of himself, so I escorted him safely away from the vicinity. There are witnesses who will verify that."

"Why did he come looking for you?" Case asked.

"I don't know, but he was belligerent."

"You were Brady's best man," I said. "Why didn't you go out with the other groomsmen for Brady's bachelor party?"

"They weren't my friends, they were Brady's. I was the best man because Mandy wanted it that way. I did it as a favor to her, because Brady certainly didn't want me around."

"You drove him home that night, correct?" Case asked.

"Yes, but that was days before the rehearsal dinner . . . and I'm not sure what you're getting at."

"Did you cancel the rehearsal dinner at the Waterfront Hotel?"

He studied Case as though trying to figure him out. "Yes."

"Did you cancel the reception at the hotel?" Case fired.

"I tried, but my father intervened."

"Did you also try to cancel the wedding?" Case asked.

He slammed his fist on the table. "I had good reason!" He took a deep breath, as though to control his temper, and said, "I know what you're trying to do. But there's a big difference between canceling a reception and killing a man."

"Understood." Case picked up his coffee and held it, letting the steam rise. "Do you have a gym membership to Fitness First?"

"Mandy and I both have memberships. How is that relevant?"

"Just out of curiosity," Case said, "is there a gym at the Waterfront Hotel?"

"Yes," Mitchell said slowly.

"Why not use that gym?"

He pressed his lips together and looked away, as though

trying to control his temper. "Because Mandy wanted a personal trainer."

"Did you also have a personal trainer at Fitness First?"

"No. And again, how is that relevant?"

"Just curiosity on my part," Case said. "I was wondering why you felt the need to accompany your sister to the gym."

Mitchell shoved his coffee away. "You want to know the truth? Because I didn't trust Brady. Okay? Now, does that make me a killer? No. Just a concerned brother."

"Do you have your gym pass with you?" Case asked.

"You're asking if the pass in Brady's apartment was *mine?*" Mitchell rose abruptly "Okay, that's it! I want you and your partner to stay away from me. And if I see you anywhere near my sister, I swear to God I'll file a harassment complaint." Mitchell glared at us, his nostrils flaring. He turned and left the coffee shop, pushing past several people standing in line, letting the door bang closed behind him.

Case raised his eyebrows. "I'd say I hit a nerve."

"You hit something, all right. Were you implying that Mitchell could be the *other woman* we're looking for?"

"He does have a gym pass." Case took another sip of coffee. "Remember the picture frame that's missing from Brady's hutch? Who was in that photo?"

"Mandy, Brady, and Mitchell."

"Don't you wonder why Mitchell was in that photo?"

"It is rather odd."

"It's bizarre." Case enumerated on his fingers. "Number one. Mitchell was around whenever Brady was with Mandy, even at the fitness club. Number two. He wanted Mandy to call off the wedding. Three. He had a spat with Brady at the bridal shower. And four. He cancelled the reception at the Waterfront. Four strong indications that we could be on to something."

"Except that Mitchell wasn't at the beauty salon, Case. He didn't have direct access to the scissors."

"He had Mandy."

"*If* the two of them collaborated."

"We've seen how close they are." Case finished his coffee and set the cup down. "I know he's hiding something, Athena."

"This is Friday. The prosecutor will be calling for a grand jury on Monday, and we're still working on theories. What are we going to do?"

"Keeping working."

"On what?" I asked. "My hope was to show Mandy the gym pass and try to persuade her to help us. Now we can't go anywhere near her."

"Finish your coffee," he told me. "We need to get to Mandy before Mitchell does."

As we hurried out to his Jeep, I said, "I'm sure Mitchell was on the phone with his sister the second he left the coffee shop."

"We have to try."

I slid in through the open Jeep and buckled my seat belt as my phone rang.

"Thenie," my sister Maia said hurriedly, "I'm at the jail. You need to come here ASAP."

"Maia, I'm right in the middle of something. Can it wait?"

"I need you to come to the jail right now," she whispered.

"Why? What's wrong."

"Mama got arrested, and I can't reach Pops. You've got to come now."

CHAPTER TWENTY

Case dropped me off at the jail and pulled into the parking lot to wait. I quickly made my way inside, going through the now-familiar security checks and then following a jailer back to the holding cells.

"Mama!"

My mother rose from the bench fastened to the wall and walked nonchalantly to the bars, her dignity still intact. I noticed she was alone in the holding cell. "Athena, don't panic. I've called your father, and he's on his way with Kevin."

"What are you here for?"

"A *chazos* charge. Nothing for you to concern yourself about."

"*How* stupid?" I asked. And why did I know all the bad words?

"All I'll say is that I'm certain I'll be released when

Kevin gets here. He's a fine attorney, and still single, by the way."

"What did they say they were arresting you for?"

"Something silly." She fluttered her hand in the air. "Instigating a riot."

"Instigating a riot? In a *jail*? Mama, did you bring food? Is that why you were arrested? I told you not to do that."

"It wasn't about bringing the food. Well, in a way it was. We, the warden and I, had a disagreement. Yiayiá and I made a big pan of pastitsio for everyone, but the *chazos* warden told me to take it back home, and I said that was wrong. If he would only have some, he would understand that this jail needs to have some good Greek catering. Then everyone here, and I mean *everyone*," she said, loud enough for it to carry to both ends of the hall-way, "would be well fed."

"And that's what got you arrested."

"You might think so, but no. Then I said to everyone within earshot, 'If you agree, please indicate,' and all the women started making noise—whistling, calling out things, clapping . . ."

"So you did instigate a riot."

Mama shrugged. "Call it what you will. Selene did not get her food today, and neither did anyone else." She raised her voice on the last half of the sentence and got a round of enthusiastic applause and hoots.

"Mama, don't make it worse. Do you want to spend the night here?"

"For bringing good food?" she asked in a loud voice.

"Okay, I'm outta here. You can wait for Dad and Kevin. I'm going to talk to Selene."

"Tell her I'm sorry the warden is such an *anóitos*, and I'll make sure she gets good food later today."

"Whether he's a fool or not," I said quietly, "the warden runs this place. His building, his rules. Get it?"

"Why did I think you'd understand? You *or* your sister?" She walked back to the bench and sat down, folding her arms in front of her. "Go see Selene."

I was shown to the visitors' room, where a very angry Selene took a seat on the other side of the glass divider.

"Can you believe it?" she asked, holding the phone to her ear. "It's bad enough that I'm here. Then in comes Mama to embarrass me *and* herself, all because she thinks I shouldn't eat the food here. What more can I say? She got herself arrested, and now poor Dad is going to have to come bail her out *and* get Kevin involved." She huffed angrily. "I hope you have some good news for me."

"I understand how you feel about Mama. She just doesn't get why everyone doesn't love her food."

"She gets it, Thenie. She's just being an *anóitos* herself. But what about the news?"

"Do you suppose she's going to have to have a hearing? She told me to say you're still going to get your Greek food today, by the way. Someone will bring it over."

"Athena, you're stalling. You don't have any good news, do you?"

"Actually, we've made some progress. We're homing in on a piece of evidence the police missed, and we're starting our second round of interviews, getting specific about what we ask."

Selene studied me for a moment, then shook her head. "You're not fooling me, Thenie."

"Honest, Selene, everything I told you is the truth. We just don't have one solid suspect. But we do have three strong possibilities—Nora, Mitchell, and Mandy."

Selene set the phone down and put her head in her hands. She looked up with tears in her eyes. When she finally picked up the phone, she said, "I thought I'd be out of here by now. I'm not even allowed out on bail!"

"Being denied bail isn't unusual with a charge of murder."

She let out a moan. "I can't believe this is happening."

"Don't give up hope, Selene. I'm doing everything possible, turning over every stone. Something's going to break soon, I can feel it."

With a frustrated sigh, she said, "I hope so, Athena."

My heart was heavy when I left the jail. Case tried to console me as we drove out to Hampton Hills again, but it didn't work. Monday was breathing down my neck.

We pulled up to the sprawling pink-brick house ten minutes later, but this time there was no silver Porsche in the driveway, and all the maid would say was that Miss Mandy was out.

"What do we do now?" I asked as we climbed back into the Jeep.

"Well," Case said, as he turned on the ignition, "from what the groomsmen said, we know Mandy does two things—shops and sits by the pool."

"We don't even know if the maid is telling the truth. Mandy could be watching us from her bedroom window right now."

"Or she could be sitting out by the pool," Case said. "Why don't you sneak back there and check?"

"I'm sure she would be more than willing to answer questions after I climb the fence and break into her back-yard swimming pool."

"Okay. Forget about her pool," Case said. "I have an-other idea."

"Are you going to give me a clue?"

"Two words," he said as he pulled the jeep out of the driveway. "Waterfront Hotel. Let's see if we can find out what really happened at Mandy's bridal shower."

The three-story Waterfront Hotel, located almost at the southern edge of Greene Street, fronted Lake Michigan and was one of the most popular places to stay in a city that had numerous hotels, guest houses, and bed-and-breakfast inns.

Case turned into the circular drive and pulled up to the main entrance, where he handed the keys to a valet. As he escorted me inside, he said quietly, "Wow, would you get a load of this place?"

"I don't think I've ever been inside. It's gorgeous."

The lobby was done in black marble and gold, with a lavish waterfall behind the reception desk. To the left was a bank of elevators, so we headed up a wide hallway to the right, passing a glass-fronted gift shop and stopping at the menu display in front of the restaurant.

"Let's grab a seat," Case said, "and see what we can learn about Mitchell."

"And get some food," I said. "I'm starving."

When the hostess came to seat us, I nudged Case. "Ask to be seated outside."

As we followed the hostess into the dining room, I looked around. White satin drapes hung from the ceiling between the large open windows that looked onto the lake. A giant crystal chandelier hovered over the center of the room. Below it was a gold champagne fountain encircled by crystal glasses. The dining room was half full, with no sign of Mitchell.

Outside was a different story. Every table seemed to be full, and the upper-class diners were clinking glasses and laughing between bites of oysters on the half shell, and crackers topped with caviar, while tropical music played in the background. A set of white wooden steps, outlined by glowing string lights, led the way down to the pool area and, beyond that, to the wide expanse of lake.

After a five-minute wait for a table to be cleared, we were shown to our seats, which had a magnificent view of the enormous infinity pool and lake beyond it. As I sat down, Case walked past the table and stopped at the railing overlooking the pool, turning back to mouth the word "Wow."

After a quick bit of surveillance, he joined me. "I feel extremely underdressed. You'd never guess from the front what a little slice of paradise this place is."

A waiter came by to take our drink orders. While Case was perusing the beer list, several other diners were waving at the waiter, trying to get his attention. The guy looked flustered.

"Are you the only server working today?" I asked.

"You'd think so, wouldn't you?" he asked. "Someone called in sick, and the other waiter is serving a private client right now. Just another wonderful summer in Sequoia." He turned to the group next to us, who had a table full of appetizers and entrées, but empty wineglasses. "I'll be right with you."

I ordered a chicken Caesar salad, while Case took his time looking over the menu. He turned to the group next to us and asked, "What do you suggest?"

"Just order already," I muttered under my breath.

Case finally asked for the seafood platter. "I hope you're not too hungry," he said to me afterward. "We might be waiting a while."

My attention was diverted by a man's voice coming from the main dining hall behind us. "Do you hear that? He sounds familiar."

Case peered over my shoulder, then tilted his head down, shielding his eyes with his hand. "It's Mitchell," he said quietly.

"Did he see us?"

"No," Case answered. "I don't think so."

The diners' chatter came to an abrupt halt as we heard Mitchell castigating the poor waiter. It went on for several long minutes before Mitchell finally shouted, "Pick up your paycheck at the end of your shift and leave."

Case looked up again to see what had happened and then reported, "Mitchell walked away, and our waiter seems to be in shock."

The chattering and clinking resumed as the commotion inside ended.

"Mitchell must oversee the wait staff," I said.

"Speaking of," Case said as another waiter brushed past our table with a silver chalice of ice in one hand and a bottle of champagne in the other. He trotted down the steps to the pool and walked toward what looked like a private VIP area. Part of the pool had been roped off and white lattice installed. The waiter set the champagne down behind the lattice, where part of a chaise longue was visible.

At the same time, I noticed Joni and Paulette bouncing up out of the water to grab their towels. They, too, disappeared behind the lattice.

"I think Mandy's here," I said.

Case turned to see. "Looks like a cabana down there."

"What do you know? Her own private section of the pool."

"Excuse me," Case said as our waiter started past us. "When you have a minute, I'd like to ask you a few questions."

The waiter, a short, slender, twenty-something man wearing a white shirt and black pants, rolled his eyes and turned toward the table full of impatient diners next to us before Case added, "It's about Mitchell Black."

The waiter paused mid-step, turned around, and gave Case a curious look.

"We're investigating the death of Brady Rogers," Case said. "Do you have a minute to talk?"

"Excuse me, son," said a white-haired man wearing a pink polo shirt at the table next to us. He shook his empty glass, showing off his thick, gold Rolex. "We've been mighty patient up until this point. I suggest you stop your—"

"Pardon me, sir. Someone will be with you shortly. These people need my assistance right now." He pulled out the seat next to us and plopped down. "Some people have to learn patience. What do you want to know about Mitchell—pardon me, *Mr. Black*?"

I scooted forward in my chair to avoid the shocked looks we were being given. Unaffected as usual, Case carried on.

"We couldn't help overhearing, and we're really sorry you got fired," he said.

"Yeah, well, I've been asking for a day off. I guess I got my wish."

"Is Mitchell your boss?"

"Worse. He's the boss's son. He's also supposedly the hotel manager, but I haven't seen him manage anything in more than a month. Now he's back, and he's making a mess of things. Mitchell knows how busy we are, but when Mandy shows up, she gets her own personal waiter." He shook his head in frustration. "Ever since Daddy left Mitchell in charge, the two of them have been treating this place like their own personal holiday resort. I'll be glad to watch it fail."

"Then Mandy is here now?"

"Mandy is always here," the waiter said, getting friendlier by the second. "Apparently, she has nothing better to do."

"You heard that Brady Rogers, her fiancé, was murdered, right?" I asked.

"Everyone in *town* has heard, so you'd think she'd behave a little more respectfully. Well, take a look at what's going on down there. Booze, boys, and sunbathing. That's some grieving fiancée. But honestly, after what happened at the bridal shower, I'm not surprised."

Now we were getting somewhere. "What happened?" I asked.

The waiter glanced over his shoulder then said quietly, "Brady showed up at Mandy's bridal shower so drunk he could barely talk."

He glanced around again to be sure no one was listening, then leaned in on one elbow. "Brady was spouting off in the bar about how Mitchell was going to bankrupt the hotel because he was spending all his time dogging Brady and not doing his job. Mitchell almost got into a fistfight with the guy. Nobody knows this, but I over-heard them arguing in the hallway. Heard some pretty in-teresting stuff."

"Like what?" Case asked.

The waiter lowered his voice. "Brady kept saying the deal was off. He was in love with Mandy, and the deal was off."

I slid to the edge of my seat and leaned on my elbows. "Do you know what the deal was?"

"I don't know if this is true," the waiter said, "but I heard a rumor that Mitchell had paid Brady a hefty sum of money."

"To call off the wedding?" I asked.

The waiter shrugged. "As I said, it was a rumor."

"And Brady said the deal was off," I said.

"Yeah," the waiter said. "But then Mitchell started threatening that he would find a way to stop the wedding, one way or another."

"What's your opinion of Mitchell?" I asked. "I know he has a temper. Do you think he's volatile enough to have killed someone?"

"Oh, God no," the waiter said. "I've seen Mitchell faint over a papercut." He laughed at his own comment. "He talks a big game, but he's all show. I know he man-aged to cancel the rehearsal dinner here, but old Daddy Warbucks stepped in and overruled him about the recep-tion."

"Is there anything else you heard Mitchell and Brady fight about?"

"They didn't have time. Mandy charged in to break up

the commotion, and after that, it was just a mess. Mitchell finally strong-armed Brady out of the building."

"Interesting," I said to Case.

"That's enough gossip," our waiter said. "I need to get back to work, make a few tips, seeing as today is my last day."

"Before you go," I said, "do you have any idea whether Mandy knew about this so-called deal between her brother and Brady?"

"Why don't you go ask her?" the waiter said, nodding over to her area. "She's sitting right down there."

CHAPTER TWENTY-ONE

I glanced down at the pool area to see Mandy sitting on the edge of the pool in her black one-piece suit, dangling her feet into the water, sipping champagne and laughing with her friends.

"Does she usually stay for a while?" Case asked our waiter.

"She'll be there all afternoon," he said.

"Good. Then let's eat before we go talk to her," Case said to me, and handed our waiter a hefty tip.

"Coming right out," the waiter said with a big smile.

"You know what I find interesting?" I asked. "All this time, I figured Mandy and Mitchell would've been working together to commit the murder. But now it sounds as though Mitchell might've acted independently."

"He couldn't have. He didn't have access to the scissors."

"Maybe he didn't use Mandy to get the scissors." I nodded toward the pool. "Look at those women out there enjoying Mandy's largess. Either one could've taken the scissors for him. Mitchell could've offered a very large chunk of money."

"But you didn't get that feeling when you talked to them, did you?"

"No, but I wasn't with them long enough to really dig deep."

"Still, Athena, it seems like a long shot."

"I know. I'm getting desperate because we're running out of time."

Case studied them. "You know what surprises me? That they're here during a weekday. Don't they work?"

"Maybe Tonya is the only one with a job." I took a sip of my drink. "I'm going to the gym tomorrow. Maybe I can find out if any of the bridesmaids or Mitchell have recently replaced their gym passes."

We ate leisurely as the tables around us slowly emptied out. I looked down at the pool area and saw Mandy get up and go behind the lattice screen. What would she do when we showed up to talk to her? Would she have us thrown out? Would she call Mitchell? Would he make good on his threat? I reached for my drink as my mouth went dry.

"Is your food okay?" Case asked, pushing aside his empty plate. "You haven't finished."

"I'm nervous, Case. I'm afraid of what Mandy might do if we bother her, especially if Mitchell instructed her not to talk to us. And don't forget his threat to file a harassment suit."

"Then maybe I should go fishing alone."

"Fishing? Don't you mean swimming?"

"Fishing for information."

"Oh, you mean *flirting*," I teased.

"Okay, yes, I'll need to use my charm."

"Aren't you forgetting something?" I asked. "Like a bathing suit?"

"Are you finished eating?"

I pushed my plate away.

"Then come with me."

I followed him through the restaurant to the gift shop, where he found swim trunks to purchase. Just as we were about to buy them, I spotted Mitchell Black walking past the shop, talking with one of his staff.

"Case, Mitchell's walking around. We'd better go."

"I have a better idea." Case picked up a baseball cap and put it on. With his sunglasses, he was barely recognizable. Then he found a pair of oversized women's sunglasses and a white lacy head scarf and handed them to me. "Remember when I had to pretend to be a Greek fisherman? This time *you* get to play dress-up."

I tried on the sunglasses in front of the mirror on top of the sunglass rack. "Are you still griping about your disguise?"

"My feet have yet to recover from those boat shoes."

I tied the scarf around my head and turned to pose for him. "How do I look?"

"Like a tourist. You can stay at our table and watch for Mitchell while I head down to the pool to talk to Mandy. I'll have my phone with me. Text me if you see Mitchell heading my way and I'll leave at once."

"I'm not sure this is such a good idea, Case. I mean, seriously, what makes you think Mandy will talk to you?"

He smiled. "Didn't I charm you into talking to me when you thought I was trying to steal your statue?"

"Yes."

"Then have a little faith, baby. I know what I'm doing."

Case paid for the trunks, hat, scarf, and sunglasses, then headed for the men's changing room. I sat back down at our table, with a glass of complimentary champagne supplied by our waiter, to watch the pool area. I took a sip of very dry bubbly and adjusted the obnoxiously large sunglass frames that were pinching the bridge of my nose. I repositioned the scarf over my hair and tried to relax as the sun roasted the back of my shoulders.

The pool was mostly occupied by women with dark tans and children with loud voices. Case strode out of the changing room into the pool area, whipped a white towel over one bare shoulder, and pulled his sunglasses down over his eyes. His dark blue swim shorts fit tightly, and his tan skin gleamed in the sunshine.

I watched him place his towel over the pool chair nearest Mandy's VIP area and reach into his pocket for his phone. He typed something, tossed his phone onto a towel, then looked over at me with a smile. My phone dinged immediately.

Relax and enjoy the show.

I took a deep breath and sat back, trying to do as he suggested. The tables were continually filling with new diners, as the lone waiter struggled to keep up with their orders. I glanced around to check for Mitchell, but he was nowhere to be seen. I looked back at the pool area just in time to see Case make a big splash in the deep end. Joni and Paulette were quick to scream and then quicker to giggle as Case pulled himself up and rested his elbows on the concrete next to where the two women were sun-bathing.

I couldn't hear what was happening, but I could see their gestures, and it didn't take long before Case was being invited to join the women for champagne. I saw Case extend his arm as he was handed a glass, and then out from behind the lattice came Mandy Black, clinking glasses with him before circling around him like a hungry wolf. They were certainly not the actions of a woman who'd just lost her fiancé. And there was definitely no sign of her being tranquilized today.

I looked around for Mitchell as my thoughts began to circle back to the night of the rehearsal dinner—Mandy, seeming to know that Brady was already dead, Mitchell, checking the time and looking perturbed—and, for some reason, Tonya popped into my mind.

I sat up straight. Not only had she popped into my mind, she had also popped into my line of sight, her blond ponytail bobbing along as she made her way through the tables, talking on her phone as she glanced around, clearly looking for someone. She was dressed in a flirty pink sundress with white sandals and a white seashell necklace, with a small white straw purse hanging from her shoulder.

I checked to make sure my scarf was in place and then scooted my chair so that I was hidden behind a large man having lunch at a table in front of me. Was Tonya here to find Mandy and the bridesmaids to talk to them, like she'd promised? It occurred to me then that I'd forgotten to ask my mother about Tonya's alibi for the day of the murder.

My phone rang. I was so startled that I reached for it too quickly, tipping over my glass of champagne. My stomach sank as the glass hit the table, the fizzy liquid rushing out around the empty dishes and silverware. Even worse, before I could catch it, the glass rolled off of the edge and crashed to the ground, causing everyone's gaze to turn toward me. I hid my face and whispered hurriedly into the phone, "Hello?"

"Athena? It's Bob. Can you talk?"

With my head ducked down, I said, "Go ahead."

"I had a look at the nine-one-one log on the day of the murder," he said.

As I sat up, our waiter stopped by the table to sweep up the shards of glass. "I'm so sorry," I whispered to him. Then I said into the phone, "What did you learn, Bob?"

"Tonya Upton placed a call at six-fifteen asking the police to check on Brady, but she made no mention of foul play."

Then Tonya had been telling the truth. "Okay, Bob," I said, relaxing just a bit. "Thank you so much."

The waiter stepped away, and the surrounding glares subsided. I looked around for Tonya, but she had gone. I tipped my sunglasses down my nose, scanning the pool area, but didn't see her there either. I was just about to type a message to Case, telling him that Tonya was on her way, when I heard a woman's voice behind me.

"Athena?"

I turned to see Tonya with a very surprised look on her face. I pulled the sunglasses off. Clearly, they hadn't disguised me very well.

"It *is* you. What are you doing here?" She noticed his empty plate and the bottle of champagne chilling at my side and said, "Are you on a date?"

I didn't know how to answer. To keep it simple, I said, "Yes, I'm on a date."

"With whom?" she asked. "Your handsome partner?"

I really didn't want anyone to think Case and I had anything but a professional relationship, but I tried and failed to come up with the name of one of the men my mother had mentioned. So I blurted, "Yes, with Case."

She glanced around. "Where is he?"

I was drawing a blank. Where was the quick-thinking reporter I'd once been?

Snap to it, Athena, I told myself. *One of your suspects is right in front of you. Take advantage of it!* "He's in the bathroom. If you have a moment, can I ask you some questions?"

She smiled and took Case's seat. "Of course. Go ahead."

"First, I want to let you know that I checked on your phone call to the police, and you were telling the truth. I'm sorry if I sounded like I doubted you."

She shrugged it off. "No need to apologize. I would do the exact same thing if Selene were my sister."

"That reminds me," I said. "Have you or the others had a chance to talk to the detectives yet?"

"I haven't spoken to the girls about it yet, but that's why I'm here on my day off. They're usually hanging out by the pool." Tonya turned in her chair and eyed Mandy's private cabana. "I see them now."

The bridesmaids were splashing their feet in the water, but Mandy and Case were nowhere to be seen. Where had they gone?

"I just thought of something," I said, trying to regain Tonya's attention before she spotted my partner. "We found Selene's gym pass."

"Does that help your investigation?"

"It could. Mandy told us that she found a gym pass in

Brady's apartment that wasn't his. I'm guessing you knew about it, too."

"Yes, and he told us it was Selene's. That's what started this whole mess in the first place. Where did you find it?"

"In Selene's gym bag," I said. "So the pass Mandy found was not Selene's."

"Wow," Tonya exclaimed. "Have you shared this with the detectives?"

"Not yet. But it's obvious that Brady was lying about whom he was having an affair with, which means he was covering for someone."

Tonya's smile disappeared, and a wily expression took its place. "You're not on a date. You're working on the investigation." She glanced around at the pool area. "You think it's one of them, don't you?"

"We haven't eliminated anyone yet," I said as tactfully as I could.

She leaned forward on one elbow, setting her chin in her palm. "Let me help you."

I was not expecting that.

"Mandy, Joni, Paulette, and I are all members of the gym," she continued. "I'll ask them to show their gym passes to the detectives. That way, you can eliminate us as suspects."

"Thanks," I said hesitantly, "but what I really need is the pass Mandy found at Brady's apartment. I want to find out who Brady was protecting."

"I don't know what happened to it," Tonya admitted. "But I'll try to find out and let you know."

She smiled again as though we were old friends and she had just solved all of my problems. I didn't allow myself to completely trust Tonya, but I wasn't about to turn down her offer either. I gave her my number, thanked her for her help, and asked her for one more favor, very curious to see her reaction. "What about Mitchell? Do you think you can convince him to show the detectives his pass?"

"I can certainly try."

"I'd appreciate it."

Hearing Mitchell once again berating someone, this time directly behind me, I pulled the sunglasses back over my eyes and made sure the scarf was covering my hair.

Tonya turned to look behind her. "Where's Case? He can't have been in the bathroom this long."

"Actually, he's down at the pool."

She studied me for a moment. "You don't want Mitchell to see you, do you?"

"He doesn't want us near Mandy."

"Did he threaten you?"

"With a lawsuit."

"I'm not surprised." She glanced around again, then said quietly, "I'll distract Mitchell You get Case out of here."

She had barely finished talking when Mitchell passed right by the table and headed down the white steps, making straight for the pool. I watched Tonya bolt from her seat and hurry after him, calling his name. Mitchell turned toward her just as Case appeared from behind the lattice. I texted him: **911. Get out now,** but he was too busy talking and laughing with the sunbaked bridesmaids to hear the ding.

Mandy came out and handed him something I couldn't see. He smiled and pocketed the item, then turned toward his towel and phone lying on his lounge chair. I twisted a lock of hair so tightly I almost pulled it from my scalp. *Check your phone, Case!* If Mitchell saw Case now, all hell would break lose.

Only a few yards away stood Tonya and Mitchell, chatting away. Case walked casually in their direction to grab his towel, unaware that if Tonya moved an inch, he would be directly in Mitchell Black's line of sight.

CHAPTER TWENTY-TWO

Case looked down at his phone, and instantly his head came up, swiveling in my direction. He saw me pointing and followed my finger to where Mitchell and Tonya were standing. That's when I realized that the two were directly in front of the door to the men's room, Case's only escape route. I watched as he dropped his phone into his pocket and quickly stepped back behind Mandy's VIP area. What was he doing?

A minute later, Case stepped out from behind the lattice and executed a perfect dive under the water. Not long afterward, Mandy stepped out and called a greeting to Tonya and Mitchell. As the two walked the length of the pool toward Mandy's private section, Case swam in the opposite direction. When he reached the far end, he swung himself up and out of the water, then strode quickly into the changing room, pausing long enough to motion for me to meet him inside the hotel.

Except for his slicked-back hair, I never would have guessed Case had just been swimming. He met me outside the men's restroom, and we proceeded outside to the valet station to pick up his Jeep.

"You frightened me half to death," I said. "Thank God Tonya was there. She distracted Mitchell so you could leave. I don't even want to think what would've happened if he'd seen you."

"It wasn't me I was worried about," Case said. "Mandy made it clear that she did not want her brother to find out she was talking to me."

"Is she afraid of him?"

"I think it was more about appearances."

"Because she wasn't acting like a grieving fiancée."

"She was flirting rather heavily," Case said. "At least Mandy was more clear-headed today. She seemed relieved to hear that you found Selene's gym pass. And look what she gave me." Case pulled out of his pocket a white gym pass the size of a credit card with the Fitness First logo on the front.

My eyes opened in surprise. "Is this the pass Mandy found under Brady's bed?"

"You bet," Case said.

"She had it with her?"

"In her purse. She was going to stop at the garden center today to give it to you. See that symbol in the right-hand corner? That indicates that the pass belongs to a member, not an employee."

"Which definitely indicates it wasn't Brady's."

"Right."

I slid the gym pass into my purse. "I've changed my mind. I don't think Mandy's the killer."

"Don't be too hasty. That could be what she wants us to think."

"I don't know, Case. I'm ready to put Mitchell at number one. He hated Brady. He paid Brady to call off the wedding. He could've gotten a key to the apartment from Mandy's purse. He could've paid one of those women to steal Selene's scissors—or even hired one of the waitresses here to slip into the salon. What waitress couldn't use some extra cash? And he can come and go from the hotel without anyone questioning him. To me it adds up to one big motive and opportunity."

"Let's not count Mandy out yet," Case said. "She had a motive, she had easy access to the scissors as well as to Brady's apartment, and she disappeared for a while after she and Tonya went to the church."

"Then why would she give us the pass?"

"To throw us off her trail. All the pass proves is that Selene didn't leave hers at Brady's apartment. It doesn't clear Mandy as a suspect."

I removed my scarf and brushed my hair out of my eyes. "Hopefully someone at the gym can tell us who it belongs to. If it belongs to Nora, then I'd move Brady down to number two and leave Nora at number one."

"And then there's Tonya," Case said. "Something about her bothers me."

"Fifteen minutes ago, I would've agreed with you. She had the opportunity to grab Selene's scissors, but I have yet to pin down a motive. Why would she want Brady dead? And after what she did for us today, I'm actually starting to like her. By the way, Maguire confirmed her story. She was telling the truth."

"Have you checked her alibi with your mom?"

"I completely forgot to ask. And Mom's a little tied up at the moment."

"Is she still in jail?"

"When I last heard." I took off my sunglasses and rubbed the bridge of my nose.

As the valet pulled up in Case's Jeep, I felt a chill run up the back of my neck. I turned and looked back at the hotel. There were a few people here and there, but no one I recognized, and nobody seemed to be watching us.

Case gave the valet a tip and then walked around to get into the driver's side while the valet opened the passenger's door for me. As soon as I climbed inside, I felt the back of my neck prickle. Again I glanced around and again saw no one I knew. "Case, I think we're being watched."

He looked back at the hotel as he started the motor. "Did you see someone?"

"No, but I felt like someone was watching me. I felt the same way on my way to the coffee shop this morning. It gave me the creeps."

"Keep your eyes peeled," he said. "Someone out there is a murderer."

I pulled Selene's gym pass and the gym pass that Case had given me from my purse and studied the two. They were identical in every respect save for the bar code on the back. "I wonder who this belongs to," I said.

"Do you want to head over to Fitness First?" Case asked. "See what we can find?"

I looked at the Jeep's digital display and saw that it was almost 1:00.

"I've got to get back to the garden center in case my

dad is still trying to get my mother out of jail. And that's a sentence I never thought I'd be saying. Would you be able to run over to the gym with me this evening?"

Case gave me a sidelong glance. "I made plans with Lila to interview men for the captain positions for my new boats."

"How about afterward?"

"Lila suggested we grab a bite to eat afterward."

Of course she would. "Then I'll go to the gym myself," I said, trying not to sound jealous. "I'll let you know what I find out."

When I arrived back at Spencer's, my father was still at the jail, and the garden center was jammed with customers. Along with tourists browsing in the aisles, Delphi was helping people in the outdoor area, Drew had a line at the register, and Mrs. Bird was perched on an outdoor sectional with my son, Nicholas.

"Mama," he shouted and jumped up to greet me. Then he ran back and grabbed Mrs. Bird by the hand. "Can I show her Oscar, Mom?"

"I don't think she's here to see your raccoon, Niko."

"Quite the contrary, dear," the feisty elderly lady said with a wink. "I've never seen a pet raccoon before. We can take care of my business when your son and I are done."

I watched them exit through the back doors then turned to see my father and mother walk into Spencer's, my mom talking a mile a minute.

"Are you okay?" I asked her.

"Better than most of the women there," she said. "Do

you know how long they hold some of those poor women before their initial hearings?"

"Aren't they only allowed to hold them for forty-eight hours?" I asked.

"Some have been there a week, Athena. A week!" She sighed sharply. "It's so unfair, and what can we do about it? Nothing."

My dad gave me *the look*, lifting his chin to signal he needed a break. I let him slip away while I changed the subject. "Mama, do you remember someone coming early to the diner to set up for the rehearsal dinner?"

My mother tapped her chin. "A pretty blond woman came in around ten, and I let her out back to set up."

"Was she back there the whole time?"

"I don't know. The diner was busy. I didn't check on her."

"Did you see her leave?"

Mama shook her head.

Which meant that Tonya could have slipped out through the back alley and made the quick five-minute jaunt over to Brady's apartment. She would've had plenty of time to make it back to the diner to continue setting up for the rehearsal. But I still didn't have a motive for her.

I sent Case a quick text to fill him in on Tonya's alibi, then watched my phone, waiting for his reply. Oddly, he didn't respond.

Mrs. Bird came back into the barn rubbing her hands together. "All right, missy. Let's go work up some plans for my garden."

There went my afternoon.

Before we went into the conference room, Drew came trotting up. "Hey, Athena, I've got a varsity meeting at seven this evening. Will you be able to stay until closing?"

"Sure."

And there went my evening.

"*Because I say so* is not a good answer," Nicholas said to me. He'd already changed into his pajamas and brushed his teeth, all the while laying out his reason for bringing Oscar indoors at the garden center.

"No matter how friendly he seems, sweetie, Oscar is still a wild animal," I said.

"But what if I can prove that he's not wild anymore?"

"What if we got you a hamster instead? I used to have a hamster when I was your age."

Nicholas huffed and turned on a reading light above his bed. He reached under his pillow and pulled out a book. "You can't teach a hamster to do tricks."

I gave him a hug and told him I would think about it. I read him a few chapters, and once he'd fallen sound asleep I left the door open an inch and tiptoed out. On my way to my bedroom, I pulled out my phone and typed to Case: **Where are you? Text me when you get this.**

I hit SEND and waited but after fifteen minutes there was still no response. At first, I'd figured that he was out with the boat captains, or even worse, Lila, but after several hours with no answer, I became convinced it was more than that.

Are you OK? I texted.

No reply again. My thoughts kept returning to the feeling I'd had all day that someone had been following me. But maybe it wasn't me who had been followed. Maybe Case was in trouble.

With the maybes threatening to overwhelm me, I phoned him, but the call went straight to voicemail. At that, I grabbed my purse, tucked my phone in my back pocket, and headed out the door. Something was definitely wrong.

All the way to the *Páme*, I kept swiveling around for a look behind me. Tourists were out in flocks, crowding the sidewalks, weaving in and out of shops, standing outside restaurants and bars in groups, listening to the music that blared from the bands playing inside, so it was hard to tell if I was, indeed, being tailed. Fortunately, I wasn't getting that funny feeling of being watched. Was I just being paranoid?

I checked the phone to see if a message had slipped in while I was in the crowd, but nothing was there. As I walked, I texted Case again: **Coming to the *Páme*.**

I was halfway to the marina, and still no word. I thought of calling him again, but instinct told me not to ring his phone in case it put him in a compromising situation.

With a queasy feeling in my gut that was growing stronger by the minute, I sidestepped laughing, chatting throngs of people and plowed onward in the growing dusk, the ten-minute trip seeming to take twice as long. I hurried along the long boardwalk that fronted the lake, counting the piers until I reached pier 3, then almost trotting along the row of docked vessels, heading toward slip 26.

When I reached the slip, I slowed down to have a look around. No one was behind me, and even though the lights on the pier were dim, I could see that no one appeared to be watching from the shore either. I approached the *Páme* cautiously but didn't see anyone lurking in the shadows. I walked to the end of the pier to have a look from a different angle and again saw nothing suspicious.

I checked my phone again. No message, no returned call. Something was fishy, and it wasn't just the lake. I returned to the boat and stepped across onto the deck. Moving quietly, I glanced around the upper deck. No one was near the steering wheel or hiding under the outside table. No one was lurking near the door to the galley below.

I went around to the opposite side of the boat and crouched down to peer carefully into a window. From my vantage point, I could see the small kitchen table and two chairs, the kitchen counter, a small upholstered chair, and a portion of the sofa that wasn't below the window. And then Case walked across my field of vision and sat down in the chair, holding a glass of what appeared to be white wine in his hand. He certainly didn't look like he was in danger. Was his phone out of charge?

But then he nodded, as though someone were talking to him, and got up to retrieve a bottle of white wine from the kitchen counter. He walked across the room and stopped almost directly in front of the window. I was about to tap on the window, but then he held out the wine bottle as though ready to pour from it.

A woman's hand stretched an empty glass toward the bottle.

Lila!

My stomach twisted. I edged away from the window, feeling jealous and angry and, simply, foolish. I felt as though I'd been hit upside the head. To think I'd been worried. What an idiot I was.

But as I started to walk away, I paused. It wasn't normal for Case to ignore my calls and texts. Something was off. Something else told me to go back to the *Páme*.

I climbed onto the back of the boat and crept down the stairs to the galley door. Taking a deep breath, I tried the handle. The door opened smoothly, and I stepped inside.

There sat Nora Modelle, with her bloated body stuffed into a very revealing black sundress and wearing black sandals, and, more importantly, with her hair straight and long and colored light brown like mine.

"Hello, Thenie," she said in a low, breathy voice.

CHAPTER TWENTY-THREE

I glanced at Case, who looked relieved, and said, "I hope I'm not interrupting."

"Not at all," he said, his tense face relaxing into a smile. "We were just having a conversation about genealogy."

Nora winked at him, as though he was telling an inside joke.

"Wine?" Case asked, moving back toward the tiny kitchen.

Smiling at Nora I said, "Sure."

Her mouth twitched in annoyance. It was obvious she felt I'd interrupted. I wondered what exactly she'd had in mind.

As Case took another glass from the kitchen cabinet, Nora rose and said curtly, "I should be going."

"Are you sure you don't want to stay longer?" I asked. "I have so many questions for you."

She shook her newly colored locks. "Sorry. I have to be up early tomorrow."

"That's a shame," I said. "Maybe we'll stop by the library soon."

"Make an appointment next time." She downed the rest of her wine, picked up her purse, and headed for the door. "Thanks for the hospitality, Case. Really good to see you again, *Thenie*."

The tone in her voice left no doubt as to the sarcasm in her statement.

"I like your new hair color, by the way," I said with a big smile.

She shot me a dark look before opening the door.

Case walked her to the upper deck and then returned, shutting the door and leaning against it. "Thank God you showed up."

"The mystery of why you didn't return my texts is solved, and you're welcome," I said. "Poor Nora must've gotten tired of looking like Mandy. Now she's trying to look like me."

"She said she'd done some research on my family." He handed me a piece of paper that had a genealogical tree of the Donnelly line. As I studied it, he poured my glass of wine and brought it to me.

"What an excuse," I said, feeling almost giddy with relief. "She didn't even know what first names to use."

"It's a very general tree, obviously a bid to get my attention."

"Even though she thinks we're engaged," I said.

"Maybe *because* she thinks we're engaged," Case

replied. "Remember, she stalked Brady, too, when he was engaged to Mandy."

"So it's kind of her MO. She changes her identity and stalks engaged men." I held out my glass and clinked with his. "Let's hope she doesn't kill them as well."

"Don't think that thought didn't run through my mind," Case said as he sat down in the chair.

"Why didn't you text me? I would have come to your rescue sooner."

Case held out his phone. The screen was dark. He shook out a few drops of water from the charging port. "I jumped into the pool this afternoon with my phone in my pocket." He gave me a sheepish smile. "I'll have to get a new one tomorrow morning."

"Put it in a bag of rice," I said. "Delphi does it all the time."

He looked around at the small cupboards above the tiny kitchen area. "I'm not sure if you're aware of it, but there's not a whole lot of room for dry goods."

"What about salt? Anything to dry out your phone until you get a new one."

"Don't worry about the phone. It's history. I will need your number, though. And don't be surprised by an unknown caller. I'm going to get a new phone number to stop all the spam calls I've been getting."

"Do you have a piece of paper? I'll write down my number for you."

Once again, Case looked around at the cupboards.

"Forget it. I'll write the number on your hand. What else did Nora tell you?"

Case took a drink of wine and leaned back in his chair. "She blames Selene, not Mandy, for her breakup with Brady because, in her opinion, Mandy was nothing more than Brady's meal ticket. She said Brady had his eye on Selene before Mandy came along. And Selene, according to her, flirted back."

"How would she know any of this?" I asked.

"Probably because she stalked Brady at the gym."

It made me wonder whether Nora had been stalking me.

"She knew about Selene's complaint to the gym manager," Case continued. "She told me she thought Selene tried to get Brady fired because he started seeing Mandy."

"In other words, my sister was the jealous one. So Nora didn't see just Mandy as her enemy, but also Selene. And Selene would make the perfect patsy because of her history with Brady. All Nora had to do was wait for Selene to go to lunch and then drop by to pick up her credit card. Voila. Scissors gone."

"Maybe Nora subscribes to the theory that if she couldn't have Brady, no one could," Case said.

"And there's my poor sister taking the fall for her. But how do we place Nora at the scene of the crime?"

"She'd had to have been watching Brady to know when he was at home."

"And how do we find that out?"

"Maybe one of Brady's neighbors saw her. We'll have to check into it."

I glanced at my watch, finished my wine, and rose. "I have to get going. I'm going to use your restroom and then stop at the gym on my way home."

"I'll walk you to the gym."

"Aren't you worried about Nora following you?"

"I'll drive you to the gym."

Several minutes later, I came out of the bathroom holding a long, silky Gucci scarf.

"What's this?"

"It appears to be a scarf. Where did you find it?"

"In the bathroom. Nora must have left it. We'll have to drop it off at the library when we go back to see her."

"It might not be hers."

"Who else's could it be?" And then I remembered who I'd seen wearing silk scarves. "Lila Talbot was here?"

"She stopped by after our dinner."

Before I could stop it, the green-eyed monster reared its ugly head, and I found myself blurting, "I'm trying to solve a murder and get my sister out of jail while you entertain millionaire heiresses on my *pappoús*'s boat?"

It came out more bitter than I'd intended. I tried to turn away, but Case stopped me, holding my shoulders, looking deeply into my eyes. "Is that what you really believe?"

I tried to back up, but he moved closer so I couldn't look away. "You think I'm not committed to this investigation?"

I gently removed his hands from my shoulders. "I don't know what you're committed to right now."

"Stop it, Athena. Talk to me. Ever since I decided to stay in Sequoia, I've felt this growing distance between us. What did I do?"

"It's getting late and I'm tired. We don't have time for this now."

He gripped my shoulders again. "Then make it fast. What have I done?"

I drew a deep breath to calm myself. "You're letting Lila call the shots."

A sudden rocking of the boat tipped me off balance. But for Case's firm grip, I would have stumbled.

He gazed down at me intensely. "I decided to stay in

Sequoia because of you, silly woman. I like *you*, Athena, not Lila. And I thought you liked me."

"Then why are you so cozy with Lila? Why was she on the boat with you? Why is her scarf here? Did she leave it so I'd find it?"

"Hold on a minute. You're way off base. There's no reason to worry about Lila Talbot."

"No reason? Do you know her at all?"

With a sigh, Case leaned his back against the kitchen counter, folding his arms across his chest. "I didn't invite Lila here. She invited herself over. She wanted to talk about my business. You know how she is."

"Yes, and I know how you are, too."

"What does that mean?"

"Flirting with suspects, flirting with receptionists, flirting with Lila . . . Is that the only weapon in your arsenal?"

He straightened, looking angry. "You're saying all I am is a flirt? That's how you see me?"

I knew I was being unreasonable, but I couldn't seem to stop myself. "Well, you're certainly not a white knight."

"You want a white knight?"

"Yes, as a matter of fact."

"Great. Then I'll be your white knight."

"You can't, Case, not when Lila has her claws so deep in you that they're almost coming out the other side." I felt my eyes well up. "I know it's just a matter of time before you and she . . ." I broke off and looked away, blinking back tears.

"Athena, listen to me," he said softly. "Lila is not the person you're making her out to be. Trust me on that. Maybe you're right about one thing. Maybe I do rely on my charm too much. But there's only one person I care about. That happens to be you, in case you haven't figured it out."

I wiped a tear off my cheek. "Really?"

"Really. I have absolutely no desire for Lila." He stepped closer to me. "I'll say it again. I like *you*, Athena. I uprooted my entire life to stay here, to be near you. I gave my grandfather's statue to you and your family. I wouldn't do that for anyone else."

I gazed up at him, my heart swelling with joy. He had done all that for me, and there I was doubting him.

"I felt a real connection to you before we started this investigation," he continued. "Where did that connection go?"

"I felt a connection to you, too, and then you disappeared. Then when you finally surfaced, you seemed bowled over by Lila."

"Lila introduced me to her finance manager and we discussed business. That's it."

He held my shoulders again. "Lila knows how I feel about you. And for all I care, she can take her money and walk. I like *you*, damn it. What do I have to do to prove it to you?"

I was stunned by the intensity of his feelings, by the knowledge that he had come back to Sequoia because of me. I gazed into his eyes, wanting desperately to tell him how much his words meant. But I couldn't get the words out.

He inched closer, his hand lifting to caress my face. His touch was gentle, loving.

Another wave hit the boat, and I rocked backward. Case stepped forward to steady me, bracing his feet to keep me from falling against the door. His arms came around me, and I held onto him until the rocking subsided.

He pulled me closer and bent his head to mine. The kiss was magnetic, electric, and the next thing I knew I was locked in a deep embrace. Everything in my head was telling me to break away, but my heart wouldn't let me.

When he pulled back to look at me, I said, "I'm sorry I acted so jealous. I just have a problem with Lila buzzing around you."

"You think I don't get jealous?" he said as he held me. "Watching you go on these dates and then having to read about them in your blog? That drives me crazy."

"Then why do you read the blog?"

"To make sure the dates are a disaster."

I didn't want to laugh, but I did. I didn't want to be in his arms, but I was. I didn't want to be so enamored of someone who could break my heart, but again, there I was, holding him tightly, looking up into his beautiful eyes, and starting to listen to his words instead of the fears looping through my head. For once, I felt my guard drop. I still didn't completely trust Lila, but I decided I should start trusting Case.

"I saved your life," he said and kissed me lightly, playfully. "The least you could do is go on a date with me."

I couldn't help but laugh. "What would my mother say to that?"

We smiled into each other's eyes. The moment was enchanting, and I wanted it to go on forever. But then reality began to seep in and with it, a flood of thoughts. And as though benefiting from a second wind, I felt renewed in our quest to rescue my sister and our ability to work as a team.

"You help me catch this killer," I said, "and I'll take you to the nicest restaurant in town."

"You can take me to the diner for all I care."

I smiled. "That's where I meant."

We were both smiling as we ended our embrace. Case patted his jeans pockets, checking for his keys and wallet. "We're going to solve this murder, Athena."

"We're this close," I said, holding my finger and thumb an inch apart.

He put his arm around me as he opened the door. "Yes, we are this close."

And we were, just like we'd been when he'd first decided to stay in Sequoia.

I reached over and grabbed the scarf lying on the table. "I'll take this."

"It's been a long day," I said as we got into Case's Jeep. "Why don't you drop me off at home? I'll run to the gym tomorrow morning."

"Sounds like a good idea."

I stretched and yawned, causing Case to yawn. "It's been a long week," he said. "What's our game plan for tomorrow?"

"It depends on what happens at the gym. If we can identify the owner of the pass, we can firm up our top suspect and take our findings to the detectives."

"If they'll listen."

"I'll talk to Maguire and see what he says."

"In the meantime," Case said, "I have another meeting tomorrow at nine with the finance manager. Then I want to head over to Brady's apartment building at eleven to interview the neighbors. Do you want to meet me there?"

"You bet. Text me after your meeting, and I'll be there."

Case held up his phone. "Waterlogged, remember? I

won't be able to text until I buy a new phone. So let's just say eleven o'clock."

Case pulled up in front of Spencer's. "Have a good night and I'll see you tomorrow."

I started to open the door, then paused. "What are we going to do if we can't nail down one of our suspects?"

"We break Selene out of jail and head for Canada."

"I'm serious, Case. We have two days."

We both fell silent on that thought. Two days until Selene was formally charged with murder unless we found a way to stop it. What if we failed?

"I'm glad you came to the boat this evening," Case said.

"I am, too."

"I didn't know how I was going to get rid of Nora."

I paused with my hand on the door handle and smiled at him. "At least she didn't stab you."

He gazed at me for a long moment, a smile playing across his lips. I halfway expected him to lean in for another kiss. But then he touched the end of my nose with his fingertip.

"*Kalinýchta,* Goddess Anon."

And then he did lean toward me, his lips meeting mine in a sweet, tender kiss that I carried all the way upstairs to my bedroom.

Later, as I sat at my desk trying to write my blog, I kept coming back to two new facts. Case and I were a true team once more, closer than I'd thought I'd ever be to a man again. And anything I wrote would be read by both Case and my father. So I had to keep it as anonymous as possible while still speaking my truth. And what was my truth? That some women couldn't keep their hands off of other women's men?

But was Case really mine? Even though he looked like that white knight of my dreams and acted like a white knight at times, he'd still said only that he liked me. And truthfully, I couldn't push him into making a full commitment when I wasn't even sure whether I wanted one. So what was I going to write about? Time was flying.

Patience, Athena.

IT'S ALL GREEK TO ME
by Goddess Anon

Patience. I seem to be in short supply these days. "Patience is the greatest of all virtues," Cato the Elder said way back in ancient Rome. "Our patience will achieve more than our force," Edmund Burke said in the seventeen hundreds. And as my Greek grandfather still says, I ypomoní eínai o adelfós tis sofias, *Patience is the brother of wisdom. Maybe that's my problem. I don't seem to be wise when it comes to taking a deep breath and stepping back. I realize that some things can't be rushed, like tourists, love, or time, but sometimes there's a very good reason for wanting to speed things up.*

Maybe that's how speed dating earned its name.

But I digress. Just wait until I tell you about the night I had.

I held out my hand, and he put the chocolate bar into it. "Remember," I said, "no chocolate for animals. It'll make them sick."

"Good morning, everyone," my dad called as he came out from his office. "Morning, Niko."

"Good morning, Grandpa," he said. He gave my dad a hug and took off toward the back doors.

I called out after him, "Not too many peanuts for Oscar, either!"

Drew arrived next, followed by Delphi. Today she was dressed in a pink, white, and orange paisley skirt and orange top with pink flip-flops. Her curly black hair was pulled up on top of her head with a pink scrunchy.

We had a quick morning meeting, after which I announced my plans for the day. "I'm sorry I haven't been here much."

"Take all the time you need," Dad said. "We're handling things just fine now that Drew's here."

"I'm going to give Drew a tour of the shrub area," Delphi said. "And after that, we're going to have a lesson on fertilizer."

As she led Drew away, he glanced back at us with a helpless look on his face.

Dad headed toward the office, motioning for me to join him. I made us two cups of coffee and sat across from him as he took his seat behind the desk. He took a sip and set the cup down. "How's the investigation going?"

"We've got it narrowed down to three suspects, but we haven't been able to single any one of them out."

"What does your gut tell you? Who killed Brady Rogers?"

I breathed in the coffee's soothing aroma as I lifted the

cup to my lips, thinking. "My gut says it was a jealous lover, Brady's ex-fiancée, Nora Modelle who had a restraining order against her for stalking Brady. She had the means, motive, and opportunity. And now I think she's stalking Case, even though she believes we're engaged."

"Excuse me?" my dad said almost choking on his coffee.

"That's our cover story. She thinks we're engaged, yet she showed up at the boat last night to see Case. I just have a strong feeling it's her."

"You like Case, don't you?"

I gave him a puzzled glance. "Yes, I like him. Why?"

My father rubbed his chin, thinking. "Does he like you?"

"He told me he does, but . . ." I let the sentence trail off.

"But what?"

"Old habits die hard. I'm still having some trust issues."

"Don't let your ex-husband play mind games with you, Thenie."

"Do I do that?"

"I know you pretty well, daughter of mine, and I've seen this side of you before. Don't let your insecurities blind you to the truth. I've noticed a drastic change in you since you moved back to Sequoia." He began to enumerate on his fingers. "You've taken back control of your life. You saved Little Greece from destruction. And you took down the most corrupt, powerful man in this town. So don't forget who you are. If this Nora woman is guilty, let the facts prove it, not your emotions."

As a child, when my dad would lecture me, I would argue back, desperate to prove him wrong, but as an adult,

I listened. "I'm going to the gym after I speak with Selene. Hopefully, the facts will back up my instincts, but you're right. I'll reserve judgment until then."

"One other thing," he said. "Your mother wants me to convince you to invite Case over for dinner."

"It's too soon, Pops."

"I'll trust your judgment on that."

After going through the usual check-in procedure, I took a seat in the visitors' side of the room and waited. Within five minutes, my sister was brought in. As soon as her hands were uncuffed and she was seated, she picked up the phone and leaned forward, her eyes shining with the most hope I'd seen since her arrest. "I've got big news."

"Tell me."

"Mandy came to see me. She believes in my innocence, Thenie."

"Is she going to talk to the detectives?"

Selene nodded excitedly. "She said she was going to tell them everything that happened in the week before Brady's murder, including the fight at the Waterfront Hotel. But she doesn't want her brother to find out."

"Why not? Does she suspect him?"

"I don't know." Selene took a deep breath. "She told me that Mitchell found out that you and Case snuck into the Waterfront, and that Mitchell had a long conversation with her. She said he lost it. He screamed at her about being a traitor and told her she'd better never talk to either one of you again."

"Does he think she implicated him in Brady's murder?"

"I don't know, but I'm worried about her."

"Okay, I'm going to the gym right now. If the pass be-longs to Mitchell, I'll take it straight to the detectives and tell them what he said to Mandy. They've got to take a closer look at him."

Maybe I was wrong about Nora.

Dark clouds were rolling in from Lake Michigan as I made the short walk to Fitness First. The summer storms in Sequoia were usually brief but could be sudden, and sometimes severe. The sidewalks and outdoor cafés had already begun to empty out, leaving a clear path for my quest.

I passed the large windows that fronted the Fitness First building and was once again greeted by the acrid smell of body odor as I entered the gym. The front desk was empty, as it had been the first time. I pulled out the gym pass from my purse and continued to wait by the desk, tapping my fingers anxiously on the counter. Didn't the gym have a manager? How was I going to find out who owned the pass?

I watched as a man dressed in black workout attire passed me and swiped his card to enter the gym area, and then I had an idea. With one swift swipe of the pass, I was inside the gym, scouting for the locker rooms. If the pass belonged to a woman, I should be able to use it to open her locker and find out who she was. I just had to find the right locker.

The women's locker room reminded me of the one in my high school. Long and narrow, it had lockers on both sides and a few benches running the length in between.

Just as I hoped, each locker had a thin card swiper in place of the usual combination lock.

The gym had been only half full, I'd noticed, and the locker room seemed to be empty, but I waited a while just to be sure I was alone. I heard the shower running and knew I didn't have much time, so I began to swipe, first the top locker, then the bottom. Row after row, I swiped the mystery pass, praying that any moment I would hear a beep or a click. Then I heard the shower stop and the soft slap of sandals heading my way.

Just as a woman turned the corner I heard a beep and, to my delight, a locker door on top popped open. I glanced inside and my heart sank. Empty. Just to be sure, I reached my hand along the bottom and my fingers caught on something. I plucked the item from its stuck position in the corner and couldn't believe my eyes. The image was dark and hard to identify, but I knew immediately what it was. An ultrasound of a fetus. And the date stamp across the top was two weeks before Brady was killed.

I stashed the small square photograph in my purse and quickly made my way out of the locker room and, finally, out of the gym. My mind was spinning. Was the ultrasound Nora's? Was that why she looked so bloated? If Nora was pregnant with Brady's child and he decided to marry Mandy anyway, it would've been a very strong motive for her to kill him.

Out in the air, heavy with the smell of rain, I called Bob Maguire and asked for his advice.

"I'm on duty right now," he said. "Why don't I stop by Spencer's later, and we can discuss what to do next?"

"Thanks, Bob," I said. "I'll be there."

I hadn't gone a block when I felt eyes on the back of my head. I turned sharply, expecting to see Nora behind me, but although I searched the faces in the crowd, I saw no one I recognized. I felt drops on the back of my head and glanced up to see heavy black clouds above me. And suddenly there was a torrent of rain.

I glanced both ways, then darted across the street to the ice cream shop. I bought a pistachio single-dip waffle cone and stood by the front window, licking the drips running down the side as I searched for that elusive face in the crowd now scattering outside. I stood there for another five minutes, polishing off my ice cream, and then gave up and proceeded on to Spencer's during a break in the rain.

And still I felt like someone was watching me.

Luckily, Spencer's was bustling with activity. Drew was ringing up customers, Dad was giving a brief history of the *Treasure of Athena* statue to several tourists taking photos, and Delphi was helping a soggy group of shoppers select garden supplies. I found Nicholas in the stockroom, listening to music and organizing boxes. I was pleasantly surprised. Everything was indeed running smoothly in my absence.

On my way to the office, Drew got my attention, and I joined him behind the register. He talked in a hushed tone as he scanned in a large pallet of flowers. "Have you ever had a problem with shoplifters?"

"Not really. Why?"

"I noticed someone standing over in the corner earlier." He pointed near the front of the store, where we kept some of our smaller gardening items: gloves, weed pullers, garden shears, knee pads. "She was acting very strange and kept staring at me. I thought maybe she was trying to steal something."

"Will you do me a favor and check the inventory when you have a chance?"

"I'm on it," he said

"By the way, did the woman have hair like mine?"

"I couldn't really tell. She was wearing a big yellow raincoat with the hood pulled up."

"If you see her again, let me know immediately."

Just before I opened the office door, I heard what sounded like someone rifling through drawers. I swung open the door, ready for a confrontation. A tiny shriek escaped my lips as a black-and-gray blur brushed past my legs and scurried for the back door, toenails clicking against the wood floor.

I held my hand over my pounding heart and stepped inside the office. There I saw everything that had been on the desk, including all the paperwork I'd been working on, scattered over the floor. The only thing still standing was the desk phone. I looked around at the mess in dismay. Nicholas was about to be in big trouble.

I turned to go find him and was shocked to see a woman standing in the doorway. Nora Modelle.

I had my stalker.

CHAPTER TWENTY-FIVE

"Hello again, *Thenie*."

Nora closed the door and leaned against it. She was dressed in a pair of white capris, a loose, pale green blouse, and white sandals. Her wet, straw-like locks were matted against her forehead and her black mascara had run, leaving streaks beneath her eyes.

I was about to ask how she'd known where to find me, but I already knew. She was the one who'd been following me, long enough that she even knew how to get back to the office. How many times had she slipped into the store unnoticed? My dad or Delphi might have even waited on her.

I casually walked around the desk, putting a barrier between us. "What do you want, Nora?"

She had a strange secretive smile on her face. "I came here to help you."

That wasn't what I was getting from her expression. Trying not to betray my anxiety I glanced down for something, anything, on the desk I could use to defend myself, but Oscar had taken care of that.

Nora took the purse from her shoulder and set it on a chair. "Don't be alarmed. I'm not going to hurt you." She leaned on the desk. "I came here to help you."

Her demeanor was confident, with no undercurrent of anger or jealousy in her tone. If Nora wanted to hurt me, she sure wasn't showing it. But I still didn't trust her.

"The game's over, *Thenie*," Nora said with a wink. "I know who you are. I know you're working with Case to find Brady's killer, and I know that you suspect me. I'm here to clear all that up."

Behaving as though I felt as calm as Nora appeared to be, I took a seat and indicated the chair beside her. "Please, have a seat."

She sat down and immediately took a jab. "You're not as clever as you think you are, you know."

I stared at her, unsure of what to say.

"I was on to you from the start, Athena Karras Spencer. I read the newspaper. I've seen your photograph. I know you solved the Talbot murder case. And now you're trying to pin Brady Rogers's death on me."

"Have you been following me?"

"Two can play at being a detective. I solve mysteries all the time in the genealogy department. That's what I was trying to tell your boyfriend last night."

"He's not my boyfriend."

"You might want to tell him that. But whatever. I'm going to show you that I couldn't have killed Brady."

Nora opened her purse and pulled out a piece of paper. She slid it across the desk toward me. "Take a look."

I picked up the paper and saw a doctor's handwritten prescription for prednisone.

"You can see that the date written on it is the date Brady was murdered."

"All this proves is that you were at the doctor's office sometime that day."

"Look at the doctor's address. He's not in Sequoia, he's in Saugatuck. I've been going to him for my eczema for the past year because no one in town was able to help me. And look at this." She took out a bottle of pills and shook it, then slid it across the desk. "Check out the date it was refilled and the address of the pharmacy. It's also in Saugatuck.

"Now call the doctor's office and verify that my appointment was at eleven that morning. It takes almost half an hour to get to Saugatuck, so I left here at ten-twenty, then had to wait twenty minutes to see my doctor. After my appointment, I went to the pharmacy in his building and then decided to have lunch before I drove home."

"You told us you were at work on Friday," I said. "Why did you lie?"

Nora leaned forward and asked cynically, "Why would I tell a couple of strangers about my doctor's appointment? Think, Athena." She sat back with a smile. "Now if that doesn't prove my innocence, then please do follow through with what I told you. I'll even use my phone to call the doctor's office."

My mind was racing as she talked, and now that she sat and waited, all I could think of was that she still hadn't proved she was out of town all day.

"Why do you have the written prescription if you got your medicine filled?"

"He gave me two scripts, one for prednisone that I didn't get filled. What else?"

"Did you follow me here from the gym?" I asked.

"I'm not a stalker."

"You didn't answer my question."

"I followed you so I could explain myself."

"Did you follow me to the gym, too?"

She shrugged one shoulder indifferently.

"Do you know why I went to the gym, Nora?"

She shifted in her chair, showing a bit of agitation for the first time. "I don't have a very good reputation at Fitness First, if that's what you were checking. I'm sure they told you that I stalked him there, but I just wanted to talk to him." She wiped away an imaginary tear. "Brady hurt me badly. He used me and left me. You don't understand what it's been like."

She was back to her "poor me" attitude. "Mandy found a gym pass to Fitness First in Brady's apartment. Do you know anything about that?"

She looked stunned. "No. Of course not."

"Really? I used the pass to open a locker. Do you have any idea what I found in that locker?"

She shook her head and for the first time looked unsure of herself.

I pulled the ultrasound picture from my purse and slid it across the table. "Does this look familiar?"

Nora picked up the picture, and her jaw dropped. "Where did you find this?"

"I told you where."

Her eyes welled up and in a hurt voice she said, "It's an ultrasound." She raised her head. "Whose is this?"

"That's what I'd like to know. Look at the date stamp

on the picture. It was taken two weeks before Brady's death. Whoever owns that locker, Nora, has a secret."

She jumped to her feet, slamming her fist on the desk. "Why are you doing this to me? You have no right to punish me this way."

How was I punishing her? Her quicksilver temper raised a red flag. "I'm not trying to punish you," I said calmly. "I'm just trying to find out who killed Brady."

She shoved the photo back across the desk and snarled, "You talked to Mandy and her friends, didn't you?" She started around the desk toward me, clenching and unclenching her fists, her face red with anger. "What did those nasty women tell you about me, *Thenie?*"

I took a step back. "Forget about Mandy and her friends. I know the truth, Nora, and I can help you."

"The truth?" she cried. "What do you know about the truth?"

I took another step back, one eye on the door. "You're pregnant with Brady's child."

"How dare you!" she cried, and then she covered her face and began to sob.

My first instinct was to run, but then the office door opened and Maguire stepped inside. Nora looked back, saw him in full police garb, and turned back to me, swiping at the tears running down her cheeks. "You called the police?"

"Put your hands behind your back," Maguire ordered.

Nora gave me a pleading look. "Please, Athena, tell him we were just having a friendly conversation."

"Friendly?" I asked.

Her shoulders sagging in defeat, she turned to face the wall and put her hands behind her back.

"Next time, Nora," I said, as Maguire cuffed her, "make an appointment."

"Let's go," Maguire said.

"I didn't kill Brady!" she cried. "You can't charge me for having a simple conversation."

"I can charge you for trespassing," he said as they left the office.

My knees suddenly felt weak. I sank into my desk chair just as my dad and Delphi walked into the room.

"How was that for coming to your rescue?" Delphi asked

"Good timing," I said, trying to smile.

"Are you okay?" my dad asked. "You look a little pale."

"I could be better. How did you know I was in trouble?"

Delphi sat on the chair across from me. "When I saw the office door closed and heard voices inside, I had a strong feeling of danger, so I called Bob, and he came right over."

"Thanks, Delph. You did good."

She smiled. "Of course, I did."

My phone vibrated. I slid it from my purse and saw an unknown number on it. Assuming it was Case I said, "I have to take this."

"We'll leave you alone," my dad said, and then he and Delphi left, pulling the door closed behind them.

I answered the call with a happy, "Hey, you finally got a phone! And wait till you hear what just happened."

For a moment, there was no response. Then I heard, "Athena?"

It was Tonya. I recognized her soft voice immediately. "Sorry," I said. "I thought you were someone else."

"I found something," she said. "I think you and Case need to see this."

"Okay. Where are you?"

"At Brady's apartment. Mandy asked us bridesmaids to help her clean out his belongings, and we found something that might clear Selene."

"I'll come right over." I hung up with Tonya and put my phone into my purse.

I found my father looking through a landscape guide in the conference room and said, "Hey, Pops. I think I might finally have evidence to clear Selene. Is it okay if I leave for a bit?"

"Absolutely. Don't worry about anything here. Just concentrate on getting Selene out of that jail."

"Thanks, Pops." I glanced at the clock on the wall. It was almost eleven o' clock, time to meet Case at Brady's apartment anyway. "I'll be back in a little while," I told Delphi as I passed her on my way to the door.

"Take an umbrella," she said.

"The storm has already passed, Delph."

"The first one has," she said. "But there's a bigger storm on the way."

Just before I reached the front door, my cousin Drew stopped me. "Remember when you asked me to check on those garden supplies? I found only one thing missing. A pair of garden shears."

I arrived at Brady's apartment building at eleven on the dot. There was no sign of Case's Jeep in the parking lot, so I waited for him in the lobby. But after fifteen minutes, my impatience got the better of me, and I decided to wait outside Brady's apartment. I saw a directory and ran my finger down the list of residents until I spotted Brady's name. Apartment 301, third floor.

My phone rang, once again with an unknown number. This time I said cautiously, "Case?"

"It's me."

"Where are you?"

"Just docking the boat. We were out on the lake when the storm came up."

"Are you okay?"

"It was dicey for awhile, but we're fine. Anyway, I didn't have any cell service to let you know I'd be late."

I could hear island music and laughing in the background. Was that Lila's voice, too? "But I have big news about my business venture," he said.

"Case, we were supposed to meet at Brady's apartment at eleven."

"I know, and I'm sorry. Where are you now?"

I walked to the elevator and pressed the UP button, exceedingly annoyed. "Exactly where I said I would be. And I also have big news—if you're not too busy."

"Tell me your news."

"I went to the gym and used the pass to check the lockers. I finally found the locker it belonged to and inside I found an ultrasound of a baby."

"You're kidding. So one of our suspects is expecting? Was there a name on the ultrasound?"

"Nope. Nothing. But then Nora showed up at the office supposedly to clear up her name, so I showed her the ultrasound and told her I knew she was pregnant. She freaked out, Case. She broke down in sobs. I'm assuming the baby is hers and she killed Brady out of jealousy. She's in custody now."

"You've already had her arrested for murder?"

"Not for murder, for trespassing. While I was talking to Nora, Delphi phoned Maguire to tell him I was in danger. He arrested her."

"Good for Delphi, and that *is* big news." He paused. "But if Nora's the killer, why are you at Brady's apartment?"

"I got a call from Tonya. She said that Mandy and the bridesmaids are there cleaning out his apartment and that they've found something that can clear Selene." I exited the elevator and followed the numbers until I found Brady's apartment.

"Did they tell you what it was?"

"I didn't ask. I'm standing outside Brady's apartment right now."

I heard a loud thump come from inside. I pressed my ear to the door but didn't hear anything.

"Wait a minute, Athena. Something's not right about this. Why are they having you come there instead of taking whatever it is to the police?"

"Maybe they plan on taking it to the police after they show me, or maybe they want me to take it. I don't know. It's Mandy and three others, Case. Why are you worried?"

"I don't like it. Wait right there. I'm on my way."

"You're being a little over-cautious," I said, but the phone call had ended. I slid the phone into my back pocket, and continued to listen at the door. Odd that I didn't hear the muffled sound of women's voices, but maybe they were in the bedroom.

I glanced at my watch. How long would it take Case to get there? I leaned against the wall, waiting, drumming my fingers against the old wallpaper, but finally my curiosity got the better of me. I double-checked the number on the door, then reached for the handle. The door opened silently into the living room, where light streaming in from a large window illuminated stacks of packing boxes. I stepped halfway inside and called out "Hello?"

No answer.

I closed the door and looked around. The apartment had been stripped of decorations and dressings. The hutch that had once housed the missing picture frame had been emptied, its doors standing open. It certainly looked as though they had been cleaning up and packing, just like Tonya had said.

I heard another thump, quieter this time, and proceeded through the living room into the drapery-darkened dining area straight ahead. In the dim light, I saw something that brought me to a halt—a large, multi-tiered wedding cake placed in the center of the table. At the top of the cake was a small figure of a bride with the groom missing.

Next to the table were opened gift boxes of varying sizes and silver wrapping paper torn and scattered around the floor. There was even an opened bottle of champagne beside the cake, with several glasses sitting full. One glass had been knocked over, the liquid pooling along the edge of the table. I glanced around at the mess, a frozen tableau of a celebration gone wrong. It looked like a spaceship had landed and swept up everyone.

I heard a voice that seemed to come from the hallway off to my right. I waited a minute, listening, then turned the corner and walked down a hallway into a darkened bedroom, the drapes on the two windows drawn. Everything was eerily quiet. Where were the women?

Case had been right. There was something off about this.

I pulled out my phone to call him and see where he was and remembered I didn't have his new number. Before I could pull up RECENT CALLS to find it, I noticed something on the nightstand directly in front of me—the gray marble picture frame. It was exactly as I'd imagined but was way too large for the small nightstand. And instead of the black-and-white photo of Mandy, Mitchell, and Brady, a new photo sat in its place.

I put my purse down and picked up the frame, feeling the heft of it. I couldn't make out who the two people in the photo were until I flipped the frame over. At the bottom was an engraving etched in the stone: *For Brady, with all my love forever and ever, Tonya.*

Tonya? I inhaled sharply as I absorbed the meaning of those words. Turning the frame over again, I recognized a younger Brady sitting on a worn, print sofa, and a brown-haired, girlish Tonya on his lap. They were both petting a large dog and laughing. Tonya's hair was short, and she was heavier, but she looked happy. In fact, they both did.

I heard a soft thump again and traced it to the other side of the bed, only to find Mandy lying on the floor with her eyes closed as though she'd rolled off while taking a nap.

"Mandy?" I set the frame on the floor, gripped her shoulders, and raised her up, trying to get her to sit up on her own. "Mandy, what happened?"

Her head rolled to the side, and her eyelids fluttered open and then closed again. "Mandy, talk to me," I said, laying her back down. "What happened to you?"

She opened her eyes and tried to talk, but her words came out slowly, as though she were on tranquilizers again. "A-thena." Her pupils were large, dark circles, and she slurred my name. She wasn't looking directly at me, but over my shoulder. It was clear she couldn't focus.

"A-thena," she said again. With more urgency this time, she said, "A-thena, be careful!"

Chapter Twenty-Six

The nerves along my spine tingled a warning. I turned quickly to see Tonya in the doorway behind me. She was dressed in a white lace-and-satin wedding gown, her face veiled. Her appearance was ghostly, the full-skirted gown flowing behind her as she came toward me in an angry rush.

A feeling of pure fear washed over me. I lunged onto the bed and scrambled over it to get to my purse. I pulled my phone out and hit the MICROPHONE button as I dashed for the door. "Call nine-one-one," I shouted, but Tonya was faster, catching my arm in her strong grip, squeezing with incredible strength, causing the phone to slip from my hand as I winced in pain and tried to pull away.

I could hear Mandy start to cry as I wrestled to break free, but Tonya had me backed onto the bed in seconds, kneeling over me with the white dress spilling over my torso. I fought as hard as I could, but my strength was no match for hers. While one hand pressed my wrists into my belly, her other reached for my neck.

"Stop," I cried breathlessly, attempting to pull my hands free. "Think what you're doing!"

"I know exactly what I'm doing," she ground out. With one hand gripping my neck, she yanked open the night-stand drawer and retrieved a small silver revolver.

My heart was racing as she pressed the tip of the barrel against my throat. I was so frightened I could barely breathe. "Please, Tonya, don't do this."

"Shut up." She removed her hand from my throat and backed off the bed. The gun wasn't pointed directly toward me now, but she knew that the threat was enough to keep me still.

My cell phone began to ring. She picked it up from the floor, backing away until she was on the other side of the doorjamb, then leveled the gun at me while she read the text message. Then, with my phone still in her hand, she put one finger over her veiled lips as she backed out of the door.

Had the message been from Case? Was he nearby or still miles away?

I rolled off the bed and dragged Mandy up to a seated position, desperate for answers. "What happened? Where are the others?"

Mandy shook her head, alternately sobbing and panting like a frightened animal. "I don't know. Tonya said they'd be here."

I stroked her hair and whispered that everything was going to be fine, that Case was on his way. But now there was no way to warn him that I was in trouble.

I heard a thud from outside and knew Tonya was still

in the apartment. Was she setting a trap for Case? The room grew even darker as a loud rumble of thunder shook the walls. Delphi had been correct. A bigger storm was approaching.

"Tonya killed Brady," Mandy whispered, trembling. "I tried to fight her off but she made me drink a glass of champagne while she told me everything. I don't remember anything after that."

"You'll be okay. Don't worry." I cursed myself for not following Case's instructions. Tonya had fooled me completely. How could I have gotten it so wrong?

I looked around the room for something to block the door. A yellow rain jacket, like the one Drew had seen someone wearing at the garden center, was lying in a wet pile near the closet. I hurried over to the dresser and tried to push it across the wood floor, but it wouldn't budge. I tried the window next but couldn't get it to open. I came back to Mandy, who was attempting to stand up.

"I'm dizzy. Help me," she said.

I eased her onto the bed just as Tonya opened the bedroom door and entered. She had a roll of duct tape in one hand.

I swallowed hard.

"Where's your *boyfriend*?" she snarled. Her voice was like steel now. "I tried the phone number from your contact list, but he didn't answer."

Thank God, she knew nothing about Case's dead phone. "Tonya, please talk to me. Tell me why you're doing this. What are you trying to prove?"

"She thinks this is her wedding day," Mandy spit out. "She's a murderer and a cheat."

"Mandy, please," I said quietly.

"Yes, *Miss Black*," Tonya sneered, "shut up."

A loud clap of thunder sounded nearby and heavy rainfall pounded against the windows as Tonya tossed the tape to me and gestured with the gun. "Tape her mouth shut."

The absent look in Tonya's veiled eyes terrified me. She was not the helpful, loyal friend anymore. She was a cold, calculating killer, and it showed in every move she made. I knew I didn't have the physical strength to stop her. Instead, I would have to slow her down, keep her talking, and pray that Case would be there soon.

Mandy made small whimpering sounds as I gently placed the tape across her lips, and tears fell in steady streams down her cheeks. "It's going to be okay," I whispered.

"Now toss the tape back."

My phone rang in Tonya's hand. She set the tape aside and looked at the number. "Who is this?" she asked, holding up the phone so I could read the screen. "There's no name on it."

I flipped through several answers in my head before saying, "My son just got a new phone and I haven't recorded his number yet. I was talking to him earlier. You can check RECENT CALLS if you don't believe me."

She ignored the incoming call and swiped through my call log. After finding Case's name on the list, she thrust the phone at me. "Call him. Tell him to meet you here."

As I took it she said, "One wrong word and I'll kill Mandy."

I was a shaking mess, but I tried my hardest not to show it. I nodded and waited for Case's voicemail, knowing that his old number was useless. "Case, it's Athena. Meet me at Brady's apartment. I-"

Before I could get another word out, Tonya snatched

the phone from me and headed out of the room. "Tonya," I said, "please talk to me. Help me understand."

She continued down the hallway and disappeared into the dining room. In a few moments, she came back, a glass of champagne in one hand, the revolver in the other. "Want the truth, Athena? Here it is. I didn't want any of this to happen."

"Then stop. Think what you're doing. It can't end well."

"Back away." She waited until I'd moved to the foot of the bed then she set the glass on the nightstand. "Now put your hands behind your back."

I had no choice but to obey. My hands were taped behind me, and I was forced to sit on the bed next to Mandy's prone body. Tonya gazed at us, a smile playing about her mouth, then began to twirl slowly in her dress, stopping in front of the dresser mirror. She raised her arms, showing off the delicate lace that covered her shoulders and arms. "How do I look in Mandy's gown?"

At that, Mandy screamed in rage, but through the tape, it came out muffled. Paying no attention to Mandy, Tonya twirled again, her long blond hair no longer in its usual ponytail, but long and silky down her back. "It should've been mine, you know." She picked up the picture frame and gazed at it lovingly. "He should've been mine, too."

I thought back to what my dad had said about letting my emotions take control and instead tried to play off of Tonya's emotions. "You both look so happy in that picture. When was it taken?"

"Years ago," she answered without looking up, "before we moved to Sequoia. This was when we were the happiest, when we had nothing." She held up the photo so I could see. "Brady, me, and a big dog in a single-wide trailer. Can you imagine? But look at us in this picture. Not a care in the world. We never should have left."

"You were happy there," I said. "Why did you leave?"

"Stop it, Athena. Don't pretend like you actually care." She set the frame down on the bed. "I killed Brady, and now, sadly, I have to kill both of you, so why don't you ask the real question?"

I breathed in deeply, contemplating how hard I really wanted to push her.

"See? That's your problem. You never just come out and say what you want to say. But there's nothing you can tell me now that can make things worse. So go ahead. Ask me."

"Why did you frame my sister?"

"Because I could."

That was all I'd planned to ask, but as my anger grew, so did my list of questions. "Why didn't you just leave town after you killed Brady? And why did you go out of your way to help us? And now what? You're going to kill us, too? And Case? And leave three dead bodies here? Do you really think you're going to get away with this? Come on, Tonya. You know it can't end well. Do yourself a favor and give up."

Tonya's laughter stopped me. "There you go. Finally. Good for you, Athena."

I stared at her, not knowing what to say.

"You know, I admire your tenacity," she went on, "even though your detective skills are somewhat lacking." She moved around the bed toward me. "I wasn't going to stick around after I killed Brady. Everything was going according to plan, but then you came along"—she pointed the gun at me—"and you had me worried."

As she continued to talk, I heard a noise like a rap on

the door and gave a start, but then I realized it was just the crack of thunder. I chewed my lower lip. Case didn't know I was in danger. Was there any way I could warn him?

"And when I found out that *you*, the *famous* Goddess of Greene Street, were investigating, I thought maybe I had met my match." She shrugged. "Looks like I was wrong."

"Is that why you cozied up to me? So you could keep an eye on me?"

"Partly," she answered. "Let me ask you something. I know you suspected me at first, but you didn't suspect a thing when I called you over here. At what point did you change your mind about my being a suspect? Was it at the Waterfront yesterday? Was that when things changed?"

"Yes," I answered honestly. "You had me completely fooled. I even started to like you."

She smiled. "Thank you."

"So what's the plan now?"

She glanced at her watch. "Don't worry. I'll explain everything in due time. We have to wait until your partner gets here."

Mandy began to struggle and scream again. Tonya picked up the glass of champagne from the nightstand and walked around to her side of the bed. "It's time for bed, Mandy." She yanked the tape from her mouth and held her head back by the hair as she poured the liquid down her throat. Mandy coughed and tried to spit it back at her, but Tonya only tugged her hair harder until she was almost crying. I noticed she had placed the gun near the picture frame on the nightstand, not far from where I sat.

"Have you been drugging her this whole time?" I asked.

"Not until today. After Brady's death, the doctor gave her something to ease her anxiety. Fortunately, Mandy carries her pills with her, don't you, Mand? See, I know everything about Mandy's life." She put the tape back over Mandy's mouth. "Everything."

Mandy struggled as hard as she could, but Tonya held her shoulders until she quieted down, and then finally Mandy lay still, her chest shaking with silent sobs. Tonya sat quietly beside her, listening to the rain pouring down, the lightning and thunder now coming in steady waves. "There you go," she said to Mandy. "Off to dreamland."

I had to keep her talking so I wasn't next. "When did you decide to kill Mandy?"

"It doesn't matter." Tonya stroked Mandy's hair as the drugs began to take effect. "She never loved Brady. She just wanted to own him, like the spoiled child she is. I was the only one who truly loved Brady. Who truly understood him."

"Why don't you leave now, while you have the chance?"

"Because of you, Athena. Everything happening right now is because of *you*. Does it make you happy knowing that this is all your fault? If you would have just let it go, no one else would've gotten hurt."

At that my Greek temper flared. "No one would've gotten hurt? You framed my *sister*. That's not my fault and there was no way I was going to let that go."

"No, of course not. You'll be loyal until the end." She rose and wandered to the window, moving the curtain aside to look out. "You know, Brady and I came to this town with a plan. It was a brilliant plan, and it was working flawlessly until Brady deviated from it."

"So you killed him," I said in disgust.

"He didn't have to die. I gave him an ultimatum." She shrugged. "He made his choice."

She was truly a cold-blooded killer. "And now you have a new plan."

"We'll get there," she said. "Let me start at the beginning." As she began to talk, she sat on the edge of the bed and pulled the veil away from her face. My shoulders were hurting from my arms being tied behind me, so as she talked, I very subtly moved my hands in circles, trying to loosen the thick tape.

"It started small," she said. "Brady would train women at the gym, and they would flirt with him and buy him things. At first, I got angry. We'd argue, and I'd kick him out, but he would always come back. Then it dawned on me. We could make a fortune off of these women. But not in our little town. We chose Sequoia instead—a nice, wealthy tourist town with plenty of rich, lonely women."

"That's when he met Nora."

"Not at first. But yes, ultimately he met Nora, and plenty of other women besides. But that wasn't the big score." She tapped Mandy's leg. "Mandy Black was our honey pot. And Mitchell only sweetened the deal. He offered Brady five thousand dollars to stop dating his sister. That's when we decided that Brady should marry her."

Tonya's eyes begin to well up, but she blinked them away and continued. "He wasn't supposed to *actually* marry her. In fact, Mitchell later offered him ten thousand dollars to call off the wedding, but that wasn't enough for Brady. He got greedy. He wanted more. Then Mandy found my gym pass in Brady's apartment." She turned to gaze at Mandy. "My only mistake."

She gave Mandy's ankle a push. "She came to me in hysterics, determined to find the owner of that gym pass. Luckily, Selene had just filed her complaint. Her name was fresh on everyone's mind because Brady wouldn't shut up about it. He finally agreed to tell Mandy it was Selene's pass, and I thought she would leave it at that."

I jerked as several loud cracks echoed around us. Tonya stood up, still talking. "Mandy left everything up to me. All of the wedding planning, the flowers, the cake, this dress . . ." She smoothed out the fabric as she walked toward a full-length mirror in the corner of the room. "I basically planned my own wedding. This dress fits me way better than it does her. She didn't even care. I picked out my own favorite flowers, my style of cake . . . She let me take control of everything except the one damn thing she wouldn't let go of."

"Brady," I said.

"I meant the stupid gym pass. Mandy wanted to confront Selene about it, but I couldn't let that happen. Not until we got the money from Mitchell. If Brady would've just taken the ten thousand, we could've fled this place, and no one would've gotten hurt. But then something happened that changed everything."

She swiped a tear on her cheek as she continued to look at herself in the mirror. She arched her back slightly and let her fingers caress her belly. And that was when I knew. Tonya was the one who was pregnant. It was her locker that I'd found. It was her ultrasound that had been stuck inside.

Now I understood what motivated Tonya, what drove

her emotions. Her baby. But I couldn't play my hand just yet.

As she admired her belly in the mirror, I said, "What happened?"

"I told you. Brady deviated from the plan."

"Was that the night of the bridal shower? When Mitchell confronted Brady?"

She swung to look at me. "*That* was when I knew that Brady had made his choice—Mandy over me. How could I let him get away with it?" She went back to stroking her belly. "So while Mandy and the bridesmaids were toasting their perfect future, I was planning my own."

"You made sure Jill got sick, didn't you?" I said.

"Now you're starting to see conspiracies," she said with a laugh. "Well, you're wrong. Sometimes things just fall into place. It wasn't in my original plan, but I used the opportunity to my advantage. I convinced Mandy to substitute Selene as a bridesmaid, purportedly to test her relationship with Brady. And then I made sure Selene would look guilty."

She smiled at her reflection. "It was pretty damn ingenious, actually. I used a tissue to grab her scissors off her tray so I wouldn't leave fingerprints. I took one of my old T-shirts and used it to wipe off the scissors before I dropped it in the dumpster behind the salon. I dumped Brady's cell phone in the trash bin behind Selene's apartment building. And then I made sure I'd have an alibi for the time of the murder. I planned everything down to the last detail"—she turned to me—"except for you."

"You had me fooled, Tonya. You even had the police fooled. But you could've left last night and been across the country by now."

"You were getting too close," she said. "When I found out that Mandy still had that gym pass, I knew it was just a matter of time before you tracked me down." Tonya opened the closet and pulled out a pair of garden shears. "Selene killed Brady with her scissors. It seems fitting that you would kill Mandy in the same fashion. Wouldn't you agree?"

I closed my eyes against the horrible images in my mind. "Tonya, leave town. Leave right now. Who's going to stop you? Do you really want to be responsible for more deaths?"

"I *am* leaving town, but not just yet. I need to tie up some loose ends first."

"You're going to kill Case, too."

"No," Tonya said slowly. "You are." She set the garden shears next to Mandy and picked up the gun. "Right before you shoot yourself."

CHAPTER TWENTY-SEVEN

Tonya looked at me with sad eyes. "I'm really sorry it has to be this way."

I glared at her, wanting to break free from my bonds and claw her conniving eyes out. But I reined in my emotions. That wasn't how to reach Tonya. She was going to be a mother. I had to play off her maternal instincts. "Let me call my son," I said. "Let me hear his voice one last time."

"Sorry, Athena. I can't do that."

"Then send him a text from me. He'll get one last text from his mother telling him I love him. That's all I ask."

She shook her head in disgust, and for a moment I thought I'd failed to convince her. Then she said, "Okay. You're a good sister. I'm sure you're a good mother, too. I'll get your phone." She paused at the door. "You know, it's a shame that this is how it had to turn out." She gave me one last, sad glance before leaving the bedroom. She came back with my phone and showed me the unknown number. "Is this his number?"

"That's it," I said. "Please text, 'I love you, Niko.'"

Surely, Case would understand the message.

She typed in my words and hit SEND as another jolt of lightning lit up the bedroom. Thunder quickly followed, along with a short, faint ding from outside the room.

"What was that?" Tonya asked, turning her head toward the hallway.

"I didn't hear anything." Was that a text signal? Could Case be in the apartment?

Tonya turned to give me a cold look, then left the room, closing the door quietly behind her.

I turned to Mandy and whispered her name, but she was out cold. I pulled my arms taut against my back and, with extreme pressure, tried to separate my hands, feeling the thick tape pull around my wrists. The blood rushed to my head as I gritted my teeth and rolled my wrists until I felt the tape bunch in the center, freeing up enough space to squeeze one hand through.

My arms tingled, and my hands were red from lack of circulation, but I was free. I reached for the heavy picture frame at the edge of the bed and tucked it behind me, resting uncomfortably on it as Tonya opened the door and entered the room.

She tossed a phone onto the bed near me. "Whose phone is this?"

I didn't know what to say. I gazed from the phone to Tonya, then noticed a dark shadow in the hallway behind her. "Maybe it's Mandy's."

Case. He must have hidden when he heard the phone ding.

Tonya picked up the gun and pointed it at me. "Why would her phone be in the living room?"

"I don't know. Listen to me, Tonya, you can't shoot us here. You know that. Someone will hear you. So leave the gun and get out while you can."

She stepped closer, and so did Case's shadow. Holding the gun steady in her hands, she said, "I can't do that."

"You have to. I know your secret. I found something in the back of your locker."

She thrust the barrel at me. "Stop playing games."

"I used your gym pass, Tonya. I found the ultrasound photo. I know you're pregnant."

Her eyes widened.

"If the police find you here," I said, "they'll put you away for life. Do you know what happens to a baby whose mother is in jail?"

Tonya's eyes went blank as she put one hand on her flat belly. With a quiver in her voice she said, "Brady told me that if I didn't get rid of the baby he would leave me for Mandy." Her tears flowed down her cheeks, and she wiped them away. "We were supposed to get married and have children. *That* was the plan. But when he was faced with the reality of it, he ran right into Mandy's arms. What kind of man does that?"

"What about *my* son, Tonya? He's ten years old, and he's my whole world. I can't imagine what you must've gone through, but think what my son will have to suffer if I die."

"You have a loving family. They'll take care of him. I have no one, *no one*, Athena, to take care of my child. I refuse to let Brady ruin both of our lives."

"But you don't mind ruining my son's life? You might

think you're clever, Tonya, but all you really are is a cold-blooded killer."

"Cold blooded? I came to Brady with a picture of our unborn child. He looked at the life growing inside me, a life he helped create, and told me to destroy it. Then he shoved me away for a woman with money. How is that for cold-blooded? He was a monster, Athena. He deserved to die."

"You created that monster. What did you expect to happen when you told the love of your life to sleep with other women for money?"

"He wasn't supposed to sleep with them. That wasn't part of my plan. I didn't know he had his own."

I was sick of hearing about her plans. "Tonya, listen to me. If you have a gun in your hand when the police show up, they will shoot you. You can't take that chance. Not with the baby."

"When the police show up? What are you talking about? The police don't know I'm here."

"That text you sent to the unknown number? That wasn't my son's number. That was my friend Officer Maguire's phone number."

She lowered the gun and I could see the uncertainty in her eyes.

"What are you going to do, Tonya?" I asked. "Leave before the police come, or stick around so they can arrest you?"

A flash of lightning lit up the room, illuminating Case standing in the doorway. My heart pounded in fear. Tonya still had the gun. What if she turned now and saw him? What else could I say to keep her attention on me?

"Tonya," I said gently, "what will you name the child if it's a girl?"

"What?" She gave me a cold look. "Don't be nice to me. It's too late for that."

She moved around the bed, her wedding gown flowing behind her. "This was supposed to be my wedding day, Athena. Did you know that?"

She set the gun down on the nightstand and picked up the garden shears. As she straddled Mandy, I watched with a pounding heart as Case crept into the bedroom, halting when a floorboard creaked.

Instantly, Tonya turned, lifting the shears high above her head. "One more move, Case, and she dies."

I pulled the heavy picture frame from behind me and swung it with all my might, cracking the frame against the shears in Tonya's hands, splintering the glass. Tonya shrieked in pain as she dropped the shears. Case lunged across the bed and pulled Tonya's arms behind her back, dragging her off the bed and onto her feet, where he strong-armed her hands behind her back.

As she cried out in pain, I said, "Be careful. She's pregnant."

With a cry, Tonya sagged to the floor in a pool of white fabric, her body heaving as her emotions poured out. I could feel the pain engulfing her, the pain that had driven her so fiercely, escaping her body in violent waves. I put the gun on the nightstand and went to her. After all the heartache she'd put me and my family through, the horror she'd put her friends through, and the life she'd taken, watching her writhe in such horrible pain still made me feel sorry for her. She had the rest of her life to pay for the crimes she'd committed.

As Case stood silently by, ever watchful, I held her hands in mine and let her cry.

"Police!" I heard. "We're coming in." And then Maguire

and three other officers burst into the room, weapons drawn.

Case stood beside me as two of the men pulled Tonya to her feet. She was crying uncontrollably as they marched her out of the room.

Maguire went over to check on Mandy, lifting her eyelids and checking the pulse in her neck. "What happened to her?"

"She was given tranquilizers," I said. "I don't know how many, but the bottle is in her purse."

"I'll call for an ambulance." He spoke into his shoulder radio and then went to find the missing purse.

Case pulled the loose duct tape off my wrist then picked up my hands so he could see the bruises. He lifted each wrist in turn, pressing kisses on them. "I was so worried about you, Athena. I was afraid I wouldn't—" He took a breath. "Are you okay?"

"A little shaken."

He smiled. "A little?"

"I was worried that you wouldn't understand my text message."

"I was in the apartment when that message came through. I hid behind a stack of boxes. I thought for sure Tonya would spot me."

"The ambulance is here," Maguire said from the doorway. "I'm going to have to ask you two to step out."

As we cleared the room, Maguire said, "I need you both to give statements. Are you okay with doing that here?"

"Sure," Case said, as he put his arm around me.

That's when I noticed that he was soaking wet, drenched from head to toe. I had to laugh. "How's that Jeep with no doors working for you?"

In the living room, we were greeted by paramedics who checked us over and offered Case a wool blanket. "Let me," I said, accepting the blanket.

I wrapped him tightly and pulled him close. "Thank you for coming to my rescue."

At first, he smiled, giving me the charming, dimpled smile that only Case Donnelly could, and then he kissed me and everyone else disappeared—officers and EMTs—all vanished as a second kiss was followed by a third. He pulled the blanket around both of us, enveloping us in the soft wool.

"Excuse me, you two," I heard from behind, "are you ready to give your statements?"

I turned to give Maguire a smile. "I'll let Case go first."

While Case gave his statement, I texted my parents to let them know what had happened, telling them we would meet them at the Parthenon. By the time I had finished, the rain had died down, and the dark clouds had passed, revealing a bright blue, sunny sky.

"I guess it's time I meet the whole family," Case said as we left hand in hand, walking past curious onlookers in front of the building.

"Be brave," I told him. "You'll survive."

"My sweet girl."

Mama was the first to greet us, her arms outstretched, her gold bangle bracelet jangling as she enfolded me in a tight hug. Case was next to get one.

"Someone bring this man a towel," Mama said. "Come in. Come in, both of you. Tell us what happened."

And by us, she meant everyone. The entire family—

aunts and uncles, cousins, sisters, even a few of the regular customers—had gathered at the Parthenon to greet us. Yiayiá and Pappoús were next to dole out hugs, and then I heard my little boy's voice, and I started to cry. He came in through the back door with my father, both of them beaming at me. Nicholas ran into my arms, and I held him as long as I could, my love for him threatening to overwhelm me.

Maia and Delphi emerged from the crowd, clearing the way for a table they had set especially for Case and me, a spot near the center of the room where everyone could crowd around and hear our tale.

"Quiet, everyone," Uncle Giannis said. "Let the Goddess of Greene Street talk."

At the end of my story, after relating my suspenseful final few moments with Tonya, I let Case finish with his heroic rescue. I took his hand under the table, and he squeezed mine as he said, "But Athena's the real hero. A little impulsive, walking into a room alone with two of our top suspects, but a hero nevertheless."

I leaned close to him to say *sotto voce*, "Need I remind you *why* I had to go in alone?"

Case smiled at everyone as he said quietly, "We can discuss that later."

I gave his hand a gentle squeeze. "And just so you know, *you're* my hero."

As Maguire entered the diner, I called out, "And here's another hero," which brought a round of applause.

"Thank you," he said, "but I was only doing my job." He crooked his finger at us, motioning for us to meet him outside.

At that, Mama rose to inform everyone that dinner was on the house and the food would be out shortly. The menu she described was suspiciously similar to that of the rehearsal dinner.

Case and I met Maguire on the sidewalk outside, where I found Charlie Bolt, a newspaper reporter from the *Sequoian Press*, waiting. He was the same reporter who'd covered the Talbot murder investigation.

"Excuse us a minute, will you, Charlie?" Maguire asked.

"I'll be right over there when you're finished," Charlie said.

"Sorry to interrupt your celebration," Maguire said to us, "but I thought you'd be happy to hear that Selene will be released as soon as the judge signs the order."

"That's fantastic, Bob," I said and gave him a hug. "What about Tonya?"

"Tonya gave her statement, admitting to everything," he said. "And Mandy is awake and doing fine."

"I can't even begin to thank you for everything you've done," I told him. "You've gone above and beyond the call of duty."

"I was very glad to help." He held up his hand in greeting to someone behind me, and I turned to see Delphi glance behind her and then blow him a kiss through the open doorway. He blushed and continued. "Do you want to press charges against Nora?"

"No," I said, "but I would like to know what was behind her little attack."

"I think I can clear that up," he began. "Nora was upset when we took her away, but she was more than willing to explain. She told us she had been pregnant a few months back, and apparently, Brady was the father. He convinced her to end the pregnancy, which she did reluctantly, and then he left her for Mandy anyway. She said in her statement that when she saw the ultrasound, it brought back the trauma. She wouldn't go into it any more than that."

"Wow," I said, glancing at Case. "That Brady was something else, wasn't he?"

"Now you two go enjoy your celebration," Maguire said. "You've earned it. We can save any further discussion for another time." He turned to the reporter who was leaning casually against the Parthenon's wall. "You're up, Charlie."

"And so are you, Athena," Charlie said with a smile, "I'd like to interview you for an article in tomorrow's paper. Would you mind taking a quick trip down to Spencer's so I can get a photo of you with the statue of Athena? My car is right there." He pointed to a small Toyota.

"How about we meet you down there?" Case asked. "Athena and I have some things to discuss."

While Charlie started for his car, we began the four-block walk to the garden center. As we walked, Case took my hand and gave it a squeeze. "Before we get there, I need to talk to you about my business venture."

The tone in his voice gave me a knot in my stomach. "You didn't get the loan?"

"I did, but it's not enough to fund the business, even with Lila's help. So I've decided not to pursue it. Besides, I've found something I like better."

Better? As in, staying in Sequoia better? "And that would be?"

Case turned to face me, his eyes sparkling with excitement. "A private-eye business. A detective agency right here in Sequoia. What do you think about that?"

I smiled in relief. "I love it."

"I'd have to research what I'd need to do to get my investigator's license, of course, but that should be no problem. And with some financial help, I could open up shop right here on Greene Street."

My heart soared with happiness. He really was putting down roots in Sequoia. "You would make a great private eye, Case. It sounds like a wonderful idea."

"Naturally, I'd want you to work with me whenever you could. The Greene Street Detective Agency wouldn't be complete without the Goddess on payroll."

As we paused outside Spencer's, I leaned in to give him a kiss, feeling happier than I'd felt in a long time. "I think I could manage that part-time."

He kissed me back, but then his smile wavered just a little as he said, "You trust me, right?"

"Of course, I do."

"And we're good now?"

"Yes," I answered slowly. "Why?"

"Because there is one condition to getting my private eye business off the ground, and that's about that financial help I mentioned."

Behind me I heard a *click click click* of high heels, and suddenly, a hand clasped my shoulder. I turned to see Lila Talbot standing between us, one hand on my shoulder, the other hand around Case's back. She pulled us together into a tight-knit trio and smiled.

"Hello, partners."

*Keep reading for a special excerpt of the first
Goddess of Greene St. Mystery.*

STATUE OF LIMITATIONS
A Goddess of Greene St. Mystery

New York Times **Bestselling Author**
Kate Collins

First in a new series!

In this delightful new series by the New York Times *bestselling author of the Flower Shop Mysteries, Athena
Spencer comes back home to work with her crazy big
Greek family at their garden center. But she never
expected that a return to her roots would mean protecting
her family from murder . . .*

After her divorce, Athena has returned to coastal Michigan to work in her family's garden center and raise her son,
while also caring for a mischievous wild raccoon and fending off her family's annoying talent for nagging. Working
alone at the garden center one night, Athena is startled by a
handsome stranger who claims to be the rightful owner of
a valuable statue her grandfather had purchased at a recent
estate sale.

But she has even bigger problems on her plate. The
powerful Talbot family, from whom her *pappoús* bought
the statue, is threatening to raze the shops on Greene
Street's "Little Greece" to make way for a condo. The recent death of the Talbot family patriarch already seemed
suspicious, but now it's clear that a murderer is in their
midst. Athena will have to live up to her warrior-goddess
namesake to protect her family from a killer and save their
community from ruin . . .

Look for STATUE OF LIMITATIONS *everywhere
books are sold!*

PREFACE

IT'S ALL GREEK TO ME
blog by Goddess Anon

Chaos Reigns

I've read your comments and I'm truly flattered. I know many of you want me to reveal my true identity, but trust me, it's better this way. My life has been nothing but chaos lately, and I can't give you any more details than that. But I can give you a little backstory.

First of all, I come from a big, noisy—and nosy—Greek family consisting of several annoying siblings, a meddling mother firmly committed to the idea that I should marry a nice Greek boy, a father who, although not fully Greek, has totally embraced the culture, and my grandparents Pappoús (or Pappu, as we pronounce it), and Yaya (actually it's spelled Oiaoiá, but I'll keep it simple).

Secondly, when I was young, I prayed for a handsome white knight to come along to rescue me, and guess what? Nothing. Ever. Happened. I finally figured out I'd have to do it myself. So, at the ripe old age of twenty-four,

I packed a suitcase, moved to the closest big city, got a studio apartment, a low-paying job at a big company and worked my way up until I reached a level of success that made me happier than I'd ever dreamed possible.

I also met and married a very successful, non-Greek businessman, which caused all kinds of uproar back home. So along with a wedding gift, my mother gave me her prediction of my future with this man: he'll break your heart; after your divorce you'll never be able to support yourself in the city; then you'll come back home where you belong.

Oh, how I prayed that she would be wrong but, once again, my prayers went unanswered, because, much to my consternation, it turned out that she was right.

Ten years later, my corporate job was eliminated and my husband divorced me, leaving me in debt up to my ears but unchaining me from a bitter marriage where I'd felt invisible and wary of ever getting close to a man again. So, with a young child to support, I packed up our belongings, along with my pride, and returned home into the welcoming—or should I say gloating—arms of my family.

Now my child and I not only live in the big family house, but I also work for the family business, which at least enables me to earn my own money so I can move into my own place one day. In the meantime, my child, who'd been so distraught by the divorce, does seem to be blossoming here in the midst of our eccentric but strong fam—

CHAPTER ONE

Monday 8:10 p.m.

My computer monitor flickered briefly, and the screen went black. The lights in the ceiling high above my desk made a buzzing sound and then they, too, went dark. The window beside my desk offered little help. The bright May sun had set fifteen minutes ago.

Muttering under my breath, I reached for my cell phone only to remember that I'd set it on the oak console table on the opposite side of the office. A bolt of lightning momentarily illuminated the room, enabling me to make my way around the old oak desk and across the wood floor to the table. At a sudden heavy thud from somewhere outside the room, I paused. Standing in the dark beside the table, I waited, listening.

Hearing nothing more, I did a quick mental inventory. My father John Spencer, who owned Spencers Garden

Center, and my youngest sister Delphi, had left when the shop closed at eight. I'd turned on the CLOSED sign and bolted the door myself. Then, with no one around, I'd retreated to the office to write my blog—my way of releasing my pent-up frustrations. The store was completely empty, so what had caused the noise?

I located my phone, switched on the flashlight, and shined it at the open doorway. Thunder rumbled in the distance as I quietly peered out into the huge garden center.

The office where I worked was on the right side of the shop behind the L-shaped checkout counter. I could see that the cash register hadn't been touched; the bolt on the big red doors was still thrown; nothing on any of the shelves had been disturbed; none of the outdoor wall decor was askew; and no windows had been broken. That was a relief. But I still had to track down the source of the noise.

Over a century ago the garden center had been a barn on the very northern edge of Sequoia, Michigan, the last building on Greene Street. Now, with a brand-new arched roof, big picture windows, a high-beamed ceiling, cream-colored shiplap walls, and a shiny oak floor, Spencers was one of the most attractive buildings along the mile stretch of tourist shops. I'd always loved being there—I had a natural green thumb—but I'd never expected to make it my life's work.

Another thud turned me in the direction of the outdoor garden area, located on an acre lot behind the barn, and then I had my answer. It was Oscar, our friendly neighborhood raccoon, who liked to steal shiny objects. He'd pilfered any number of items from the area where we kept garden décor. I wasn't about to let him take another one.

Using my cellphone's flashlight as my guide, I headed toward the back exit, walking down the left side past rows of indoor plants, garden supplies, tools, and small decorative pots. Circling the long, oak plank conference table at the rear of the barn, I pushed the glass door open and stepped outside just as the electricity came back on. Hanging lanterns around the perimeter of a ballroom-sized area right outside the building illuminated a cement floor and a wide aisle down the middle that divided the area into two sections. The left side was filled with shelves overflowing with flowering annuals, perennials, and vegetables, while the right side contained stone, clay, glass, and cement garden sculptures, water fountains, large decorative planters, wrought iron benches, and patio furniture.

I caught movement from the corner of my eye and backed against the door with a sharp gasp.

A man was crouched at the base of a life-sized marble statue of the Goddess Athena, now lying on her back in the grass. He had an open pocketknife in his hand and his cell phone was propped nearby, its flashlight aimed at the statue's base. He jumped to his feet, obviously as shocked to see me as I was to see him.

"Drop that knife and don't move a muscle." I thrust my phone forward, the beam pointed at his face and my trembling finger on the home button. "I've got the police on the line."

If only that were true.

The hanging lights flickered, threatening to go out again.

"Okay," he said in a calm voice. "No problem." Moving slowly, he placed the knife on the ground and raised his hands above his head. "I'm sorry. I didn't mean to alarm you."

"You broke into our shop. What did you *think* that would do to me?"

"Hold on a minute," he said in a rising voice. "I did *not* break into the shop. I was *told* to stay here until someone could help me, and that was"—he tipped his wrist to see his watch—"over twenty minutes ago."

I gave him a skeptical glance. "You've been out here for twenty minutes?"

"*Over* twenty minutes. Again, I'm sorry for alarming you, but I was just doing what I was told."

Undeniably good looking, the man had dark hair that was parted on the side and combed away from his face, big golden-brown eyes, a firm mouth, and a strong jawline. My gaze was drawn down to his expensive tan suede bomber jacket that showed off his muscular shoulders, dark blue jeans that revealed an athletic build, and noticeably pricey navy leather loafers.

His expression seemed sincere, but the truth was that I was alone with a stranger behind a big barn on Greene Street, the main thoroughfare of our small lakeside town, with only my phone and my wits to protect me. The other shops had already closed and any tourists who'd stuck around would no doubt be comfortably seated inside a restaurant or one of the local sports bars. With the storm quickly approaching, who would hear my cry for help?

I jumped at a sudden clap of thunder. With all the bravery I could muster, still holding my phone, I pointed toward the lane that ran behind the shops on Greene. "You need to leave right now."

"Will you at least give me a chance to prove I'm telling the truth? If you don't believe me, I'll go."

A strong eastern wind blew through the garden area, shifting the hanging lanterns, and causing my long, blue sweater to billow out around my white jeans. I could smell the rain coming.

Brushing long strands of light brown hair away from my face, I said, "Make it fast."

"The young woman who waited on me—I didn't get her name—is probably in her late twenties, with lots of curly black hair tied with some kind of fuzzy purple thing. She had on a purple sweater, jeans, and bright green flip-flops. She was shorter than you but had more . . ." He gave me a sweeping glance, his eyes moving from my long brown hair all the way down to my white flats. He saw the narrowing of my gaze, and finished with, "color in her cheeks."

That wasn't what he'd meant to say and we both knew it. He had just described Delphi, my airhead of a sister who, like my other two sisters Maia and Selene, had the curvaceous bodies, shorter stature, and olive complexions of my Greek-American mother, Hera Karras Spencer. I, on the other hand, was the only one who had inherited the pale, slender form and straight light brown hair of my English-American father.

It was quite likely that Delphi had gotten busy with something and had forgotten to tell me. Her absentmindedness was common enough to convince me the man could be telling the truth, but still, what did he intend to do with that knife?

I gestured toward the statue. "What were you doing?"

"Can I put my hands down? My arms are tired."

At my curt nod he said, "Thank you. I'm Case Donnelly by the way."

As he walked closer, holding out his hand to shake mine, I realized I was still clutching my cell phone.

"You might want to put that away." His mouth quirked as though trying to hide a grin. "I'm guessing the police hung up a long time ago or they'd have been here by now."

I stood my ground, my gaze locked with his.

"And your flashlight app is on, by the way."

He wasn't missing a trick. Feeling a blush starting, I turned off the app, slid the phone in my back pocket, and took his hand. "Athena Spencer," I said in a crisp, business-like voice. I'd gone back to my maiden name when my divorce had become final.

"Athena." He looked impressed. "Like your Treasure of Athena."

That he knew the statue's name surprised me since it wasn't written on any tag.

"It's a pleasure to meet you, Athena. Are you the owner here?"

His charming smile and warm, firm grip left me a little breathless. I dropped his hand and stepped back, feeling awkward and at the same time angry with him for causing it. "I'm the business manager. My father owns the garden center. Now would you answer my question, please?"

"I'd be glad to." He gestured toward the overturned figure. "I was trying to find out if the statue is authentic."

"She's authentic."

"Do you have the legal paperwork to prove it?"

Feeling my temper on the rise I said, "Yes. It's called a sales receipt."

"And does it say on this sales receipt that the statue is by the Greek sculptor Antonius?"

I paused to think. Had I seen the name Antonius anywhere on the receipt in the file marked *Statue*? I'd only noticed that it *was* a receipt because it had been sticking up out of the file when I was putting something else away. Who was Antonius anyway?

As though reading my thoughts Case said, "Antonius is a Roman artist from the early twelfth century who became famous posthumously for his sculptures of Greek gods and goddesses."

I lifted my chin. "As a matter of fact, I do know that." *Not.* "And anyway, it doesn't matter. The statue isn't for sale."

"That's okay. I wasn't interested in buying it. But just out of curiosity, may I see the receipt?"

His impertinence irritated me. "No, you may not. It's late, I'm hungry, and I was supposed to meet someone for dinner ten minutes ago."

Case studied me with a shrewdness that made me uneasy. "It's just after eight o'clock. Why isn't the garden center open?"

"All of the shops in town close at eight. You're not from around here, are you?"

Completely ignoring my question, he glanced back at the statue. "I'm betting you paid a lot of money for her."

His sudden switch of topics threw me off guard. Plus, I was growing hungrier—and angrier—by the second. I hadn't wanted to dine so late anyway, especially not with Kevin Coreopsis, the "good Greek boy" my mother was encouraging me to see, but of course, when did my wishes ever count? I would've much rather had dinner with my son at The Parthenon with the rest of the family.

"First of all, I didn't buy the statue. My grandfather did. He was going to use it at his diner, but it was too large. Secondly, how much he paid isn't your concern. Now would you please keep your promise and leave?"

"I'll take that as a yes, she did cost a lot of money. I hope your grandfather at least bought her from a reputable art dealer."

"Not that it's any of your business, but he bought her at an estate sale." Why had I told Case that?

My stomach rumbled, reminding me why.

"So, an auctioneer sold it to him? Is the auction house reliable?"

I balled my hands into fists, not about to admit that neither the auctioneer nor the auction house was one I knew anything about. I hadn't even been aware that Pappoús had purchased it until it was delivered.

"Okay," Case said, "I'll mark that down as a *you don't know*. Whose estate was up for auction?"

I pulled my cell phone out of my pocket. "Get out now or I really will call the police."

"One more question. Did the auctioneer inform your grandfather that someone had applied a thin layer of cement over the bottom of the statue where the sculptor's name should be?"

I glanced in surprise at the sandal-clad feet of the marble Athena and saw that Case had indeed scraped off a bit of what appeared to be a cement coating.

"I'll take that as no," he said. "Therefore, my question for you is, why would someone put cement over the sculptor's name unless it wasn't a genuine Antonius?"

I absorbed the information with a sinking feeling in the pit of my stomach. Had my pappoús been ripped off?

Case straightened his jacket cuffs, clearly satisfied that he'd made his point.

And indeed, he had. With one eye on the black clouds overhead I asked, "How long will it take you to find out if she's authentic?"

"Five minutes, and I won't even charge you for my services."

I stared at him in surprise.

Case smiled, revealing a charming dimple in his cheek. "I'm joking."

His teasing helped break the tension between us, and I couldn't help but smile back. I glanced at my watch. "All right, Case Donnelly, you've got five minutes."

As he crouched down to work, my nerves kicked in. What if this outrageously expensive statue was a fake, not even worth what we'd paid to move it from the Talbot's estate to the diner and then to Spencers? I felt sick to my stomach thinking about it.

I'd protested mightily that it was too big for the diner and too far out of my grandparents' budget anyway, but as always, my voice went unheard. The family had gathered behind my stubborn Pappoús because he was the head of the family and his decisions were final, regardless of what his college educated granddaughter had to say.

The problem was twofold: it was too large for The Parthenon's front entryway, and Spencers was stuck with it until we could convince Pappoús we needed to sell it, which didn't seem likely. He loved his Treasure of Athena and would often bring his lunch down and sit at one of the outdoor tables gazing at her as though waiting for her to come to life.

As Case worked, I had to admit that the statue was beautiful. I hadn't seen such exquisite detail in a sculpture since I'd toured Greek museums with my family years ago.

Standing at over six-feet tall, Athena wore a traditional flowing toga gathered over one shoulder with a clasp so that the material draped down over her small, firm breasts. Another layer of material swirled down from her waist to the sandals on her feet. Her hair was swept up beneath a helmet that covered the top of her head. Her arms were bare and slender, but her strength was evident. One hand rested on her right hip, the other hand was outstretched in greeting. She was the Goddess of War and Wisdom, strong, courageous, and independent, none of which I felt.

Case blew away the dust he'd scraped off, uncovering a small brass plate attached to the bottom of one of Athena's soles. I knelt down for a closer look as he wiped off the brass with his palm. "There's your marking."

I squinted at the etching but couldn't make sense of it. "Is that in Greek?"

"You don't read Greek?"

"I usually skipped Greek school. Does that mean the statue's an authentic Antonius?"

"She's authentic, all right, and worth a small fortune."

As he hoisted the sculpture back to its standing position, I stared at it in awe, my heart racing as the words *small fortune* echoed in my head. We owned an authentic Greek Antonius? Surely Pappoús wouldn't mind selling now. And just think what they could do with that money to spruce up the interior of their outdated diner.

Case held out a hand to help me up. "There's one more thing you should know about her, Athena."

"And that is?"

He brushed dirt off the statue's exquisite marble face. "She's mine."

ACKNOWLEDGMENTS

I'd like to thank my son, Jason Eberhardt, for going above and beyond the call of duty in his efforts to make this book glimmer. His talent for suspense will make him a great writer one day, and I hope his experiences with me will be the impetus for charging fearlessly forward.

I'd like to thank Jack Gillen for his expertise on boats and for helping me understand what it takes to own and maintain a boat. It isn't for sissies, is it, Jack?

I'd like to thank my hair stylist, Amber Milenkoff, for helping me understand the stylist's life (and for her darned good haircuts, too).

As always, I'd like to thank my daughter, Julia, for her constant support and encouragement, and to Doug for being there to support and encourage her, too.

I'd like to thank my editors, Tara Gavin and Elizabeth May, for being a dream to work with. (Yikes. I ended with a preposition. Don't hate me.)

I'd like to thank my agent, Jessica Faust, for being the pillar in the background, always ready with an encouraging word or whatever type of support I need.

To all the hopeful writers out there, believe in your work and don't let rejection shake your faith. If you love it, send it out. It'll find a home. If you have uncertainties, join a critique group, and have them give it a go. Don't be afraid of criticism. Instead, learn to work with it, and you'll produce a better manuscript.

RECIPES

Greek Omelet

This delicious egg dish is the perfect start to any day. With a bit of prep the night before, it takes no time at all to whisk them up. Just ask Athena. Enjoy!

INGREDIENTS
8 eggs
¼ cup (60 mL) water
¼ tsp (1.25 mL) pepper
⅓ cup (75 mL) minced onion
¾ cup (175 mL) chopped, seeded tomato
½ cup (125 mL) crumbled, feta cheese
¼ cup (60 mL) chopped, pitted Kalamata olives
½ tsp (2.5 mL) dried oregano

Whisk eggs, water, and pepper in medium bowl. Set aside.

Spray non-stick skillet with cooking spray. Heat skillet over medium heat. Add onion; cook, stirring frequently, for about 1 minute. Add tomato; cook for 1 minute. Stir in feta cheese, olives, and oregano. Set aside.

Spray 8-inch (20 cm) non-stick skillet with cooking spray. Heat skillet over medium heat. Pour one-quarter of egg mixture into skillet. As eggs set around edge of skillet, with spatula, gently push cooked portions toward center. Tilt and rotate skillet to allow uncooked egg to flow into empty spaces.

When eggs are almost set on surface but still look moist, cover half of omelet with one quarter of filling. Fold unfilled half of omelet over filled half. Cook for a minute, then slide onto plate.

Repeat 3 times for 3 more omelets.

Source: Get Cracking. www.eggs.ca

Kourabiedes

These Kourabiedes (Greek Butter Cookies) are a classic Greek cookie. Some call them wedding cookies, some call them Christmas cookies, I call them delicious! They're buttery, crumbly, and not too sweet. *Opa!*

INGREDIENTS
1 lb unsalted butter, room temperature
½ cup powdered sugar plus another cup for coating
1 Tbsp almond extract
1 large egg
⅛ tsp baking soda
5 cups all-purpose flour
¼ tsp salt

Preheat oven to 350 degrees. Beat butter in the bottom of a stand mixer on a medium-high speed for 20 minutes.

Add egg and almond extract, mix until combined.

Sift ½ cup powdered sugar, baking soda, flour, and salt together in a large bowl. With the speed on low, add mixture a little bit at a time until completely incorporated. If the dough is too sticky, add a little bit more flour.

Roll about 2 tablespoons of dough into crescents and place on a baking sheet lined with parchment paper or silt pad.

Bake for 15–20 minutes until very pale brown and cooked through.

If you're serving the cookies right away, let them cool slightly and toss in powdered sugar. Serve within 24 hours. If you want to bake them and serve later, store in an airtight container in the fridge. When ready to serve, pop in a warm oven until warm, then roll in powdered sugar.

Source: www.cookingforkeeps.com